Christmas Australis

CHRISTMAS AUSTRALIS

A FRIGHTENINGLY FESTIVE ANTHOLOGY OF SPINE JINGLING TALES

V.E. Patton . Darren Kasenkow
Emily Wrayburn . Lyn Webster
Andrew Roff . Natasha O'Connor
Madeleine D'Este . Belinda Grant

True Dialogue
Publishing

Compiled and published 2019 by Veronica Eileen Strachan as V. E Patton
True Dialogue Publishing
Cover by Creative Girl Tuesday 2019
Edited by Peter Dunn

ISBN: 978-0-6485134-5-2

A catalogue record for this book is available from the National Library of Australia

This Anthology of original Australian fiction has the #6amAusWriters of Twitter to thank for its creation. The #6amAusWriters are a brilliant, supportive, and yes, occasionally sleepy, group of writers who rise with the sparrows to make time in their lives to work on their craft.

See you there sometime…

Contents

Ghostly Greetings from the Epica

Welcome aboard dear reader, to the weathered planks and creaking masts of a ship that sails the forever mysterious waters of eternity. Where dreams that have been and will be merge together in a cosmic dance that sways to a never ending tune and winds from forgotten realms fill tattered canvas sheets with empty promises of landfall.

The Southern Cross above is forever my companion. And while rumour has it the Incas thought the bright stars a mystical symbol of the Heavens, the living, and the underworld, it is for me a sparkling treasure that assures I am still very much a part of this world—even if I'm also afloat in a whole new hemisphere.

Now it must be said, that though these dishevelled galleys echo with distant whale songs and the constant rattling of rusting chains, you've chosen the perfect time to venture upon the salt soaked wood of a vessel built of pure heartache. After all, the magic of Christmas reaches even the loneliest decking of a lost, convict ghost ship.

Jacob Bloodsworth is my name, though I can't remember the last time I've actually heard it called aloud, and the ship you've stumbled upon is none other than the *Epica*. Historic records may insist the first fleet of scoundrels to venture the unforgiving seas to New South Wales in 1787 numbered eleven, but as your eyes adjust to the light of the stars, I'm sure you'll agree there was indeed another. As for the absence of any crew, I'm afraid it's a mystery I too ponder over and over again as the waves continue to lash what has become the only home I'll ever know.

How did it come to be that I sail these eternal waters, you might venture to ask? Well, the Old Bailey would have you believe me guilty of stealing nine linen shirts, two pairs of silk stockings, four handkerchiefs and eight ounces of chocolate, but truth be told it was closer to thirteen ounces—even if I do still profess my innocence.

I was quite sure the gallows pole would be the choice of destination bestowed by such wise and worldly men. Imagine my utter surprise when hands strengthened with hate bustled me upon this very ship for the long journey to the land down under. It was a harrowing choice of eventuality that received its name, so it was whispered amongst the filthy passengers of equal professed innocence, from the disheartening fact that it was a place where men go to die. Only, the *Epica* never quite made it and my death seems to have been withheld.

For two hundred and fifty gruelling days or more we sailed monstrous oceans that cared not for our company. A lack of food left us skin and bones; sleep was only achievable in snatched moments huddled in a ball on the cold unforgiving wood.

Then, on one particular night, when rumours of landfall began to drum from tired lips and hunger drove the meekest of men to fight the last of the withering giants, an exceptionally large full moon emerged and with it a sense of calm upon the waters unlike anything seen before.

And then there was nothing.

I awoke perhaps the next morning, or perhaps a thousand years later. Every plank of the ship was empty and no matter how loud I cried out there was only the squawk of a gull or a flapping of the sail to respond to my sudden desolation. Before long, I understood my journey would forever be without end.

So welcome aboard! I can't tell you how many circumnavigations I've ventured along the outline of the Australian coast, all in a ship that has me yearn for innocent times of bread larceny and pocket pilfering long gone. But, it's always such a heartfelt gift to have someone like you join me at such a special time of the year. You see, it's only at Christmas that a guest of unbridled wonder such as yourself can grace these hallowed halls of the vessel I call home. As the wondrous Southern Cross would observe, it's only at Christmas that eerily illuminated bottles from ocean depths unseen bubble to the surface ready to be grabbed by my salt-cracked hands. Each glowing, glass float holds within its carefully moulded form the greatest gift of all—a starlit dark and festively inked tale upon carefully scrolled paper. Can there be anything more wondrous to electrify the hypnotism of eternity?

Gather close, for the first bottle has broken through the mystical blue. Let's see, what do we have 'ere? Hmm, this tale looks to be a right jolt of the kind that could stun a penguin! And it all seems to start so very innocently…

Peace on Earth

By V. E. Patton

*For Nana and Grandad Brethie, who gave me
the best Christmas memories a child could have.*

"**W**hat are those sparkly dots on the photo?"

The vegetable knife slipped from Kate's nerveless fingers and disappeared into the sink full of potato skins. She closed her eyes and took a deep breath. A cornucopia of aromas tickled the back of her throat; Christmas smells. With the humid bouquet of rich food, wine and drying pine tree came the memories, Family memories. She took another deep breath; she wasn't ready for those.

Not Jack, please not Jack. I was just wearing him in.

"Which sparkly dots?" she asked, aiming for calm and nonchalant as she fished out the knife. She kept her back to her boyfriend of five months, her heart pounding as she waited for his answer.

What was I thinking bringing him home to meet the Family? And at Christmas!

Jack slipped his arms around her waist, nuzzling her neck.

"The ones around your Nana's head. Almost looks like she's got jewels on her Christmas cracker crown," he laughed.

Kate tried not to howl; a feral frenzy gnawed at its shackles deep in her belly.

Bloody Family.

"See what I did there? Nice alliteration, don't you think? Christmas. Cracker. Crown," Jack said.

She leant back against his chest, breathing in his clean, homely smell. Lynx and London.

She scented him with her other sense; he still smelt clean and homely—and human, deliciously so. Kate's mouth dried and her throat tightened as she felt the frenzy roiling into something wilder. With an accustomed ferocity, she slammed it back into its box. She clamped her teeth together and patted Jack's hands with her own damp ones.

It'd been a risk bringing him here, but they'd promised to be on their best behaviour. Though if Jack could truly see the dots, then he'd opened the Pandora's Box that was the Vizard Family Christmas Secret.

And then what? Whose side am *I* on?

Best behaviour! They promised!

Kate mentally face palmed herself for being so gullible. When was her Family ever on their best behaviour? Jack tightened his hold, sensing her tension. She wondered if he could hold his own with this crazy lot and survive the festivities—and the Secret.

She always capitalised Secret, because in her mind it was a Big Deal. Too big really. Hard to hide when the whole mob got together over Christmas lunch. Too much food, too much drink, emotions unleashed, boundaries crossed.

Unfiltered Family.

She shuddered. And what if it wasn't just the Aussies? What if the Other Cousins came? And Great-Grandad B?

Her belly did a flip-flop. She shouldn't have come. Her eyes flashed to the dusty green Bakelite clock above the sink that had tick tock-ed heedlessly through so much of her childhood. The timepiece wore a slightly askew crown of tattered tinsel. Kate had to admit that her life had felt exactly that since she'd left the Family fold for the real world—slightly askew.

Was it too late to do a runner back to the city?

She moved from patting to grasping Jack's wrists, her mind whirling with the pros and cons.

But her sister Shirl, the one who was next to her in the Family line-up, had begged her to come. Shirl had promised that only the immediate Family of six siblings and their progeny would be there. And that they'd all be good; keep *IT* under control.

It'd been three years since Kate had made the trek home for Christmas. She'd told herself that things must have changed in that time. Things in the rest of the world had changed after all. There was peace on earth for one thing. Well, an uneasy peace perhaps, but still peace.

And it was such a long way to drive back. Home was four humid hours from the safety of crowded Melbourne. Three on the highway, then Nana's place was another hour on the dusty corrugated track, shaking Kate's bones till she thought her joints would pop.

She should've turned back when they'd hit the locked front gate.

"That doesn't mean us does it?" Jack had asked, waving at all the hand painted warnings decorating the rusty iron, telling people to stay out, stay off, beware of various fauna, and get lost. "They don't seem like a very welcoming bunch. Are you sure I'm invited?"

Kate had laughed it off and assured him the Family would love him.

And now that he could see the sparkly dots, she had absolutely no doubt. They would love him to pieces.

Am I ready for that? I've lived apart from Family for so long. Kept the Secret contained.

Family comes First. Especially at Christmas. Her Mum's oft-quoted maxim rattled into her brain.

And Blood Will Out. The Vizard motto.

She let go of Jack's wrists and blinked to refocus her eyes. She snuck a sideways glance at Jack as he moved away to hold the photo album up under the light at the window. He did look mighty fine in his '*I hate Christmas*' T-shirt. A brave garment to wear in this house. The glare of the morning sunshine emphasised how it hugged his scrawny arms and rounded shoulders quite nicely. She did love the nerdy types. They spiced up the conversation so tastefully.

Yeah, good picking Kate. Got yourself a good one—for now.

Maybe someone else would bring a friend to distract the attention from Jack. Kate knew this was a slim hope, only she and Shirl were still single, and Shirl was here on her own.

Maybe it was a fluke, just this one photo.

She sighed and stopped the back and forth in her head, taking another look at Jack's silhouette. Nana did so hate those beefy blokes Shirl used to bring home. They'd turn their noses up at the Family's little weatherboard bungalow plonked in the middle of the paddock with all the add-ons and the outside toilet. Then they'd spend all day blustering around and telling everyone how fabulous they were at this or that sport or drinking game. They'd all been a bit tough to swallow.

When Kate had introduced Jack to Nana this morning, she'd seen the smile reach her grandmother's eyes when Jack spoke of his appreciation of her hospitality in his ever-so-proper English voice.

Nana. She looked so much older now. In the three years Kate had been away, her grandmother seemed to have aged thirty. She'd faded, stretched thin. Though her eyes were the same sparkling brown they'd always been. The same sparkling brown as her daughter, Kate's Mum, and the same as Kate's own.

Family comes First. Especially at Christmas.

He's an adult for goodness' sake.

Kate took a deep breath and released her emotional grip on Jack. He didn't need her smothering.

"You should ask Nana about the photo and the sparkly dots on her crown," Kate said to Jack. She picked up the veggie knife again and reached for another potato.

"Okay gorgeous." Jack kissed her neck one more time and her skin tingled.

Dammit. He makes me feel good. Maybe he's worth fighting for. Kate thought she could manage her Nana and siblings at least. And there had been no mention of Great-Grandad B coming.

Shirl came in from the lounge room, and by the tilt of her sister's nose, Kate's *other* sniffing must have pricked her senses. She raised an expressive eyebrow at Kate.

"Whaddaya up to Jack?" She drawled, taking a swig of her champagne. "Kate can't get all these spuds done on her own you know. The rellies will start showing up soon. If you're gonna make that damn English veggo rubbish, you'd better get started."

Kate could see the glints in Shirl's eye and smell the augury in the aether. Kate shook her head, a warning in the glare she threw at her sister.

"It's Cranberry Mushroom Nutloaf," Jack said, a little miffed at Shirl's tone. "It's almost done and I'm sure it'll be a hit. Old family recipe."

'Old *Family* recipe, eh?' Shirl's smile got a little feral. 'We have a few old *Family* recipes ourselves."

When Kate glared at her, Shirl added, "Oh, we Vizards love our veggies too."

"Jack's just asking me about the dots on the Christmas photos is all." Kate headed Shirl off the food tack, but then realised she was heading from frying pan to fire. Revealing he could see the dots was a big mistake.

"I've seen dots like this before you know," Jack mused, taking the bait instead. Kate met Shirl's startled gaze over Jack's head.

"Winner, winner, bunyip dinner," Shirl laughed.

"What? Turnips?" said Jack looking back and forth between the women. "Are we back to veggies? I thought your family were all vegetarian Kate."

"Well some of us more than most," Shirl laughed again. "Now, don't mind Kate. She's a worrywart. Tell me Jack, where have you seen sparkly dots before?" She flung an affectionate arm around his skinny shoulders, which exposed her impressive cleavage to his purview.

Jack appeared to be rethinking his admission. Either that or Shirl's barely contained décolletage had thrown his brain into a tizz. His cheeks flamed as he looked up at Kate with a mute plea for succour. The flush was not an attractive look with his pale skin and flaming curls. Kate scented the sourness of his discomfort.

"I s'pose you'll think I'm daft," Jack said. He paused and tried to step away from Shirl. She leant in and sniffed his neck before releasing him.

When Kate kept smiling at him, he threw caution to the wind.

"OK, I got some shots like this when I took photos up at the old Beechworth Sanatorium." He paused. "The tour guide said they were spirits."

"Spirits? What spirits?" Nana asked, wandering into the room.

"In some photos I took Mrs Vizard," Jack explained. "But since then, almost every selfie I take has these sparkly dots in them. I thought it was the lenses at first, but I've tried all sorts and can't get a clean shot."

"You never told me that before? I thought you were just selfie-shy," Kate said, drawing out a chair and seating herself at the kitchen table. Jack stood up straighter and she could see Shirl checking him out in light of this new information. Kate could see Shirl's form quiver. Kate mouthed *'best behaviour'* at her sister behind Jack's back.

"Did you believe them?" Nana asked Jack, "about the spirits?"

He shrugged. "I don't know Mrs Vizard. I like to keep an open mind."

"Do you think a pesky spirit has got into your camera?" Shirl asked.

The doorbell jangled and interrupted their interrogation before Jack answered.

"Get that will you Jack?" Kate prompted, trying to extricate Jack before he got in too deep.

Jack seemed a little anxious about her request, but obligingly took off for the front door, squaring his shoulders. He'd left the photo album open and Kate ran her eyes over the images, grimacing at the memories they evoked. Was she ready to peel the scab off this particular wound? Would she have a choice?

"Nan?" Kate's voice was her attempt at neutral. "Do you think he could be—you know?"

"Let's not count our chickens," Nana said, sitting down at the table and helping herself to a glass of champers and a shortbread biscuit. "Not at Christmas. Anyway, I thought you'd given up thinking about your Family responsibilities? Didn't want to have anything to do with that shit. Wasn't that a direct quote at your mother's funeral?"

Kate wilted with shame and her eyes misted with sadness.

"We miss her too, Kate," Nana whispered and drew her granddaughter into a hug. "She was my daughter, my little girl."

"I've missed you, Nan. I'm sorry I stayed away so long. And okay, I have missed Family Christmas too," Kate admitted, giving her Nana's frail form one more squeeze then letting go. She wiped her eyes on her Christmas apron. "You know I always felt envious of people who had all that northern hemisphere White Christmas stuff. It's like they have the bloody monopoly on the season. We have to wear their cold weather traditions, no matter how stinking hot it is here."

Her sister and Nana watched as Kate pulled herself from her melancholy, swiping at her tears again. Her Nana passed her a tissue and Shirl poured them all another champagne.

"But I tried it and it stunk. I was freezing and wet, and no one knew how to do Christmas right. I missed the dam, and the sun, and too much food, too much grog, screaming kids and a dried out tree and—well, everything."

Nana patted Kate's arm as she accepted the glass of bubbles and dabbed at her own eyes with another tissue.

"Blood is always thicker than water," Shirl said, "no matter how annoying."

"You do know that saying is misquoted don't you," Kate said. "Jack told me it's from the bible. The real version is *'the blood of the covenant is thicker than the water of the womb'*. So it actually means blood that's shed in battles is a stronger bond than genetics. It was in the middle of an argument about whether or not to come up for Christmas. Then I got into a rant about the patriarchy subsuming the creation role of women and mothers yet again, and well…"

"Jeez you must be hard to live with Kate," Shirl teased. "Why does he put up with you?"

"Actually, he makes me think about things differently. And it's just, well, I guess I've got used to him. And I like him." Kate took a deep breath. "So, I was wondering… if… is Great-Grandad B coming?" She finished in a rush.

Nana's reply was hindered by a torrent of her offspring bursting into the kitchen like an exploding tap. The open door exposed the women to the noise of the rabble coming in the front door which had risen to rock concert decibels. A few carloads of relations had obviously arrived at the same time.

And if he does come? Kate asked herself. *I'll just take it one step at a time.*

Jack came back into the kitchen with a kid hanging from each arm and one around his neck. He looked more stunned that someone who'd made a successful croquembouche on their first attempt. Kate couldn't help laughing at him. This was her Family; he'd have to learn to sink or swim.

The next hour was a cacophony of greeting and teasing and cooking and drinking—lots of drinking. It was thirty-two degrees Celsius already and only ten-thirty in the morning. The air conditioner struggled with the crowd, rattling its fan back and forth from the darkened lounge room. The kitchen was a sauna with all the roasting and cooking going on. Kids screamed as they chased each other around the house, doing laps and getting under everyone's feet.

"Get outside you bloody kids," Bob yelled at them as the pavlova he was decorating with strawberries and passionfruit got sucked into the wake of a racing child and almost hit the floor. Luckily, Maureen's hands made the save.

"Can we go down the dam? I'm sooo hot," one of the kids groaned.

The whines multiplied tenfold as all the mobile kids took to bemoaning the heat and the need to swim.

"I'll take them. My hands aren't much good for cutting and cooking these days," Nana said. She laboured out of the corner chair and wriggled her arthritic fingers at her offspring.

"Are you sure Nan? They can be a handful," Louise said, her hands sticky with brandy cream sauce and her eyes a little glazed from checking the quality of the brandy.

"I think I can manage five ungrateful brats," Nana laughed, "but I'll leave you the babies."

Those same five ungrateful brats charged around her in a circle, yelling their agreement at the top of their lungs.

"Yay, Nana's taking us for a swim," and various versions of the same chant emerged from five young throats.

"Can you tell us a story on the way Nana?" asked the youngest, already yanking at the collar of her new Christmas frock to begin disrobing in the crowded kitchen.

"Stories have to wait till after lunch loser," the oldest informed her. "Cousins, then lunch, then stories, then pressies."

"Yeah, then all the oldies fall asleep on the couch and dribble," chuckled a third child. All the kids giggled and the parents rolled their eyes—but no one denied it.

"Get your togs and towels. Sunscreen on all of you," said Bob, owner of the youngest and oldest of the five.

"Do I have to sunscreen?" Blue's dark eyes and matching skin were the envy of his two fair skinned cousins.

"You betcha. Skin cancer capital of the world this place," said Shaunie, one of Blue's dads. He ruffled his son's unruly curls then herded his brood into the front room in search of bags and togs.

"Do you want to go Jack? Have you seen our private beach?" Shirl asked, sliding a hand over Jack's shoulder and down his arm, giving his biceps a little pinch on the way.

"Hardly a beach Shirl. It's a muddy dam," Kate scoffed, glaring at her sister.

"But it's *our* muddy dam," said Nana.

"Come on, Nana. We want to swim before the cousins get here. They'll make the water all yucky," Blue grumbled.

"Cousins? Shirl, you told me they weren't coming this year. That they couldn't make it through." Kate's belly roiled again, fright and fear battling anger at her sister's manipulation. "And anyway, I need Jack to help here."

With the mention of cousins and the possibility of the Secret and all its consequences emerging now real possibilities, Kate was vacillating between flight and fight. If she sent Jack off unguarded, Nana was more likely to start the twenty questions again or to spill the beans.

Shirl smirked at Kate's glare.

"Make it through? How far do they have to come?" Jack asked trying to interpret the staring match between Kate and Shirl. Kate broke first, turning to Jack.

"A long way Jack. They have to come a long, long way," she finally said, dropping her eyes.

The cousins are coming. If Jack tried to bolt when they arrived, the stink of his panic would have all hell breaking loose. And no baker escapes from a croquembouche without fingers—or worse—burnt from toffee.

"You'll be fine without him, Kate. We won't be long, the kids'll cool off and we'll be back in time for lunch," Nana said. She shuffled over to the sink where Kate had started chopping broccoli. She put her crooked fingers on Kate's arm.

"I'll look after him. The day is young and I'm not dead yet. I'll need your help with the cousins. It's been too long, and they were very insistent. Someone must have told them you were coming."

Tears sprang into Kate's eyes. She put her knife down and hugged her Nana, breathing in the scent of talcum powder, feeling her Nana's paper thin skin and the stuttering connection to the aether.

How could I have left her to manage all this on her own?

Her Nana pushed her back and gazed into her eyes, love and light glistening in their chocolate depths.

"Like I said. I'm not dead yet. And it's only the cousins. No one has seen Great-Grandad B since your Mum passed."

Loaded with towels and hats, and slung with bags of chips and bottles of water the swimming troop trekked out the back door, setting the tiny cow bell jangling. No matter how many times she heard it, Kate still loved the tinkle of that bell. They put it up each year to announce the festive season's comings and goings. Its constant ringing was an integral part of Christmas from the first of December to the New Year.

"That bloody bell. I'm going to get rid of it, right now," Louise said as the bell clanged another burst of dissonance. "It's doing my head in."

A chorus of '*no*' greeted her from everyone present and they all laughed. Glasses were re-filled, and the preparations picked up a pace, people wove around each other in their annual festive dance. With no strangers present, the aether began to buzz, and everyone's edges blurred. Kate had been away from them all for so long. Yet this moment was more than familiar; it was a part of her, she was part of it. Despite how annoying her Family could be, she *had* missed them.

She let the festive magic drift under her skin.

Maybe it will all be fine. It's just the cousins.

***

The back garden hummed with heat, the roses and hydrangeas heavy and drooping on their stems, even the agapanthus' moptops sagged. Jack's nose crinkled with the rich floral fragrance and the underlying humid decay.

"It must use a lot of water to keep it looking so good," Jack said.

"I'll have to put the sprinkler on after lunch or I'll lose half the garden to this heat," Kate's Nana replied. She tucked a strand of silver hair behind her ear and adjusted her wide-brimmed straw hat.

Jack was hot and sticky, sweat sliding down his back. Perhaps he should have stayed in the house helping Kate. At least it was mildly cooler inside. He yearned for some of the energy the five kids were expending chasing each other around the abundant fruit trees that peppered the large backyard.

He was envious of the kids' camaraderie too. His own childhood had been a lonely affair. He'd always wanted to be part of a big family. At least his English diet of good manners helped him make connections with people quickly, particularly in the Antipodes where common courtesy was more hit and miss. Though burdened with three quarters of the kids towels and buckets for the trip to the dam he still asked, "Can I carry anything for you Mrs. Vizard?"

"No, I'm good. But you can stop calling me Mrs. Vizard. Nana will do," she smiled. "Unless your own Nana would object?"

Jack heard the query in her voice and shook his head. "No, no grandparents and only one parent left. Though Mum still lives in London," he explained, picking up and re-packing a plastic floatie that had fallen out of his collection.

"What's Kate told you about her Family Jack? Has she let you in on all our misfits and melodramas?" Nana asked.

"I don't think so," Jack responded politely, humouring the old lady. "She doesn't really talk about her Family much. She filled me in on the list of who's who on the way here, but that's about it."

"Well, you're in for a treat then. The Vizards are something special. Especially at Christmas."

Jack thought Nana's smile held a hint of mischief as she trailed after the whooping kids who were finally heading towards the back gate.

When they made it to the dam, the sun beat down mercilessly on their skin and the trees were too spindly to provide much shade. Jack scooped soil into the plastic bag and wound it around the bottom of the beach umbrella, though there was barely a breath of wind. The kids screeched as they flashed over the burning mud and charged into the water, shedding thongs and hats and t-shirts like a tree sheds its autumn leaves. Nana laughed at their antics, splashing and dunking each other.

"Be careful you lot," Jack warned, worried about the littler ones holding their own in the muddy water. His experience with child minding was all virtual, gleaned from movies and social media.

He shielded his eyes against the glare that skipped diamonds across the water. The dam was bigger than he'd expected, the size of a public swimming pool at least. A sprinkle of tall eucalypts marked the far shore and a scraggly line of wattles and native shrubs grew on this side. The trees around the dam were eaten up to stretching height by foraging cattle. Though behind the fence that led back to the garden, the flora was wild and overgrown. Nana had explained that in the winter, it was a briskly flowing creek. In summer only this dam remained and often by the end of January it was barely a wading puddle.

The kids were like a pod of dolphins swimming and diving around each other. Jack blinked. For a moment he almost thought he saw a dolphin, but that would be ridiculous this far inland, and in a freshwater pool.

Yikes, I need to slow down on the beers.

"Don't fuss Jack, they won't come to any harm in the water. They've got great instincts, they know their way home," Nana said, sitting down in her aluminium chair under the umbrella's shade.

Jack thought her response a little odd but put it down to advancing age and the glass of champagne he'd seen the woman scull before they left. His lack of social experience extended to older people.

His mind registered how bizarre it was to be wearing his shorts and a T-shirt on Christmas Day. Back home in England, he'd have layered up with coats and hats and gloves if he was outside. And he would've spent the morning shovelling snow off the path and loading wood onto the fire.

"It's a scorcher isn't it?" Nan said, seemingly reading his mind.

"I love the Aussie heat," he answered, turning to watch the tell-tale shimmer in the surrounding bush.

"Just as well. We need Kate at home. Her time for gallivanting all over the world is done. She's got things to learn here. Family things. I'm not going to be around forever."

Jack wasn't sure what to say to that, so he sat on a brightly coloured towel under the beach umbrella and opened the sunscreen to slather himself. Fair skin and southern sun, a fatal combination.

Today even the birds looked hot, a scatter of magpies on the shore furthest from the kids kept their feet cool in the waves, snapping and warbling at each other as they searched for a feed in the slimy mud. A single kookaburra flapped down to a low branch to eye the noisy occupants of the dam. Its raucous laughter erupted and Nana waved at the bird. The kookaburra bobbed its head and flew off.

"Old friend?" he asked.

Nana just smiled.

Suitably covered in sunscreen, Jack wandered down towards the water. Sweat popped all over his skin as soon as he left the shade, his feet crunched on yellow grass, and the dry smell of tea tree wafted towards him. The dirt dampened and his feet squelched into the gooey ochre mud of the bank.

"Watch out for yabbies," one of the kids yelled. Jack stepped back.

"And leeches," another laughed and did a backflip off the far bank, landing with an impressive splash.

Australia's reputation for being home to an overabundance of the world's most deadly fauna flashed into his mind. Jack decided discretion might be the better part of valour, and he headed back to wait under the brolly. There was only so much Jack was willing to sacrifice to ingratiate himself for his girlfriend. Being feasted on by leeches and yabbies seemed a step too far.

"Ouch!" Jack felt a stabbing pain in his foot. On inspection, a large black and red ant had a firm grip on his heel. He hopped on his other leg and flicked the offending insect off.

"Watch out for the Jumping Jacks," one of the younger kids said helpfully, "they really hurt."

Jack couldn't remember if an ant bite was life threatening. Though with his luck, he'd be allergic to it. He tended to be hypersensitive to all sorts of things.

Definitely time to retreat.

As he sat back on his towel and put his sandals back on, he glimpsed a movement, a shadow beside Nana. He turned to look —there was no one there. He glanced at Nana to see if she'd noticed and jumped to his feet. The woman's skin was grey, her eyes closed, and her arms hung lax at the sides of her chair.

"Nana, Nana, are you okay? Mrs Vizard! Can you hear me?" He patted at her soft cheeks, then lifted her hands back into her lap, pumping them up and down a few times. He held his palm in front of her mouth. She was still breathing —barely.

One of the older kids must have heard him shouting and wandered up to the umbrella.

"You have to go and get help. I think your Nana's sick," he said, trying not to panic the kid and still patting ineffectually at Nana's hand. He couldn't remember which kid this was. The introductions had been a madhouse.

"I'll mind her. You go," said the girl, the calm look in her honey brown eyes belied her young years. "You'll be faster. You've got longer legs. A bit skinny but," she added. They both peered at Jack's white hairy legs sticking out of his baggy board shorts. He glanced from the kid to her great-grandmother. The grey hue to the older woman's skin was turning a dusky blue and his stomach dropped.

Minutes mattered.

"I'll be back as soon as I can," Jack said, sprinting for the start of the path tucked in amongst the tea-tree.

Less than fifty metres into the bush, Jack realised his mistake. Every dusty shrub and curve of sandy soil looked exactly the same. He tried to retrace his steps to start again. Now he couldn't find the dam, the gate, or even the fence. He stopped to take a ragged breath and laid his hand on the scratchy bark of a tree.

"Ouch." As he pulled his hand away an ant half as long as his finger had another chomp.

"Freaking feral country," he growled, flicking the offending insect away. The bite stung like crazy, the insect's pincers still in his skin. He picked them out and sucked at his wound. So now he was twice bitten as well as lost—and the old lady was still dying.

"Shite!" He checked his watch. Surely someone would be coming down to call them back for lunch soon. They must've been at the dam for long enough. He threw his pride to the four winds and began to yell for help. His screams dropped into the scorching midday heat unanswered, menace brewing in the ensuing silence.

He swatted flies away as the sun broiled his brain. Somewhere in his frantic flight he'd forgotten to grab his hat—or had he lost it? It'd only taken them a few minutes to get to the dam in the first place, it shouldn't be this hard to find his way back to the house. Panic stalked his resolve.

Jack second guessed his decision to run for help. He should've stayed with Mrs Vizard or insisted one of the kids went; they'd know the way at least. What if the old woman died? The kids would be scarred forever, and it would be all his fault. Years of therapy ahead for them—and himself. What would Kate say?

Will she ever forgive me for killing her Nana?

He took a stab at a direction; anything was better than nothing. The way ahead rapidly gave up all pretence at calling itself a path. Jack felt like he was forging his way through virgin jungle, branches and insects attacking on all sides.

At least the air had cooled slightly under the shadows of the foliage.

Minutes later, he blundered into chilly water. One foot snagged on a twist of vine and he tumbled headfirst into the murk. It was unexpectedly deep, and he floundered around trying to orient himself, his mind full of leeches, yabbies and worse. Reaching for a tree root to drag himself out he glimpsed a pair of red eyes glaring at him from under a submerged shelf.

He didn't wait to find out who or what owned the eyes, adrenaline shot him to the surface. He floundered to the edge, heaved himself out of the water and took a few steps back. The pool was a dozen paces wide, twice as long, and edged with rocks and ferns, almost as though it had been built rather than born.

Billabong, it's a billabong.

His mind produced the odd name and registered the moist fecundity and tranquillity that swamped his senses and calmed his fears. Colourful water lilies peppered the surface, bobbing up and down in the wake of his escape. Strange odours assailed his nose, but his noisy breathing and pounding heart were the only things he could hear.

Nothing to be scared of here.

Jack took a deep breath and wiped the dripping water from his face. He didn't remember anyone mentioning this oasis, and he wondered if it connected to the other dam; part of the same creek system. His feet had sunk into mud up to his ankles and he eased back further, cursing at his luck as one of his sandals stayed where he'd stood.

Nana's grey face swarmed to the fore. He dragged out his sandal, fixed it on firmly and turned to retrace his steps. He took one more calming breath and felt the air crackle. The hair on the back of his neck stood to attention and he spun back to the billabong, water flying from his wet hair.

The surface bubbled, a small whirlpool forming in the centre. As the vortex grew, two glowing red eyes peered at him from the darkened depths. A grimace exposed long yellowed fangs and a thrusting grey tongue. A bone-chilling yowl reverberated from its throat as a black furred monstrosity began to rise.

Jack bolted.

After crashing through the bush for a dozen paces, he glanced back to see if the thing was following, but trees obscured his view. He twisted back the way he'd come and smacked into a branch directly in his path. The impact knocked him onto his butt. The back of his head hit the dirt, giving him a second bump to match the one now growing on his forehead. He groaned and knew he should get up, that thing was coming, and Mrs Vizard was dying, and the kids. The kids!

His limbs refused to obey.

His eyes closed.

All thought ceased.

***

When Jack came to, Kate's brothers were depositing him onto a bed in a cool dark room. Kate's worried face had swung into focus as she tried forcing some sugary tea down his throat.

"Wait Kate, your Nan and the kids, they're all alone and your Nana is sick, really sick." He stopped her as she moved in with the tea again. "Kate, I'm fine, but your Nana, she was turning blue and the kids are all alone." He tried to get up. She pushed him back onto the pillows. He grabbed her arms and shook her.

"Kate! There's a monster! It's out there at the bottom of a billabong I fell into. I saw its red eyes and yellow fangs and… and…" Jack trailed off as the terrifying images tumbled through his brain and his tongue tried to catch up.

A stunned silence greeted his announcement. When neither Kate nor her brothers moved into action, Jack hurried on. "It was huge and black and hairy with these red glowing eyes," a sob bubbled up his throat. "Kate, all the little kids. We need to get them. I'm so sorry I left them. I tried to find my way back, but I got lost. It all looked the same."

Kate shushed him.

"Jack, Nana is fine. She nodded off, that's all. She's back in the kitchen now giving orders. All the kids are fine too. Though grumbling that they had to carry all their stuff and yours back from the dam," Kate laughed. She waved Bob and Shaunie out of the room.

Jack struggled to make sense of it, his head pounding and his vision blurry. When he stared at Kate, he thought he saw something weird around her head, an odd spiky outline. His heart began to race again.

"What about the monster in the billabong? It might be still coming."

"There aren't any monsters here Jack," Kate said. He thought her voice sounded a little wistful—but that couldn't be right.

"Too much sun and beer combined with a bump on the head. Almost a perfect recipe for seeing a monster in the billabong." Kate ran her hands through Jack's hair, her tone sombre.

He closed his eyes and lay back then surged up again.

"Are you sure your Nana's all right?"

"Jack, she's fine, the Vizards are hard to kill. She's a little worried about you though. What were you thinking running off into the bush?" Kate wiped his dirty hair back from his forehead with a cool washer. "The kids said you got bitten by a Jumping Jack. Maybe you're allergic. You *are* allergic to lots of things. Is it possible you were hallucinating?"

Jack could tell Kate was trying to give him an out. His story sounded far-fetched even to himself.

"Kate, your Nana was grey and I couldn't wake her up. Then she was turning blue. I ran and got lost, then got bitten by a giant ant, and then I fell in the billabong. You never told me about the billabong. Then those eyes, those red eyes—they were coming for me." Jack's head felt fuzzy and the bumps fore and aft pounded at his brain. The ant bite on his hand began to throb in time with the one on his foot. He let his head drop back onto the pillow.

"I'm sure it's only the heat and beers messing with your head. You'd better lay off the grog for a bit," Kate said. She convinced him to swallow some painkillers and tried to insist he lay down for a while.

Jack felt embarrassed by his poor showing and refused to stay in bed. Kate tut-tutted as she cleaned the bumps and scratches, then bandaged small cold packs onto his head.

"You've already got your Christmas cracker crown," she laughed at him.

Jack's smile was a little forced, but he followed her directions to a chaise lounge at one end of the verandah. Kate wouldn't hear of him helping with any more preparations.

"Relax," she instructed, handing him a glass of iced tea. "And stay put. Catch forty winks if you can."

He hunkered down in his corner, his swirling stomach still trying to process all the adrenaline. Jack tried counting the kids to see if any were missing, but they moved around too much. He kept glancing towards the path that led to the dam, dreading seeing red eyes glaring at him from the shadows.

Amongst the background babble he picked out Nana's voice issuing orders in the kitchen. His gut settled a little and his shoulders dropped.

Maybe it was the ant bite.

Jack felt himself drifting but was too wound up to doze. He stood up to examine the luncheon tables, wincing a little at his aching head.

Red tablecloths gleamed with festive crockery, cutlery, and crackers. The centre piece of golden wattle and silver tinsel was woven into a spectacular wreath around a huge red candle. He blinked a few times, his focus just a little out. He could see sparkly dots dancing everywhere now.

Jack peered at the Vizard mob as they scurried about and squinted to clear his vision. As well as the dots, he kept seeing odd echoes of people, as though there was a shadow or a second person behind their face. Well, not a person really. Some of the shadows were like animals or birds, and some of the images were more disturbing; like something from an eighties schlock horror, with a hefty dose of bogan Aussie chucked in.

He grabbed onto the back of a chair, rubbed his eyes, and blinked a few times as Shirl cackled on her way into the house. Her disturbing outline faded as Kate walked past in the other direction. He watched as she dropped her baskets of fresh-baked bread rolls onto the tables and hurried back up the verandah steps. She patted his arm as he eased back and leant on a post.

"Are you okay, Jack? You shouldn't be on your feet." She peered into his eyes and seemed to come to a decision. "I think we'd better take you to the doctor. Come on. Let's go right now." Kate urged him towards the back door, but he baulked.

"What? Miss lunch after all this preparation and personal injury? No, we have to stay. We've come all this way and you haven't been home for ages. Your family would never forgive me."

"Nor me," Kate responded, her shoulders slumping. "I wish you hadn't fallen in the billabong," she added after a brief pause.

Jack couldn't quite make the connection and sought to reassure her. A few more hours and they could head back to the city, away from all the feral fauna and flora.

"A little the worse for wear is all. Nothing a good feed won't fix," he said.

Kate blanched. "Last chance. We could still make our excuses," she offered.

"Nah, I'm good. Really. I've just been seasoned by the locals to make me feel like I'm part of the family, that's all."

"You're not trying to take Jack away from us, are you little sis?" Shirl stepped close to Jack; her cleavage pressed into his arm. She glared at Kate, who glared right back and unwound Jack from Shirl's embrace.

When Kate didn't answer, Jack took a deep breath and pointed towards the tables under the trees.

"Why are you setting so many places? Are there more people coming?" he asked, watching Bob pull glasses from a cardboard box and pass them two at a time to a queue of kids who relayed them to the trestles.

"Apparently the cousins are coming—despite Shirl promising me they weren't," Kate said, scowling at her sister.

"Oh yeah, only half the party are here so far." Shirl laughed as she headed to the table with another load of festive fare.

Jack nodded and smiled, not sure if he was missing something because of the bump on his head. Shirl's laughter sounded exactly like the kookaburra he'd heard earlier down by the dam. And when she bobbed her head at him, she'd reminded him even more of the bird he'd seen bobbing at Nana. He reached to his head and felt the bandages. His cheeks flushed with embarrassment.

He took another deep breath and finished off his iced tea. The delicious aromas from the kitchen competed with the fragrant garden, and Jack felt his stomach rumble. He hoped lunch would be served soon. The growing tension between Kate and her sister made him increasingly uncomfortable. The brilliant day that had started like a fresh-baked croissant now seemed more like week-old bread, stale and mouldy in places. He reminded himself a few hours was a small sacrifice.

With four laden trestles waiting, the family had begun to congregate on the back verandah and around the yard, a palpable air of excitement thrumming through the mob. Jack felt Kate's hand steal into his. He smiled down at her. Her brown eyes were worried. He put his arm around her shoulder.

"Are *you* OK?" he asked as Kate hugged him.

"Yeah, I'm more worried about you after your misadventures. My Family can be a bit full on at the best of times, but Christmas makes them worse," Kate said. She paused, her eyes searching his. "And I need you at your best."

Jack could see her gathering herself. "Jack, I need to tell you something about my Family. We have this Secret. It makes us different. And not everyone gets it," she began. "It's hard to be different Here."

"Your family can't be too bad if you're any indication," Jack said, planting a kiss on her nose. "I'm open-minded, remember. No skeletons I can't manage."

She stared at him as though she were trying to see through his skin.

"I hope you're right. Some of us can get a little prickly about our Secret," she muttered. For an instant Jack felt as though his arm rested on a thorny bush rather than Kate's soft skin. He pulled his arm away and blinked. Kate's nose had… no it couldn't possibly have. He wrapped his arms around her again, feeling only warm woman.

***

Kate steered Jack back to a chair and headed in to gather the final dishes. She had no idea how she was going to explain the arrival of her cousins. Nana beckoned to her as she entered the kitchen.

"Time for a chat," Nana announced.

"Ooh, you're in trouble," Shirl sniggered.

Kate ignored her. Her throat caught at the sympathetic glances she got from Maureen and Louise.

Time for a decision. Family or fella?

"Surely it's not that hard Kate?" Nana plopped down onto the couch and patted the spot beside her. "Family comes First. Especially at Christmas. And you know this is not only for us. Peace on earth comes at a price. Haven't you been watching the news, the escalating violence, the earth herself rebelling; trying to shrug humanity off her skin with earthquakes, floods, and cyclones. Something has to be done to keep the balance. A sacrifice has to be made. You know it takes enormous amounts of energy from him to hold it all together." She paused. "That's if he comes. If we get the opportunity. It may be too late to stop the dissolution of all life as we know it."

"He might not come?" Kate ignored the portent of disaster and tried not to sound hopeful as she sat down next to her Nana.

"Is this young man worth that much to you?" Nana asked. "You know the Family might drive you crazy at times, but they will always be there for you, regardless. Blood Will Out."

Kate leant forward, her dark curls hiding her face.

"Is your Jack up for that?"

"He saw the sparkles Nan. Doesn't that work in his favour? If he can see aetheric spirits, couldn't he be one of us? Maybe his blood has been too diluted. Or the gift skipped a generation." Kate knew she was grasping at straws.

Nana tucked Kate's hair behind her ear. "You know what it means when a human can see the aetheric sparkles."

Kate's shoulders slumped.

"Take a moment to think about it. At least you can help me let the cousins in. The last few years I haven't been able to manage it on my own. I'd like to see them all again before I go."

Kate looked up, the blood draining from her face. "Oh Nan, no. Not yet. I thought you'd be around for ages."

Nana smiled. "This is my last Christmas Kate." She stood, brushed aside Kate's tears, kissed her on the forehead, and headed out to join the melee.

***

Nana stood at the bottom of the steps and shooed the rest of the Family onto the verandah behind her. Once the last kid had been corralled by an adult, she turned and examined her mob. A smile tugged at her lips as she gestured to Kate who'd come out to stand beside Jack.

"It's time Kate. Family comes First. Especially at Christmas," she said.

Kate opened her senses —all of them. She could feel everyone looking at her, waiting, hopeful, their forms blurring.

"And Blood Will Out," she said. Her words drew a collective sigh from her Family and a frown from Jack. She wove her way through the crowd to stand at her Nana's side.

"Happy Christmas lovelies," Nana said and turned her back on them. She moved a few paces into the back garden away from the tables, drawing Kate along in her wake. She peered at Kate, taking her in. Whatever Nana saw, it obviously satisfied her.

Nana gave Kate a small smile and raised both her arms towards her granddaughter. Kate raised her arms in a mirror of Nana's stance, creating an arch. When their fingers touched, it seemed as if the sunlight burned a path directly into their hands.

Kate felt the aether tremble, its seductive energy thrumming through her arms, into her body and down to her feet. She and Nana clasped one pair of their hands and dropped the other towards the ground. Their index fingers of their free hands pointed at the earth and they turned their backs on each other. They began to rotate slowly, moving their fingers as though they were painting a line on the grass. When the circle was complete, Kate re-joined her other hand with her Nana.

The penultimate step.

No going back after this.

She let her aetheric connection form and she *shimmered*. Her spines emerged and thickened, and her nose lengthened. Releasing the frenzy from its constraints felt deliciously wild and freeing. A quick glance at the verandah showed her Jack with his mouth in a grimace, his brow furrowed, shaking his head. All around him, Vizards began loosing their Secret.

Too late now Jack. You're in for the full Monty.

Her Nana's soft brown eyes sparkled, she nodded as her ears lengthened and her own body began to *shimmer*.

They kept their paws high as they transformed. A blazing ball of white light sprang into life between the human-sized echidna and wallaby. Both beings threw their heads back and arms wide. The bright sphere leapt into the air and widened into a blazing ring. Within the white corona, an emerald mist writhed and curled. Kate felt a mix of pride and relief that they'd been able to summon the Portal.

The Vizard Family walked, hopped, flew, and waddled down towards Nana and Kate.

Shirl pushed a stunned Jack to sit on the top step. "Better sit this one out Jack. Your turn will come later." She chortled again and *shimmered* back and forth between kookaburra and human.

Once the Family had formed a guard of honour, Nana hopped to the centre of the Portal. She hesitated, nodded to Kate, and hopped back. Kate took her grandmother's place and raised her paws towards the mist. Jagged lightning flickered in the cloudless Aussie sunshine, thunder boomed, the Portal darkened—and bulged. Finally, an enormous black feathered wing tip emerged.

The Vizard cousins were on their way.

***

Kate put a finger under Jack's chin and closed his mouth.

"I told you it was big. That we were different."

"Who are they, what are they?" Jack stammered. "What are you?" He backed away from her hand.

"Don't be impolite Jackie boy. I was just warming up to you." Bob, who moments ago had been an enormous wombat, gave him a hearty slap on the back. "Come and meet Kate's cousins."

"Cousins!" Jack's wild eyes swung from Kate to the menagerie on the lawn.

"They're not from around here," Kate said quietly.

Jack's horror was etched on his face and evident in his revulsion at her touch. "No shit Sherlock. I got that bit," he said, his voice rising to a screech. "Where the hell are they—you—from?"

Kate folded her arms; he was fast losing her vote. That was the problem with some nerdy types. The real world was a bit too raw for them.

Let's try a little bald truth and see how he goes. He did remind me he was open-minded.

"Elsewhere. They're from Elsewhere. We only get to see each other at Christmas," Kate began. She could see Jack's mouth forming the word '*Elsewhere*'. "Nana's been the only one strong enough to open the Portal properly over the last fifty years since her Mum died. We have to be careful, there are things in Elsewhere that shouldn't see the light of day in Here. If we don't make it right, we could be letting in all sorts of riff-raff."

Jack's face paled further and Kate pushed him into a chair before he collapsed.

Louise brought out a beer and passed it to Jack. He put it straight on the table.

"No. I need to keep my head clear. I need answers. How can they be cousins? They're not… not human," Jack said. When Kate didn't respond he turned from staring at the weird creatures still emerging through the Portal and glared at her.

"Well?" he prompted.

"Neither am I Jack. That's the Vizard Family Christmas Secret."

Jack stepped back, his mouth an '*O*' of horror. "I thought the bump, my eyes, the heat, hallucinating…" His face was slack fumbling for a sensible explanation. A realisation saw that look evaporate and disgust take its place.

"We're not human Jack. Not at Christmas. Well, not fully at least. It's hard to explain. I s'pose you could call us interdimensional expats. And once a year we do our bit for peace on earth," Kate said.

"I don't understand." Jack was shaking his head.

"Well, we like it Here."

"So?" Jack queried.

"So we want to stay. And being a bitza, means we can. Nan was the first bitza by the way."

"Bitza?" Jack asked.

"Bitza this and bitza that. You know, mongrels, Heinz variety. It means we can *shimmer* from one form to the other, especially at Christmas when we're all together." Kate shrugged. "Nana's mother was human but quirky, and her father," Kate shrugged again. "Well, her father was…"

"Nan's father is an Aussie legend. That's who he *is*," Shirl interjected on her way up the stairs, tucked arm in arm with what looked like a giant goanna. Jack stepped back as the goanna *shimmered* into a wizened old man and gave him a ghastly grin, his long blue tongue darting from his human mouth.

Jack swallowed a few times then turned back to Kate. He ran his hands over his face and gathered himself for another question.

"Was? Is? He's not still alive is he?" Jack glanced at Nana; her silver hair wild as she welcomed more strange creatures through the portal. He stared at Kate. "Wouldn't that make him ancient?"

"Yep, old as the hills is Great-Grandad B. Doesn't move far from home these days," Shirl chuckled, heading back down the stairs to retrieve another cousin.

Kate gave her sister an exasperated look. "Anyway, that's why we can open the Portal between realms. At least at Christmas. It's something about all the Christmas cheer that softens the barriers. That's why we all gather. But Jack, Nana's fading. She finds her other form easier these days. It's hard for her to keep her human body intact. That's what began to happen at the dam when you thought she was dying."

"And that's why we haven't been able to open the Portal for three years. The gift only gets passed to one female in each generation. After our Mum died, that became my annoying little sister," said Shirl, now traipsing back up the stairs with an oversized red-tailed black cockatoo perched on her shoulder. "Kate's the new Portal Door Bitch."

Jack rubbed his temples, trying to make sense of what was happening.

"Not quite Jingle Bells, eggnog and snowmen are we," Kate said. "You could say my Family turn into real animals at Christmas." She'd tried for levity, Jack missed it completely, his mouth slackening as he watched the eclectic parade of beings, his questions drying up.

Louise and Maureen encouraged everyone to be seated. As the cousins approached the table, they *shimmered* to human. It was much easier to use the cutlery and pull the crackers that way. And though Kate—and likely Jack—could see hints of the creatures they'd been, now they'd pass for human, mostly. There was the odd feathered crest in a paper crown or taloned paw reaching for a roast potato.

Kate steered Jack into a seat at the table and sat down next to him. "You don't mind, do you Jack? Knowing our Secret?" She reached for his hand.

"Mind!" He flinched from her touch.

Going, thought Kate.

"Ugh, that's disgusting," he grimaced as something large and green, looking vaguely like an enormous frog, slithered and slurped its way through the Portal. Bob passed one of the kids a towel from a stack on one of the chairs and they chased after their slimy cousin.

Going. Arthur was one of Kate's favourite relations.

"That means when you and I have… that I've been sleeping with an… animal?" Jack looked like he was going to throw up.

Gone.

The Family chatter went on around them. Kate watched disgruntled as Jack's face went through a panoply of emotions until it settled finally on what looked like suspicion.

"Who's missing?" He asked.

"What?"

"Who's the last chair for?" Jack indicated the vacant place at the head of their table.

Kate shook her head, exasperated at his apparent priorities.

Why would he notice that with everything else going on? Why wouldn't he notice how much he's hurt my feelings?

"Oh, that's Great-Grandad's chair," Shaunie said as he sat down opposite Jack.

Jack's mouth formed an *'O'* again.

"He doesn't always come, but we keep a place for him just in case," said Bob from further down the table.

"We haven't seen him since the year Mum died Kate," Maureen added.

"Don't worry, Jack. You'll know if he arrives. Always likes to make a grand entrance does Great-Grandad B. He's a bit of a showman," Shirl cackled.

Kate wasn't sure Jack could take another show. In fact, she wasn't sure if he could take another minute. As an only child, this much Family was pushing his boundaries, even before it had gotten weird.

She turned towards the haze of the Portal feeling Nana placing a faint X there once the last relation had come through. She swung back to see Jack reach for his glass of beer and down it in a single go.

Maureen and Louise edged past him with an enormous white china platter. Though it was empty it needed both of them to carry it. The crowd oohed and aahed when it arrived and there was a great shuffle to make room for it in front of the empty place set for Great-Grandad.

"What's that for? Another family tradition? Another Vizard Family Secret?" Jack's tone was tense.

"It's Great-Grandad's plate. He has a special diet. Only eats once a year—at Christmas. But it keeps peace on earth," Kate explained.

"What is he, your Great-Grandad?" Jack whispered; his eyes wide.

"Bunyip," Kate said.

"So what's on a bunyip's menu?" Jack asked.

Kate grasped both his hands in hers, leant close and kissed him firmly on the lips before he could pull away. A few wolf whistles and yahoos accompanied the kiss.

"There's still a little bit of me that wishes it wasn't," she said, "but it's…"

Jack felt fiery breath on the back of his neck.

He turned.

Two familiar red eyes glared down at him from a hideous face bristling with black wiry fur. The monster's mouth opened in a gross parody of a grin.

"You," said Kate.

***

The huge white platter held only scraps. Everyone had been given their share after Great-Grandad had taken his fill.

All bar Kate.

Most of the kids had left the table to settle inside around the tree with Nana and Great-Grandad as they launched into the first of the Christmas stories, the kids mostly waiting for pressie time.

"Aren't you eating?" Shirl asked, sliding the last piece of cheesecake onto her plate. "Don't tell me you're feeling all woosie about Jack. He was fair game after he blundered into the billabong and woke Great-Grandad up. Keeping peace on earth requires some sacrifice you know."

"I know. I know. It's just, well… I'm sure it wasn't quite what Jack expected when I asked him to come for Christmas lunch," Kate said, her eyes moistening. She held up her hands as Shirl went to protest. "Yes, he was grossed out about the Secret. He and I were over, even without Great-Grandad. Family comes First. Especially at Christmas. And Blood Will Out."

Her eyes roved the scraps, and she sighed wondering how she was going to explain Jack's disappearance to his mother.

"Blood Will Out," Shirl agreed. "Besides, he was very tasty. I knew as soon as he admitted seeing the sparkly dots that he'd have just the right amount of fear and adrenaline from seeing our Secret to make him luscious." Shirl licked her fingers.

"No, it's not that."

"Well, what's got your knickers in a twist? It's about time you had to throw a partner Great-Grandad's way," Shirl pouted. "Well?"

"It's hard, living apart from Family; awkward. I wanted to fit in. So, I've been a real vegetarian for three years," Kate said.

Shirl choked and spat her mouthful of cheesecake all over the table.

"But Shirl, you don't understand. I'll feel like I've failed if I give in and eat meat."

"You are hilarious," Shirl guffawed, *shimmering* back and forth between her human and avian forms. When Kate's eyes teared up, Shirl sobered and pushed the platter closer.

"Actually, there's almost no flesh on the fingers. I don't think they really count as meat," she stated.

Kate let the reek of seared blood and bone stir her Secret. She *shimmered* and reached for Jack's pinky; the skin singed to a perfect toffee glaze by Great-Grandad.

"I suppose just one wouldn't hurt."

She stuffed the finger into her mouth and crunched. Her eyes closed in ecstasy.

"Oh Jack, I was right. You *are* delicious."

***

About V.E. Patton

V. E. Patton spent as much of her childhood as she could lost in a good book. She spent most of her adult life lost in a good job as a nurse, midwife, CEO, coach and facilitator (amongst other things). After years of encouraging her children and clients to follow their dreams, she finally got around to remembering what she wanted to be when she grew up – so at fifty-five she began writing.

Ochre Dragon: The Opal Dreaming Chronicles Book 1, was her first fantasy (in a book). She hopes you get lost in it – and Book 2 Soul Staff, which should be out early in the new year.

Her alter ego Veronica Strachan has a children's book written with her illustrator daughter Cassi – Chickabella and the Rainbow Magic, as well as a memoir Breathing While Drowning: One Woman's Quest for Wholeness.

She really is a vegetarian by the way and lives in central Victoria, Australia with her ever-patient husband, one of her three adult children and a menagerie of animals (none of the animals turn into people at Christmas though).

You can find more of her stories and books, and sign up for an occasional newsletter at www.veronicastrachan.com.au

Epica Intermission

There were great friendships and even greater enemies made down in the stifling bowels of the ship whence our journey began. The rules of life change you see, and with this change comes too, a new and formidably corrupt world to test one's ability to survive.

Convicts are a motley lot on the best of days and this ship's fill was no different. Vagabonds and thieves mainly, but also a scattering of sinister men with souls burning from secrets who chose silence as their trick. Still, a common need can bring together even the most distant brother and sister, and so it was that on a Christmas Eve that marked the whispers of landfall any day our motley crew of convicts determined to stage a mutiny.

Men, women, and children, regardless of the sickness and exhaustion, thundered out from below in a show of unity that would have made the King himself proud. With the continent visible by eye, the tyrants in uniform must have been preoccupied with the idea of real food and solid drink, for they were in every way unprepared for the sudden skin and bones army that swarmed the decks and stripped away the sharp blades of power. I can look you in the eyes right now friend and tell you 'twas mayhem, but as for who emerged victorious remains a result I'll always yearn to know. You see, deep in the scrabble for the chance to become masters of their own destiny, I suffered a shocking hit to the head that was quick to terminate any future memory. When I did finally awake, all was as you see now.

Just a moment, there's another glowing gift rising. Well, I'll be. I guess this will truly be a treat, for judging by the scrolled ink we're in for a real chain rattler! Allegiance sure does test the direction of one's spirit…

Secret Santa

By Belinda Grant

Dedicated to Barbara Clarke, my Mum

The Milky Way sparkles like silver tinsel as we make our way along the causeway towards the storage section of the Claudius.

I don't know if it counts as December 25th when we're no longer circling our Sun. It should feel like any other day. But it doesn't.

My steps slow, and I rub sweaty hands along the pant legs of my coveralls.

"Mary?" Nick slows his own steps, placing his hand upon my shoulder, his gorgeous pine-green eyes scanning my features. I never need to explain what I'm thinking to Nick, he reads me like a book.

"It's just a day. We just need to stay in our lane, okay?"

The warmth and care in his voice still takes my breath away. I nod, but I can't help glancing at the array of silver badges glittering across his chest. Can you get that many commendations from the Admiral for playing it safe?

Dangerous thoughts. I distract myself with a question. "Why did they keep it all?"

"For repurposing I guess? Don't want to throw away something you can reuse later; we have to make do with what we brought until we arrive at the new planet."

"Who do you think'll be celebrating?"

"Does it matter?"

It scares me that he can ask that question.

We continue to walk. My hand brushes my sidearm and I flinch. Sixteen feels too young to wield it; the weapon is one more reminder of how far I am from home. I breathe in and out, and listen to the humming of the engine. It's only been six months since I was defrosted, but already I barely notice the sound. It fades into the background the way that bird songs once did. Nick reaches for my hand. He is warm and steady, and I imagine a current running between us; love and trust flashing along our limbs. I chew on my cheek, repeating in my mind: "Just a day. Just a day." I have to do this. Maybe not for the Admiral, or because I believe in the ban. But for Nick.

He's all I have left.

We slow as we enter the storage wing. No more talking, Nick directs me with his hand pointing. Left, right, right, left. Music swells towards us. A deep baritone singing of snow.

The sound shouldn't move me, knowing what I must do. But the tune seeps through my soul, to old memories of kneeling under a tree by candlelight, Mum's voice harmonising to Mariah and Bublé. That tinge of anticipation, the warmth of familiarity. Love as tangible as the boots on my feet.

It pours out from behind a storage room door. Nick blows me a silent kiss, for once unaware of my churning feelings. We draw our guns and raise them as I hit the green button with my elbow. The door slides across with a hiss.

The room is filled with twinkling lights and plastic trees. Buddha statues and menorahs. And faces transitioning from joy to horror.

Chatter stops, a glass of mulled wine hits the floor. The air is thick with cinnamon and citrus.

"Put your hands up and nobody gets hurt," I call over the music. A lie. There's a world of pain in store for anyone caught here.

Nick marches forward, gun swinging across the gathered revellers. "You've breeched religious-observance ban of '55. You're all under arrest. Approach Agent Jones to have your mag-cuffs activated." Nick's voice is steady and strong, and venom runs below it. When did he start believing?

Between the plastic trees and neon reindeer are so many people from my batch. Belle, Ali, Meera, Gabe. Friends who I sat beside as we cried for what had happened while we slept.

I look to Nick and he raises his eyebrows. I can read him back. *Do they matter more than your safety? More than me?*

I steady my gun.

"Please Mary," calls Belle, her voice soprano high. Her face is creased with hopelessness. She knows I'll choose Nick every time.

Then I see it. A dented copper angel on the top of the tree. Memories flash.

Mum. Bopping in the kitchen, her sundress dancing around her hips. A prawn dipped in pink sauce in one hand as she stirs the gravy with the other. I'm sitting on the stool, I know I should be helping, but I'm too angry. How can she dance, how can she act like it's Christmas without Dad?

She turns and sees my face.

There is just a wink of hurt before it's gone. She puts down her spoon and reaches across the bench to touch my face.

"He's gone. It hurts me too. But it's Christmas and we're still a family. You and me. Always."

I nod and reach for my own prawn. We tap them together for cheers and a sprinkling of pink goo flickers across our dresses. And we laugh for the first time since he left.

Then forward to when they brought me her belongings.

I'm red and raw and cracked in a million pieces and Nick's familiar voice is all that is keeping me together. I run my hand over her things: books and clothes, and a dozen framed photos of us, eyes glowing with the real light of our own sun. A million years from the hell I've woken up to.

Nick's voice echoes in the dorm along with the then unfamiliar hum of the ship.

"They defrosted the parents in '55, I guess they wanted them to settle into the ship, get their quarters ready before they woke their kids. But that was when the military council decided to impose their religion ban. Your Mum sided with the protestor." Nick blinks, the words catching in his throat. "Things got violent. Admiral thought it would be better to wake those who lost their parents after peace was achieved."

As I listen to his voice, I feel something cold and metallic at the base of the bag. A little angel ornament from our tree. Contraband in this new world. Why had she saved it?

Then Nick leans over and strokes my cheek. "I won't let that happen to you, I promise. Let's just stay in our lane and we'll be safe, okay?" And he reaches for my hand and looks at me with those eyes and I push the angel back under her clothes and try in my fear and pain to believe him.

The record moves to the next song and I'm brought back to the present as organ music floods the storage room.

I see Ali inching back, but he's no soldier and it's too obvious that something's hidden behind the biggest tree.

"Don't move." Nick's gun rises higher, and the group look at each other with fists forming. My own gun shakes like a bell.

My heart is in my mouth as I switch it to stun mode. The trigger is cold against my finger. Stacatto breaths bust through my lips. I blink my eyes and steady my hand.

I shoot Nick.

There's talking and movement, but it fades like a dream and all I see is Nick, collapsing to the ground.

I drop down to my knees and I'm crying and touching his clammy face and he will never, ever, ever forgive me.

Then I look up at them all, eyes wide with shock. Meera recovers first, putting out her hand to bring me to my feet. "Thank you, Mary."

Regret and uncertainty crest around me.

Joe steps forward and pulls me into a hug. His breath smells of peppermint. "Welcome to the Secret Santas."

I take a few breaths, and let the old hymn calm my nerves. I've chosen my new lane. It better be worth it. "I assume this isn't just a party?"

Belle goes to the biggest tree, pushing it aside to show a gathering of weapons where the presents should be. "This isn't about one day. It's time to finish what our parents started. Her eyes fill with tears but her voice is steady. "To fight for what they died for."

I keep my eyes averted from Nick as someone ties him up and claims his weapon.

"Are you in, Mary?" Ali asks, but the whole group is watching. Waiting

I look at the angel on the tree and can almost hear Mum's alto voice rising out of the choir's harmonies.

I reload my weapon and nod my head. "Ho Ho Ho."

***

About Belinda Grant

Belinda Grant is a writer of Fantasy novels and mostly Sci-Fi short stories. She adores Speculative Fiction for its ability to pull us out of the world we know, but to also give us a new perspective on it. She has been short listed in the AWC Furious Fiction competition, and when not writing, looks after four kids, (who seem to have all inherited Mum's elaborate imagination). Christmas is trapped in a bitter war with Spring for the title of her favourite time of the year.

Epica Intermission

You may think I'm a scoundrel missing even the simplest of manners, but I haven't yet offered you a rum due to the small matter of the barrels being empty. Can you imagine endless nights on a ship like this without so much as a drop of fortified spirit? It can drive a convict mad I tell you, but then until your arrival madness was the only company I had while counting the stars over and over again.

A purple bottle this time, and thankfully it comes with nothing beneath it hungry for my arm! Now, should the galley hold stores or the barrels sweet rum, you can be assured the greatest of hospitality would have been extended in honour of your presence, but alas my temporary company and sharing of Christmas whispers is all I have to offer. But then, who needs food and drink when from the depths come such wonderful moments of imagination?

So let us see what imagination brings thee. Perhaps you might place this bottle with the others while I unravel these delicate papers? Ooh, I sense something very interesting for us both here. Considering we are merely strangers crossing paths in a galaxy full of riddles, this story will surely provide food for thought…

Christmas Bells

By Lyn Webster

For Ken, Ethan, and Megan, the first readers of
my stories and still the most important.

Sara was crossing the last field when she spotted the flash of red among the tall grasses in the ditch. She hadn't been to this spot before. Although she visited the forest often, she usually walked the longer way around, following the road. Today, with the midday sun beating down, she'd taken a shortcut across the grain fields.

Drawn to that jubilant scarlet, she veered off to the edge of the long, shallow gully that ran alongside the field. Grass and weeds clothed the bottom and sides, lush and green, refreshing after the bleached growth that bordered the road. Moisture lingered in the long depression, despite the dry summer.

And from among the chorus of green, that clear red sang out, an irresistible invitation to the gardener who still lived inside her, even now. Even here.

As eagerly as a child, she half-slid down the low bank. There it was: a cluster of small narrow bells, hanging from the top of a thin, wiry stalk, half-veiled by grass. There were more of them, scattered over the floor of the ditch and halfway up the sides. A whole colony of glowing red bells, hidden down here, waiting to be discovered.

She moved closer, pushing aside the blades of grass to reach the first cluster. Fully revealed, it stopped her in her tracks. Her pulse quickened as she recognised the narrow band of yellow encircling the delicately fluted lip of each flower. Heart pounding, she checked the narrow, grassy leaves at the base, the finely arched red stems holding each bell, the tips of the dark anthers showing below the golden edging. There was no room for doubt in her mind. She knew these plants.

She'd searched them out each December for the past three years - ever since she'd moved to the village of Wattleford, at the age of twenty-three, to start her gardening business. Tucked safely away in the deep gullies and damp rock crevices of the summer-baked mountains near her new home, they'd flamed like beacons of hope for the future. They were fragile, endangered, and the emergence of each new clump had been a source of joy to her.

Her botany lecturer back at university had called them *Blandfordia*. To Sara they would always be Christmas Bells. Australian Christmas Bells.

***

A wave of homesickness broke over her, strong enough to leave nausea in its wake. She sank down in the bottom of the ditch under the blazing sun - the wrong sun, even if it did look exactly the same - and bent her head over her drawn up knees, sucking in breath after breath, fighting for control.

She'd never broken down like this in all the months she'd been living in Algarth, not even on that first, terrifying day. And she'd had more than enough reason to fall apart back then. One moment, she'd been sitting in a back garden in Wattleford, and the next, she'd been transported -

somehow - to a forest in a whole different world. A world that looked a lot like the one she'd come from, with blue sky and a yellow sun and plants and animals she recognised: oak trees and birches, sheep, deer and cattle, chickens and blackbirds. And human beings, even if their level of technology was more mediaeval than modern, supplemented by a system of magic that proved she was no longer in the universe she knew.

She'd coped with all of that, and she was still coping with it, every day. It was just that nothing she'd seen until now had reminded her so acutely, so painfully, of home as these unmistakeably Australian plants, the precious Christmas Bells that owned a piece of her heart.

Tears dripped through her fingers and fell onto the coarse fabric of her work dress. The sun began to sting the back of her neck - she'd forgotten her hat again. She stood, feeling light-headed and still faintly sick.

As she raised her head, the bells drew her gaze once more. The pitiless light dazzled her tear-filled eyes, transforming the view into a mad, alien kaleidoscope of green and red. No comfort for her there. No comfort anywhere in this place.

Swiping the tears away and fixing her eyes firmly on her dusty boots, she made her way across the floor of the gully and up the opposite slope. If a bold flash of red shouted for attention from the corner of her vision, she ignored it.

She spent some time wandering in the forest, her thoughts as dark as the shadows beneath the dense canopy. Despite the heat, she took the long way back to the farmhouse, via the road.

***

She woke the next morning to rain drumming on the roof and pouring down the windows. Mena was alone in the dining room, her auburn head bent over a steaming plate of eggs and ham. She looked up with a smile as Sara entered, the fine wrinkles crinkling at the corners of her smoky grey eyes, and welcomed her as warmly as she did every morning. Sara returned the older woman's greeting and filled a plate for herself at the sideboard.

A loud banging erupted from the direction of the kitchen. Mena jumped up and hurried out. Sara abandoned her own breakfast and followed.

The rain slashed in as Mena opened the door to admit the bulky figure of a man. He backed into the room, his head and shoulders bowed forward over something he was carrying. As he cleared the doorway, Sara recognised the still form of a young girl, maybe fifteen or sixteen years old. The first man was gripping the limp figure under the arms and another had her ankles. Water sheeted off all three of them and puddled on the stone flags of the floor.

"What's happened?" Mena stepped forward.

"Drowning," the second man grunted. "River's up. You the Folk Healer?"

Mena nodded. She bent to the girl and felt for a pulse. "She's alive. Bring her into the parlour." She turned and led the way.

As the men were settling the unconscious girl on the long couch in front of the fireplace, Sara turned to Mena. "What can I do?"

"Get blankets. We need to warm her up."

When she returned with her arms full of the soft woollen blankets, the men had gone. Mena was kneeling on the hearth, laying an unseasonal fire. Sara began tucking the covers gently around the patient.

The teenager's eyes were closed and her lips were blue. Sara couldn't detect any movement of her chest to indicate breathing. She might have believed the girl was dead, if not for Mena's reassurance. Mena knew what she was doing. Healing was her magical ability, her *skal*. It was how they'd met, all those months ago.

Trudging through the forest, confused and afraid, Sara had been accidentally shot in the arm with an arrow. She'd been brought to Mena, just as this girl had, and the Healer had not only treated her wound, but invited her to stay and help out on the farm. Back then, Sara hadn't expected she'd be here long. In this world of magic, she'd been hopeful of finding someone with the ability to send her home the way she'd come. But in all this time she'd never met anyone who could mystically transport the smallest object from one place to another, let alone whisk a person out of their own world and into a different one. Even worse, no one she'd questioned had ever heard of a *skal* like that.

She might have to accept she was stuck here for the rest of her life. It wasn't a bad place, but it wasn't hers. It never would be.

Enveloped in layers of fluffy cream wool, the teenager's face looked tiny and vulnerable. Sara stroked the dark strands of wet hair back from the pale forehead. A tear leaked from one of her eyes and dropped onto the girl's cheek. Sara wiped it away with a corner of blanket. *I wish you better luck than I've had in finding your way home.*

Mena lit the fire and joined them. She took the girl's pulse again, then knelt beside the couch, placed her hands on either side of her patient's head and bowed her own. After a few moments, she sat back on her heels, frowning slightly.

Sara peered at the still face, trying to detect any change. Had a slight touch of pink appeared in her cheeks? Or was that wishful thinking?

Mena leaned forward again and placed her palms over the girl's thickly wrapped chest, then, after a moment, her abdomen. This time, she stared intently off into space, as if her cloudy eyes were seeing things invisible to Sara. Or perhaps she was listening to something only she could hear.

When the Healer removed her hands this time, the girl gave a deep sigh. Her chest rose and fell with each raspy breath she took. Mena's intent face relaxed, although the hint of a frown remained in the tiny crease between her brows.

"Will she be all right?" Sara asked.

Mena nodded. "All she needs now is rest and warmth. Thank Aal, they got to her in time."

Despite the positive nature of the words, Sara thought she heard a trace of concern in Mena's voice. And there was that tiny frown, still lingering.

"Are you sure?" she asked.

Mena nodded again, and her expression smoothed into its usual placidity. "She'll wake in an hour or two, when she's ready." She rose briskly to her feet. "We should go and finish our breakfast. No sense letting the food go to waste."

This pronouncement was so like Mena that, even in her present mood, Sara couldn't help smiling. One minute, the woman was miraculously dealing with life and death, the next, she was concerned about a few eggs and slices of ham.

Over their cold and not very appetising breakfast, Sara reflected that it was only she who thought of Mena's *skal* as miraculous. To Mena herself, it was just another part of her, like the enhanced Strength displayed by some of the farm hands, the blacksmith's Metal Shaping, or the Beast Speaking that allowed the stable master to communicate with his charges.

None of them had been born with their *skals*. The abilities appeared in the years between eighteen and thirty-five. If Sara had belonged in this world, she might have some wonderful power of her own by now. But Algarth wasn't her world and she was never going to manifest any *skal* - yet another reminder, as if she needed one, that this place would never be home.

The bright memory of the red and yellow bells standing proudly in the ditch flashed into her mind, and homesickness jolted through her again.

She shook her head angrily to dispel the vision and the feelings it invoked. Mena shot her an interrogatory glance.

"It's nothing," Sara said, her voice rough from the effort of controlling her emotion. She had to stop thinking about her old life; it only made everything worse. From now on, if she wanted to visit the forest, she'd stick to the road.

After they'd cleared the table, Sara made to leave the room, intending to get on with some mending she'd been putting off for too long already. Mending should be safe enough - nothing emotional about mending.

Mena stopped her. "Wait a minute, come and look at what I found on my ride yesterday."

Sara followed her into the pantry. And there they were, a whole bucketful of them, glowing like a patch of flame. All the misery of yesterday rushed over her as she stared at the Christmas Bells.

Mena was speaking. Sara forced herself to concentrate on the words.

"Country people call them Harvest Bells, because they predict a good season to come. Some years there are few blooms and the harvest is poor." She smiled, gazing at the display. "I've never seen so many flowering together in one place. Right along both banks of the stream. I picked all these and there were still hundreds left."

Sara cast about for something - anything - to say in response to this.

"Are they always right?" she asked faintly. "About the harvest?"

"Always in my time on this farm, going on for eleven years now. Some say Aal created the bells as a warning to prepare for bad times, and as a promise of good times, to give us reason to rejoice. If the blooms ever fail to appear, it means disaster is coming." Her smile widened in satisfaction. "This year, they are a promise, and we will rejoice."

She turned from the flowers back to Sara. A look of surprise crossed her face. "What's wrong?"

Sara shook her head. "Nothing." She cleared her throat. "It's just… they remind me of home."

"Oh Sara, I'm sorry. I was going to put them all over the house, but I won't if it upsets you."

"No, it's okay." She had to get over this. They were only flowers, they couldn't hurt her, and they meant something to Mena. She swallowed and tried to sound normal. "They are beautiful, aren't they? Where I come from, we call them Christmas Bells."

"Christmas?"

"It's a - celebration. A summer celebration, in my country. Families get together and there are decorations and special food. And gifts."

"What are you celebrating?"

"Um, different things I suppose. Holidays, a break from work, spending time with the people you love. Some people go to church and remember the birth of a baby a long time ago."

"The birth of a baby is always something to celebrate," said Mena. "But what is church?"

This was getting complicated. "I suppose it's a place people go to get closer to God. Um, Aal I guess. They pray and sing and talk about him."

"But Aal is everywhere."

"I'm sorry, Mena, I don't really know much about church. I don't go there."

"But you celebrate Christmas? With your family?"

Sara wished she'd never started this conversation. "I don't have any family," she said shortly. "I'd better get on with the mending." She escaped before Mena could ask her anything else.

***

In the late morning, the injured girl woke with a loud cry. Mena hurried to soothe her. "You're all right, my love. You're safe."

The teenager's blue eyes darted around wildly. "Father?"

"Your father isn't here, sweetheart. Was he with you? At the river?"

The girl rolled her head from side to side in agitation. "No, no." She stopped and fixed her eyes on Mena's face. "Are you sure he's not here?"

"Only you, my love," said Mena. The reassurance seemed to calm the patient. Her head stopped moving and her eyes looked less wild.

"Will you tell us your name?" Mena asked.

"Anbid," said the girl softly.

"Nice to meet you, Anbid. I'm Mena and this is Sara."

"Hello," Sara said. She felt calmer, too. The sight of the Christmas Bells in the house had just surprised her, that was all. Now she was forewarned, she wouldn't react so strongly to them again.

***

In the end, Sara helped Mena with the flowers, arranging handfuls in containers filled from the water butt outside the kitchen door. She focused on the task, doggedly pushing away any thoughts of home. When they'd finished, she had to admit the red and yellow bells made the house more cheerful on this dull grey day. Almost like Christmas decorations. Without stopping to think, she said so.

"What else do you use to decorate at this festival?" Mena asked. They were in the kitchen again and she was stirring a pot of soup. Healing might be Mena's vocation, but cooking was her passion. Sara didn't share it, but appreciated the results. The soup smelled delicious.

She considered Mena's question. "Most people bring an evergreen tree into the house and hang all sorts of colourful things on it." No point going into the subject of artificial trees. She was sure no one on Algarth had ever seen such a thing.

"What else?"

This was harder than Sara had expected. Mena's culture had no words for fairy lights or tinsel. After discarding her first few ideas, she settled on describing a wreath she had made last year from different kinds of foliage.

Mena nodded. "It sounds lovely. And you said you eat special food, too?"

She was on easier ground here, able to choose things she'd already eaten from Mena's kitchen. "Roast meat and vegetables, followed by Christmas pudding - a steamed pudding like that delicious one you make, with even more dried fruit and sometimes nuts. And custard or cream."

Mena nodded again and gave the soup a final vigorous stir.

Sara's own choice of Christmas lunch would have been very different to the traditional one she'd described: something like cold cucumber soup, barbequed prawns with mango salsa, and Pavlova loaded with fresh fruit and cream. Impossible to convey all that to Mena, of course.

Mena put the spoon down and faced Sara squarely, placing her hands on her hips. "This year we will have a Christmas celebration," she pronounced, "with decorations and special food and maybe even gifts. It will cheer you up."

As soon as a stupefied Sara found her voice, she tried to convince her friend she didn't need a celebration; she was perfectly happy. And it would be too much work anyway. Mena overrode these paltry objections. She had made up her mind. Sara was to have her Christmas. They would begin preparations in two days' time.

Sara couldn't bring herself to tell Mena the real reason for her reluctance, it would have sounded too pathetic, too ungrateful. She'd always looked forward to Christmas, all the preparations and anticipation.

Even without family, it had been a happy time, especially in the last few years, celebrating with friends and going to parties. She'd loved making that wreath and hanging it on her door, and primping her clients' gardens to look their best for the festive season.

But a Christmas here wouldn't feel like Christmas at all. Instead, it would only underline everything she'd lost: not just an annual celebration, but her whole world.

***

By the next day, the rain had gone. Anbid was well enough to get up and Mena encouraged Sara to spend time with her. They both wanted to know why the young girl had been in the river and Mena thought she might open up more easily to someone closer to her own age. Sara was willing, but unsure where to start. She hadn't had much experience talking to teenagers, even when she'd been one herself. Gazing out of the window at the cloudless sky, she had a brainwave. She suggested a walk before the day became too hot. Anbid consented.

The two of them strolled around the area surrounding the house for a while, not saying much. Sara pointed out the various buildings, feeling like a tour guide. Anbid gave monosyllabic replies. This wasn't getting them anywhere. Sara led the way to the bench under the huge, ancient-looking oak, one of her favourite places to sit. Time for a few direct questions.

"Anbid, do you come from somewhere near here?" She tried to keep her tone light, as if she was merely making conversation.

"A few hours' walk east. It's a small farm, nothing like this." Anbid's voice was expressionless, her face unreadable.

"And your family?"

"My father lives there. And my little sister." Anbid looked away, up into the branches. "I haven't been home for a while."

Sara waited a few beats, and took a chance. "Where have you been?"

"In the city: Eorna." Anbid was still staring upwards. "I hated it at home. Every day it got worse. I had to escape. So I did. I walked away." Sara heard pain in her voice now.

Anbid had asked about her father yesterday, sounded scared he might be here. Sara experienced an unpleasant lurch in the pit of her stomach. What had Anbid run away from?

"And you ended up in Eorna," she prompted.

"Yes. It wasn't what I was expecting." Anbid's voice was high and tight.

Sara hastened to reassure her. "Well, you're here now. You're safe."

Anbid nodded. The furrows smoothed from her brow and her shoulders relaxed.

"As long as you don't fall into any more rivers," Sara added. It was a stupid remark, born of nervousness. Thankfully, Anbid took it calmly enough.

"I know. It was foolish." She lowered her gaze to meet Sara's. "Everything seemed so hopeless, you know? And then the rain... and the river...." A shudder ran through her. "Don't worry. I won't do it again."

Sara groped for something sensible to say in response to this. There was no need. Anbid was already continuing.

"It was horrible. Dark and cold. I couldn't breathe. I thought I wanted it to be over but suddenly I was desperate to reach the surface, get a breath, survive. I suppose that means I don't want to die after all." She sighed and leaned against the gnarled trunk of the tree. "I don't know what to do now. I can't go home." Her voice had risen again and her hands were trembling. "For a while, I hoped I could, but..."

"You can stay here for now," Sara interrupted. "Mena said so. She's good at taking in waifs and strays."

Anbid nodded and closed her eyes, sinking back against the tree. "I'd like that."

They sat for a while in companionable silence. Anbid seemed fully relaxed now but Sara's body was as tight as a bowstring. Her imagination kept throwing up nightmare images of what could have driven this young girl to such despair. Whatever happened from now on, they had to keep her safe.

When they returned to the house, Mena wasn't alone. A stranger stood in the middle of the kitchen, an older man with long grey hair and a weather-beaten face. Anbid was halfway through the doorway when a cry of alarm burst from her. She spun on her heel and bolted across the yard.

"Anbid!" the man shouted. He made to follow her.

Mena's brisk voice stopped him in his tracks. "Wait. Let me go, Hallin. I'll talk to her." She strode out without waiting for a response.

This Hallin must be Anbid's father, the one she had escaped from. Sara glared at him, but he was staring through the open doorway, apparently indifferent to her presence. She meant to change that. He had questions to answer.

She raised her voice to get his attention. "How did you know Anbid was here?"

He spoke without turning around. "I didn't; I only hoped. I've been to all the farms in the area, trying to find her."

"Why did she run away from you?" Anger infused Sara's words. He didn't rise to it.

"It doesn't matter now." He sounded distracted.

Her temper rose higher. "It doesn't *matter?*" She took a step towards him. "What did you -"

Without warning, he backed away from the doorway. Sara scrambled out of the way, her nerves jangling.

Mena walked in, with Anbid trailing behind her. The girl's head was bowed, her face hidden. She dragged her feet across the room to the far corner, turned around and lifted her head slightly. Her gaze darted around, finally settling on Sara. Her face was even paler than when she'd been unconscious, if that was possible. The blue-black shadows under her eyes stood out like bruises. She hunched her slight shoulders as if trying to make herself even smaller.

Sara turned her own furious gaze back to Anbid's father. His eyes, a faded blue, were staring at his daughter as if he couldn't get enough of the sight.

"Anbid?" he whispered, stretching a hand out towards the cringing girl. Her cheeks flushed an ugly red. She ducked her head again.

"Child, it's all right." He took a step towards her.

That was close enough. Sara moved to block his way. Mena shot out a hand and caught her wrist in an iron grip, jerking her to a halt.

"No", Mena whispered. "Trust me. Just wait."

Sara watched, sick with apprehension, as Hallin took one slow step, then another. Finally, when he was within arm's reach, Anbid raised her head and met his gaze. Her cheeks blazed. Tears spilled from her eyes. "It's not all right," she said harshly. "It will never be all right. You don't know -"

"It doesn't matter." He kept his voice low and soft as if he was afraid of startling her. He spread both arms out wide. "Nothing matters, as long as you're safe." His voice broke on the last word and Sara was astonished to see tears in his eyes, too.

"Father," Anbid whispered. "I've done such things ... I'm so ashamed -"

He only opened his arms wider. "Come, my daughter. My beloved one."

"I can't - you don't know -"

"Come."

A sob tore from Anbid's throat. A second later, she hurled herself against his chest. His arms went around her and they stood together, clinging to each other and weeping.

Sara turned to Mena, who still had hold of her arm. "Is she safe with him?"

"I think so," said Mena. "I don't believe it's her father Anbid is scared of." She freed Sara's throbbing wrist and turned to the stove. "Get them to sit down. I'll make us all some tea."

Sara wasn't sure Mena was right about Hallin. Nevertheless, she did as her friend asked. The four of them sat around the table and drank Mena's fragrant tea. Anbid seemed eager to talk now. She kept a tight hold on her father's arm as she began her story.

"After my mother died last year, things at home were so different. Cara, my little sister, was too young to help out much." She frowned at her father. "Where *is* Cara?"

"At home. Bertin is looking after her." He turned to Sara and Mena. "A neighbour of ours," he explained.

Anbid nodded and took another sip of the strong, sweet tea. "With Mother gone I had to look after Cara and do all kinds of things I'd never done before. Cleaning and cooking and -"

"I never asked you to," said Hallin.

She squeezed his arm. "I know, but someone had to do it." Her eyes looked far away as she remembered. "None of us were sleeping much. Cara was having bad dreams every night." She glanced back to her father. "Sometimes, when I went to soothe her, I heard you, pacing around the house."

"It was a bad time for all of us," he said.

"Yes, it was." She swallowed and went on. "I was exhausted, all the time, and Cara wouldn't stop crying. I started to lose my temper with her. And the work kept piling up. I was failing. Failing Cara, failing you, failing

Mother. No," she held up a hand as her father stirred to speak. "Please, let me finish. I need you to understand how I felt. I was caught in a trap, and I'd never be free of it, because nothing was ever going to change. Mother was gone and she wasn't coming back. There was only me. And I wasn't good enough. So, I ran away."

"Oh, child, I'm so sorry," said Hallin. "It's my fault. I was the one who failed you. I was sunk in my own grief and I didn't see what was happening."

Anbid squeezed his arm again and gave him a weak smile. "As you said, it doesn't matter now. I begged a lift on a cart going to Eorna. I thought... "She shook her head. "I don't know what I thought. I just hoped it would be better there. If I found a job..." Her voice faded away.

"You don't have to keep going, if it's too hard," said Sara.

Anbid took a sip of tea, then shook her head. "I want to. I want to tell you everything and get it over with. Like pulling a splinter." She smiled crookedly and put her cup down, ready to go on.

She spoke quickly, not lingering on the details. She told them about the friendly woman who had taken her under her wing, offering her a place to live and a job. Anbid had accepted, hardly able to believe her luck. Her new friend had led her to a small bedroom, basic but clean. As the woman left, and Anbid heard the key turning in the lock, she realised, too late, that she hadn't been lucky at all.

The real nightmare began a few hours after that. A man shambled into the room, drunk and stinking. She tried to fight him off, but he overpowered her easily. He was only the first of many.

"Once or twice, in the early days, I found enough courage to try to resist," Anbid said, her voice flat and devoid of expression, as if she was talking about someone else. "But it was no use. And then they'd beat me and I wouldn't get any food for a few days. In the end, I let them do what they wanted. But the only thing *I* wanted, was to die so it would all stop."

Sara's heart twisted. She was sick with fury. Mena was gripping the edge of the table with white-knuckled hands, looking ready to kill someone. Hallin's face had gone as grey as his hair. Tears trickled down his seamed, hollow cheeks.

Anbid hadn't finished. She let go of her father's arm and clasped her hands together on the table in front of her. Eyes fixed on those hands, she spoke about the last man, a wealthy man who said he loved her and wanted to protect her. He'd paid money for her, taken her to his house, into a room with no lock on the door. No man visited that room but him. He was gentle with her. He spoke kindly and never beat her. He delighted in buying her jewels and beautiful clothes. She ate as much as she wanted, every day.

"It was all so different," Anbid explained. "After the - others - I was… grateful. Grateful for kindness, and generosity."

Both kindness and generosity had vanished the moment her protector discovered Anbid was expecting a child. Probably his child, but not certainly. And because he would never be certain, he told her, his voice heavy with sadness, he could no longer endure the sight of her.

After that there were no more gentle words, no more delicious food, no more beautiful dresses. Only the clothes on her back and the baby in her belly and the shove of a servant, sending her sprawling out onto the street.

At this point in her story, Anbid choked, unable to go on. She bowed her head lower, resting her forehead on her clasped hands, as if unable to look at any of them.

"You're pregnant?" asked Sara gently.

"Yes." The whisper was barely audible. No one else spoke.

Sara shot a glance at Mena, who simply nodded back. She'd known all along. Her *skal* must have shown her the presence of baby when she'd first examined Anbid. That was why she'd seemed concerned.

Ugly stories crowded into Sara's head. Accounts from the history of her world, and from its present, too. Young unmarried girls had been thrown out of their families, beaten, even stoned or had acid thrown in their faces, all for the 'disgrace' of bearing an illegitimate child. How were such things viewed in Algarth? Hallin had accepted everything else, but would he accept this? Why wasn't he saying anything?

Her pulse pounded in her temples and a hollow opened in the pit of her stomach. Her heart thumped so hard against her ribs that she couldn't bear to sit still any longer. She half rose, prepared to fight Hallin off if she needed to, to protect Anbid and her unborn baby. Out of the corner of her eye, she saw Mena push up from the table too. So, she wasn't completely sure of him, either.

One beat, two, three. No one moved.

And then Hallin turned towards his daughter. One arm went around her bowed shoulders and he gathered her gently to him. She let out a sob and leaned against him.

Sara sank limply into her seat and drew in a deep lungful of air. In those last few moments, she'd forgotten to breathe at all.

"Oh, my child," Hallin said, and Sara heard only love and sorrow in his tone.

"Well, that's wonderful news," said Mena, loudly and firmly, as if by sheer force of will she could make it so. "A new life coming into the world. A reason to celebrate."

Anbid raised her head. Her brow wrinkled in puzzlement. "Celebrate?"

"Of course," said Mena. "Every child is a gift from Aal." She paused and cocked her head to one side. "Do you suppose it's a boy, or a girl?"

A hiccup of laughter burst from Anbid. It had a slightly hysterical edge. Sara was fighting the urge to giggle, herself.

"Mena is right," said Hallin, releasing Anbid from his embrace and wiping his eyes. "We have much to celebrate." He smiled at his daughter.

"You have returned safely to us and our family is growing." The smile widened. "The harvest will be good this year, I can feel it. We can hire someone to help around the house, and with the baby. Later, when you're ready, we'll talk about what you want to do with your life." He shook his head. "I never expected you to replace your mother, Anbid. She chose her path, and you will choose yours. Although I'm selfish enough to hope it won't take you too far from us."

The last tiny fragment of Sara's tension left her. It was going to be all right. More than all right.

"And now that's settled," said Mena, rising from her chair, "I don't have time for any more chatting. There's a double celebration to plan and I have a lot of work to do." She sounded pleased at the prospect.

***

They sat at two long tables under the oak tree. The sun was falling below the hills after another long hot day, painting the fields with golden light and long purple shadows. Sara sat between Mena and Anbid. On Anbid's other side perched six-year old Cara. For now, the little girl had left her grief behind and was chattering nonstop to her big sister. Anbid didn't seem to mind.

The other chairs were filled by the farmworkers and their families. Mena had invited them all to Sara's Christmas. The happy noise of the children rose, drowning out the twilight chorus of the birds.

Family lost and family found, thought Sara. *And found family, too.* She glanced sideways at Mena, whose face was still flushed with the residual heat from her cooking. She had been working in the kitchen for days and had outdone herself. Sara had never tasted goose, but the scent rising from the glistening skin of the golden-brown bird was making her mouth water.

Besides the goose, there were platters of juicy pink ham, huge bowls of roasted vegetables and soft, fresh bread. Steamed fruit puddings and cream were still to come. It was more a traditional English Christmas feast than an Australian one, but Sara wasn't about to complain.

She had taken little part in the food preparation, knowing well the limits of her skills in the kitchen. The wreaths hanging on the doors of the house were her contribution, and the garlands running the length of each festive table. She had assembled them from sprays of foliage in every shape and shade of green. She'd even found a tree whose round silvery leaves with their metallic sheen reminded her of the eucalypts at home. Rows of creamy white candles flanked the garlands, ready to be lit as darkness fell.

And in the centre of each table stood a green glass vase of Christmas Bells, fiery beacons signalling the promise of a plentiful harvest. And maybe something more. If Anbid could find a happy ending after all she'd been through, perhaps Sara might achieve her own, one day. Just because she didn't know how she'd come here, or how to get back, didn't mean she never would. She'd take the flowers as a talisman and keep hoping. And in the meantime, she'd enjoy the blessings she'd found right here. It wasn't home, but for now, it was close enough. A gentle breeze sprang up, setting the Christmas Bells nodding, as if in agreement.

Mena leaned towards her and smiled a tired, satisfied smile. "Happy Christmas, Sara."

"Happy Christmas, Mena. And thank you. For everything."

Hallin rose to make a speech, but Sara wasn't listening. She was thinking about food, family, love, and hope for the future. And the gift of a new life on its way into the world.

It all suddenly felt so much like Christmas that those nodding red bells might as well have been jingling.

***

About Lyn Webster

Lyn Webster has expended a considerable portion of her life exploring imaginary places from the comfort of her favourite reading chair. During her time as a teacher, her greatest joy was introducing her students to such journeys and equipping them to embark on their own. Retired from the classroom, she awoke one morning with a yearning to discover a new destination and share its stories with her fellow armchair travellers. After a few false starts and wrong turns, she found herself mysteriously transported, along with her protagonist Sara Martin, to the magical island of Algarth, where she's been spending most of her off-world time ever since. When not in Algarth, Lyn lives, writes, and gardens in regional Australia, with her husband and a small enthusiastic dog. Her debut novel *Greenhaelan,* is coming in February 2020. In the meantime, you can catch up with Lyn's ramblings about reading and writing at www.TwoBooks.blog

Epica Intermission

'Tis both a curse and strange gift to sail endlessly around the continent with no true idea of where I sit in eternity. Though Christmas comes as though a year has passed, the rising of the bottles leaves me with the distinct feeling there is a gulf of a hundred years or more between these new portals and the last remembered appearance of the glowing gifts of temporary escape. The planks on this ship have been weathered by harrowing winds of the future and past to be sure, cooled too with an endless night unshackled from the mechanics of the moon and sun, and now that you're aboard it would be pertinent to know with a mix of our minds and the contents of these Christmas treasures there's nowhere we can't go.

Look! There's something splashing beside this bottle. Best we use a hook to lure in the bounty - there are creatures down there that strike fear into the hearts of even the gods themselves. Ah yes, this looks to be a wonderful little journey that's perhaps right up my alley. You see it's not just time that stretches off in all directions from the wake of the ship, but also the slow bending of what we call reality…

Operation: Sugarplum

By Emily Wrayburn

For Hoffman who gave us the story and
Tchaikovsky who gave us the music.

Clara took a deep breath and smoothed her already smooth skirt.

"Okay," she muttered to herself. "Don't be weird. Don't freak him out."

She ran a hand through her hair. The humidity had made it go frizzy but there was nothing she could do about that now. She pulled it back into a messy bun and hoped for the best.

Remaining calm was easier said than done. Through the doors in front of her was boy-genius game developer, Maxwell Drosselmeier. Even the most casual of gamers knew his name. He'd finished high school at fourteen and university at seventeen. Now twenty-two, he had already had job offers from Japan to America, but he'd turned them all down. Instead, he stayed with his Uncle Josef's Australian company, Drosselmeier Industries, though he travelled often and consulted with plenty of other organisations. No one really knew whether it was all out of family loyalty or if there was some other reason.

Clara had known Josef Drosselmeier since she was a young girl and her family lived down the road from him and his wife, but she had never met Max. Max was known for keeping to himself, but when she had got wind that he would be attending the company Christmas party this year, Clara hassled Josef for an invitation.

She didn't plan on staying too long. She'd just tell Max that she was a fan of his games and that she was looking forward to the new platform he was rumoured to be building. Maybe she'd get a photo with him if he didn't mind. Then she'd leave. She was no good at back-end development, despite Josef encouraging her to learn. She wouldn't fit in with many of the people inside, despite enjoying the games they produced.

Leaving required going in in the first place, though, and she was still staring at the door. Well, if nothing else, it would be air-conditioned inside, and that was worth everything on a day like today. If she waited outside any longer, she'd start sweating, and dark patches under her sleeves was not her ideal first impression.

… not that she was trying to *impress* Max Drosselmeier in any way. But she didn't want him to be unimpressed, either. At the rate she was going, it was highly likely she would nervously spew out some embarrassing word vomit in front of him. No need to smell bad, too.

She took another breath. All right. This was it. She was going in. She squared her shoulders and closed the gap between her and the door. On the other side, a security guard was checking invitations. She didn't have an official one, but she did have an email from Josef's personal account on her phone, which he had promised would act as one. The security guard frowned at it for a moment, but eventually nodded.

"Through that way, Ms Steele," he said, pointing to a large set of double doors. Behind it, Clara could hear music and chatter. She pushed open the door and entered a dim room. There were musicians on a stage up the far end, but the music was clearly intended for atmosphere. There was no dance floor and the players kept the volume low.

There were Christmas trees dotted along the walls, with sparkly baubles and loads of tinsel. Sprigs of mistletoe dotted the corners of the room and formed the centrepieces on the tables. The tables were tall and had no seats, but empty glasses were already being left on some of them as guests went to mingle elsewhere.

A caterer walked past Clara with a tray of canapes held in front of her, and Clara snagged a mini quiche. She looked around as she bit into it and immediately saw Max Drosselmeier in a corner, holding a drink. He was leaning against a pillar, his head down as he focused on a phone. She wondered if she should just walk up to him but decided against it. She needed to find Josef. They had agreed that he would introduce her to Max. Also she had her mouth full.

She finally spotted the bespectacled older man talking to two men in suits. One of them threw back his head and laughed at something the other said, but Josef's only reaction was a tight smile. He looked like he wished he wasn't there.

Well, Clara was happy to come to the rescue. She made a beeline for Josef and cleared her throat loudly to interrupt. Josef's face lit up when he saw her.

"Clara!" he said. "How good to see you!" He turned to the two men. "I'm sorry, gentlemen. You'll have to excuse me."

He took Clara by her elbow and steered her away. "Thank heavens you arrived when you did," he said.

"Who were they?" Clara asked as they walked.

"Press. Got in here on the pretence of being from the social pages or something, but they're really trying to get the down-low on Max's new system. We've made it clear we're not talking about it yet, but they keep trying."

"Ugh."

"Indeed."

They had nearly made it to Max's pillar now. He looked up as they approached.

"Max! Someone I'd like you to meet. This is Clara. She wanted to meet you."

"Josef…" Max avoided looking at either of them.

"Just this once, Max, come on. Clara's not going to hurt you."

Now that the moment had come, Clara started to feel awkward. What was she doing? Max clearly didn't want to meet fans. The fact that he was hanging back from the party suggested he didn't really want to meet anybody.

Clara blushed and turned away, looking to see if she could make a quick getaway. Obviously, this had been a terrible mistake. She shouldn't have bothered Josef to let her come. He should have told her it would make Max feel uncomfortable.

Max took a deep breath and stuck out one hand. "Hi, Clara."

Clara shook the proffered hand, her embarrassment ebbing a little.

"Hi. I just really wanted to say that I'm a big fan of what you do. I know you were a driving force behind *The Oneiroi's Dream* and I really loved playing it. So I, um, wanted to tell you." The words came out in a rush.

Max gave her a small smile and nodded. "Thank you. I appreciate it."

Josef looked from Max to Clara and back again and then said, "Max, why don't you go with Clara and get some fresh air? Maybe up to the roof?"

"What?" Clara exclaimed.

"Why would I…" Max began at the same time, before trailing off with an apologetic look at Clara.

Josef leaned in and whispered something in Max's ear, glancing pointedly at Clara as he did. When he finished, Max sighed and looked at Clara.

"Clara? Would you like to accompany me up to the roof for some fresh air?" He looked back at Josef and raised an eyebrow. Josef raised his own in reply. Clara looked between them.

"Um. Sure?" she ventured.

She wondered exactly what Josef was trying to do, but then shoved the thought aside. She was being presented with the chance to spend one-on-one time with Max Drosselmeier. She could ask him about his creative process; where he came up with all his ideas. She followed him to the end of the room.

"What did he say to you?" Clara asked when they reached the lifts. Max pressed the up button and cleared his throat.

"He said that it might be good for me to spend time with someone my own age."

Clara blushed again. "You don't have to," she said. "I mean, you shouldn't let your uncle push you around. And you don't even know me. I could be some crazy fan girl. Or I could be from the press, like those people Josef was talking to when I got here. Trying to get the dirt on the platform you're building."

She noticed Max staring at her, smiling slightly. Oh god. She'd been rambling. What had she said? She wasn't even sure now. It had all come out in a stream.

"I'm pretty confident you're not here to get the dirt on my work," he said eventually.

Clara realised she was focused on his smile, which had grown wider as he spoke. It wasn't really fair that he was a genius *and* attractive.

"You don't?" she replied, shaking herself.

"And Josef's probably right, anyway. I don't spend enough time around people my own age. But it's too hot to go up on the roof. Would you like to see what I've been working on?"

Clara blinked. "You mean, your new system?"

"It's nearly at the point where we'll be seeking outside input on it. How'd you like to be the first?"

Clara gaped. Max was asking her to… *game with him?*

"Sure. Lead the way!"

They stepped into the lift and Max pressed the button for a higher floor. They rode in silence. Clara was too busy getting over the fact he'd asked her to be his second pair of eyes on a project and Max seemed content in the silence.

When they reached their floor, Max led Clara down a corridor of stark white walls and doors. Some of the doors had individuals' nameplates, while others had department names.

"How are you with virtual reality?" Max asked as he swiped his staff pass on a door. "Have you played much?"

Clara shook her head. "I don't know anyone with the equipment. I've played a couple of times when they've been demoing in shopping centres, that kind of thing. But that's it."

Max nodded. "I think you'll find this a bit different."

By now, they had entered a room with three rows of tables, all of which were covered in computers. But at the back of the room was what looked like a massive lounge suite with reclining armchairs. Clara saw there were keypads in the arms of the chairs, and behind them, what looked like gloves. Above that, wires led up to a round frame, which Clara suspected was supposed to go around a player's head.

"That looks… intense," Clara said.

"I guess, if anything, you're more used to something like that," Max said, nodding towards the corner of the room, where an upright stool with hand controls and foot pedals was parked. That was closer to what Clara had seen before. He turned back to the suite in front of him.

"This is the Veritas," he continued. "It's been a long time coming."

Clara smirked and raised her eyebrows. "You called your virtual reality platform 'truth'?"

Max seemed pleased that she knew the meaning of the word. "I liked the irony," he said and motioned to one of the lounge chairs. "Have a seat."

Clara moved to the side of one of the chairs and examined it more closely. Two pedals replaced the footrest of a regular reclining chair, and the keypad and joystick in the arms lit up as Max switched on the attached computer. Clara couldn't work out how to get in without climbing over the keypad.

"If I'd known I'd be doing this, I wouldn't have worn a skirt," she said.

"Oh! Lift the arm up. That leaves the side free for you to get in." Max demonstrated on his own chair before settling himself in.

Clara followed suit and managed to slide into place while Max operated the computer in front of them using the keypad on his own chair. A login screen appeared with the name NUTCRACKER above a password field.

"Nutcracker? Where does that come from?" Clara asked while he typed his password.

Max gave her a small smile. "Family trip back to Germany for Christmas when I was four. Since there were bowls of chestnuts all along the table, I figured they were for eating. But no one told me I couldn't eat them straight from the bowl. Mum swears I nearly broke my jaw, but I think she's exaggerating. Though I did break a tooth. Ever since then, she's called me 'little nutcracker'. I use it for this kind of thing so that my work's not immediately identifiable. You know, if my laptop got stolen or something."

"Fair enough."

"All right, so there are pedals for your feet. That's how you walk. Then there's the gloves for your hands. The headset is above you."

Clara pushed the pedals a few times, finding the right amount of pressure to apply. She slid one hand into a glove and with a deep, anticipatory breath, she pulled down the headset. She blinked a few times. Her nose itched. She wasn't used to having her face and ears all covered like this. She automatically reached up to scratch, but she couldn't physically reach her nose. She wrinkled it a few times, and the feeling subsided a little.

She felt around for the other glove and slipped her hand into it. The gloves were heavy, but when Clara flexed her fingers and rotated her wrists, she found she could move freely.

"Are you ready?" Max asked. "I'm going to open the game now, and then I'll join you in there in a second."

"I'm ready."

Her vision filled with purple and a cartoony castle. There were thunderclouds around it, and the occasional thunder rumbling sound effect. The 8-bit tinniness of the music reminded Clara of the Mario games she had played on her Gameboy when she had been much younger.

The title *"Operation: Sugarplum"* was emblazoned in gold to the right of the castle, with a menu beneath it. As she turned her head, Clara saw they were in the middle of some sort of wasteland. Thorny vines snaked around them, broken by pathways leading off in different directions.

"Okay," Max said, his voice now coming through the headphones. "We are not the target audience for this game. So imagine you're maybe ten. Eight? I don't know. A kid. Everybody says I'm wasting my time making a game like this for kids, but I don't see why they should miss out on the fun. It's pretty simple: Princess Sugarplum has been taken prisoner by the Rat King, and we have to fight our way to the castle to rescue her, battling various creatures on the way. Every now and then the Rat King turns up and tries to persuade us not to come any further. You have a certain amount of health for each fight. If you run out, you go back down a level, lose some gems, that sort of thing. There's stuff like a tutorial and character selection but I thought we'd skip straight to the game itself, if that's all right with you. I'll guide you through anything you need help with."

He spoke quickly, some of his words tripping over one another. Clara was surprised by the change in him. It made sense that he would be more in his element explaining his most recent project than stuck in a room full of people drinking and making merry, but even in interviews he was always reserved. She was secretly pleased that she got to witness this other side of him.

"Let's go," she said, grinning.

A hand in Clara's peripheral vision selected the word "Play". As the scene changed, Clara turned and saw a fully human figure in front of her. He was wearing a loose shirt and an open vest, and breeches with tall, lace-up boots. He had curly hair but that was where any resemblance to Max Drosselmeier ended. He had angular features, with a pointed chin and a long nose, and sharp blue eyes. A sword hung at his waist and a satchel was draped over the opposite shoulder.

On the couple of occasions that Clara had played in virtual reality before, she had had VR hands, but no actual form within the game. She looked down at herself and saw a torso and legs, and when she stretched out her arms, they were there right up to her shoulders.

"Okay, how do you even… wow. This is cool."

"You like the complete avatar?"

"I love it! But I can't see the keypad now. How do I control anything?"

Max gripped the sword at the hilt of his avatar and drew it from its scabbard.

"The sensors on the gloves will figure out what you're trying to do. Here, take this." Max took a step closer to her and held the hilt of the sword out. Clara raised her hand and as she went through the motions of grasping, her avatar took the sword from Max. She could swear she even felt its weight in her hand.

"Whoa," she breathed as Max took it back.

"The joystick rotates your view, so you will need to feel around for that. But everything else is through the gloves."

Clara nodded and slid her fingers forward. They closed around the joystick. She rotated it carefully and her view rotated with it. She rotated it back to Max and then let go. She hadn't told Max but the other reason she hadn't played much VR before was because it didn't take long for her to start feeling motion sick. Up until now, those couple of sessions in the shopping centres had been quite enough for her stomach to cope with.

She looked down at herself again and took in the flowing robes she was wearing, along with the staff or wand or whatever it was tucked into her belt.

"What's this?" she asked. It took her a couple of attempts to get hold of it before she pulled it out of her belt and examined it.

"That's your wand. You're a spellcaster."

"Awesome." She slid it back into her belt.

"You'll choose spells each time we meet an enemy. Some of them don't work on all the creatures, and you'll have to use combinations sometimes to do enough damage."

"And what are you? Some kind of fighter? With the sword?"

"Basically. But it's a kids' game, so the weapons don't really do a lot. There's no blood and gore. I'm actually going to let you do most of the work, though. It'll be good to see how someone new to the world plays."

Clara fidgeted in the chair. What if she ended up being completely useless at the game? What if she got motion sick again, and had to run for the bathroom before they even got to the first monster? What would Max think of her then? He'd wonder why he'd wasted his time.

"Come on, let's go." Max's avatar beckoned to Clara and began walking along one of the paths stretching from the clearing. Clara moved her feet, tentatively at first, now that she couldn't see her real feet. Her avatar stumbled slightly as she followed. She found a steady rhythm and caught up, and for a few minutes, they simply walked. She was certain she felt the robes of her avatar moving against her own legs and she frowned. Surely no virtual reality could be quite that realistic. She tried to ignore how it unnerved her.

The forest rustled on either side of them, and occasionally Clara saw something that looked like eyes peering out. Just like the start screen, the visuals were a little cartoony: the sky was purple and the forest was rendered in shades of black, grey and dark green. The music was a low hum in the background. The combined effect reminded Clara of Scooby-Doo episodes, though she'd never felt spooked watching Scooby-Doo.

Clara didn't know that her first enemy had approached until it landed on her shoulder and nipped her skin.

"Ow!" she exclaimed, her hand flying to her neck. She tried to swat the creature as she would a mosquito, but it was too fast. It zipped back and forth around her, darting into the trees before returning.

The scene around her paused and information about her opponent scrolled across the screen in front of her.

<u>Sprite</u>:
Fairy.
Pretty harmless, but its bite will sting.
It's very fast.
HP: 20

An arrow flashed at the end of the text and Clara reached out and tapped it. The text about the sprite was replaced with a list of spells available to her. There were only two at the moment, one to do damage and one to slow down time. She selected the second one, and the menu disappeared.

The music crescendoed, a rhythmic pulsing as it waited for the fight to begin. A glowing pattern pulsed in front of Clara. She stared at it.

"What's this?"

"Trace the pattern with your wand," Max said from behind her. "Be accurate or it won't work as well."

Clara tugged her wand out of her belt and did as Max said. The area was immediately covered in a golden glow. She saw the sprite coming towards her, now at a quarter of its original speed.

"How do I get back to my other spell?" she called to Max.

"Bottom of your view."

She looked down and saw an icon in the shape of her wand. It bounced in the corner, waiting for her. She reached down and touched it and the spell menu returned. The time-slowing spell was greyed out now, but she was able to select the other one, which caused 20 points of damage.

She traced the new pattern. A beam of light struck out towards the sprite and it tumbled backwards before blinking out of existence. Where it had been, some coloured gems tumbled to the ground.

"You'll want to pick those up," Max said. Clara ran over to the gems and bent down. As she touched them, they flew into the air, disappearing once they passed the treetops. A scoreboard at the top of the screen indicated that she now had five gems in her inventory.

Clara noticed the wand icon glowing again at the bottom of her vision, and she opened up the spell menu. She had unlocked a new spell, one that would deal 35 points of damage to ground-dwelling creatures.

Clara closed the menu, wondering if the description was a hint about her next fight.

"So you get the idea?" Max said as they began walking the path again. Clara nodded.

"Yeah, I think so."

A minute later, the air crackled and a small creature dressed in rags appeared in front of them. It had a long nose and gnarled skin. It wore a red cap and had long, dirty claws. A red bar hovered above its head with a 35 at one end.

"Stop and fight!" it yelled in a raspy voice. "Stop and fight! Stop and fight!"

Once again, the scene paused to let Clara read about her new opponent.

<u>Redcap</u>:

Goblin.

Lives in abandoned castles and other earthy dwellings.

Soaks his cap in the blood of his victims.

Will try to bite or claw.

HP: 35

Clara moved through to the spell menu and immediately picked the new spell for earth-dwelling creatures. She traced the pattern with her wand and the Redcap was bowled over by the beam of light. The force of the spell pushed Clara back a step or two and she felt a jolt go up her wand arm. She shook herself.

"It's not real," she muttered, giving her arm a shake.

The spell emptied the Redcap's health bar and it vanished, replaced by more gems for Clara to collect. She looked to see if she had unlocked a new spell, but she hadn't this time.

As they went on, they met a witch, a gnome and another goblin. Each time, the HP of her foes increased, and Clara began using combinations of spells to defeat them, just as Max had told her she would need to. She unlocked two more spells along the way, allowing her to defeat some creatures of up to 60 HP with only one hit.

Eventually, their walk led them to a clearing. In the centre stood a tall tower, with a swirling portal at the door. A cobblestone path wound from the portal through the clearing to their feet.

As Clara watched, a figure emerged from the portal. It had a long body covered in short brown fur and walked on strong hind legs. Its shorter arms ended in sharp claws and it had a pink tail that flicked as the creature looked around. Its head seemed disproportionate to its body and as it came closer, Clara saw why. It had one, two, three… *seven* heads. A gold crown sparkled on each of them.

Max noticed Clara staring. "Yeah, it looks too weird, doesn't it?"

"It's a bit weird, yeah," Clara replied.

"I told them early on in the process seven was too many. I suggested three in the early design stages. Maybe they'll listen to outside feedback."

"Can you change it at this point?"

"Well, no, but at least I'll be able to say I told you so."

Clara laughed then turned her focus back to the creature in front of her. The information about him filled her view.

<u>Rat King</u>:

Will fight with claws, spells and anything else to hand.

Can deflect spells with his own.

Will steal your gems if you let him close enough.

HP: 75

Clara chose her most powerful spell, capable of 60 points of damage. The beam of light radiated from her wand, but the Rat King held up a paw and absorbed some of the light directly into his body. His health only went down by twenty points, rather than the full amount.

A moment later, the part of the spell the Rat King had absorbed beamed out of his paw again, heading straight for Clara. She shrieked and turned and ran. The bite on the neck from the sprite had hurt enough; she didn't want to know how it felt to receive the full force of a spell.

She reached the edge of the clearing and glanced over her shoulder. She watched Max casually poke the Rat King with his sword, and the King's health went down another twenty points. Max saw her watching and motioned for her to re-join the fray.

"Sorry!" he called. "I should have warned you that would happen."

The Rat King tried to close in on Max so Max swung the sword again. Clara saw that there was little in the way of a wound inflicted even as the Rat King's health went down. She remembered what Max had said before they began playing, that there was no blood and gore since it was a kids' game. She wondered if that meant the Rat King's spell wouldn't have truly hurt her and felt silly for running away.

Clara was starting back toward the Rat King when she heard a noise outside the game. It was muffled through the headphones but sounded like footsteps.

"Hey, is someone in here?" It was a male voice, sounding concerned.

"It's just me," Max called back. "It's fine."

The footsteps came closer. "Who is this? Max, what are you doing?"

Max sighed and Clara heard him taking off his headset. His avatar still stood in the clearing, the sword hanging limply from one hand. The Rat King went after it again and Clara watched, transfixed, as he leapt onto Max's avatar and snapped at its neck, then fell back. A health bar flashed above Max's head, quickly emptying. When the avatar didn't respond, the Rat King quickly cast a spell and threw it in the avatar's direction.

When his health reached zero, Max's entire avatar shattered into pixels, replaced with a pile of gems. The Rat King greedily collected them.

Clara was still watching this when she felt a hand on her arm. She jumped.

"Sorry, Clara, I think this is it for now," Max said.

Clara pulled off her headset. Max had packed up his equipment neatly on his chair, and now that Clara wasn't wearing her own, she could see him joining a man in his forties near a bank of computers to her right.

The newcomer was wearing a suit and tie, but his top button was undone and the tie was loose. His face was red; Clara suspected he'd already knocked back a few drinks at the party downstairs. His arms were folded as he looked between Clara and Max.

"Is she authorised to be up here?" the man asked, gesturing at Clara.

"I authorised her," Max replied. "We're going to start outside testing soon anyway, so I thought she might like to be the first person to check out the system."

"Right. Is she someone you know? Or a complete stranger?"

"She's –"

"Did she sign any paperwork? You're acting like we just let anyone in for testing."

Clara wished she could sink right through her seat, rather than listen to the two men continue to argue about her.

"Well, don't let her leave without signing an NDA," the older man declared, throwing up his hands and turning on his heel. A minute later, Clara and Max were left alone again.

"Sorry," Max said, looking at the floor. "I guess that killed the mood a bit."

Clara gave a small laugh. "I should probably be going. I didn't plan to stay this long." She pulled her hands out of the VR gloves and clambered out of the chair. "Thanks for letting me play. I love it. This is going to be great when it goes live."

"You're welcome. Look, I'll get in contact in the new year and you can give me some feedback on *Operation: Sugarplum*, okay?"

"Really?" He'd been talking about feedback but Clara hadn't thought that her opportunity to provide it would extend beyond that night. When they were interrupted, she'd assumed that would be the end of it and the next time she heard anything about the Veritas would be when it was available to the public.

"Josef knows you, right? I'll get your details from him."

Max switched off the computer. As he did, there was a bright flash from behind the screen. He frowned but continued shutting it down.

"What was that?" Clara asked.

"Nothing," Max said, quickly. "I'll check all the cords back there before I start it up again."

Clara didn't think the flash had been caused by faulty wiring but she didn't argue. Max knew far more about these computers than she did.

They made their way back to the lifts and Max pushed the button to take them down again.

"So, um, do I have to sign something? Like that man was saying?"

Max scoffed. "No. You can ignore him. I'm sorry you had to see him cranky like that."

"Is he often cranky?"

"He's… let's just say it bothers some people within the company that I'm its most famous employee but also its youngest."

"Oh. Fun."

"Mmm."

The lift doors opened and for a moment they hovered in the foyer. Clara wasn't quite sure what to say. She'd already said thank you. Should she just wish Max goodnight and be on her way?

"Will you go back to the party now?" she asked eventually. Max sighed.

"I guess so. If I show my face once more, maybe I can escape."

Clara chuckled. "Well, good luck. Thanks again. And it was great to meet you."

"You, too."

It wasn't until Clara was back on the footpath and pulled out her phone to check the time that she realised she hadn't even asked him for a photo. But a night playing a game with Max was worth far more than a photo ever could be.

***

Two days later, Clara spent the afternoon doing the last of her Christmas shopping (and feeling rather proud that she was so on top of things a whole week out from Christmas). She had waited until late in the day, hoping it would have cooled down outside by the time she left the shopping centre. But as she stepped off the bus, shopping bags in hand, Clara discovered just how futile this plan had been. It might have been just on dark, but the heat was still oppressive. There was no direct bus route past her house so she had to lug her things with her in the heat for another few streets.

She'd been walking for nearly ten minutes when she first thought she heard skittering footsteps on the pavement behind her. She tried to ignore the noise. It was probably just her imagination. Or maybe the heat was addling her brain. But she couldn't help being reminded of the sound effects in *Operation: Sugarplum* the night before last. The sound bore a remarkable resemblance to that of a rat's claws on cobblestones.

The sound was still behind her after she had turned two corners so she could no longer ignore it. She bit her lip. Casting a glance over her shoulder, she saw a figure that would stand about waist-high on her. In the dim light, it seemed somehow insubstantial, flickering in and out of existence.

Clara shook her head and quickened her pace, hoping to keep it away just a bit longer. She was only a street from her house now. She just needed to get in the front door and everything would be fine.

She was rounding the last corner when she was bowled over from behind. Her bags of shopping went flying as she slammed face-first into the pavement. She screamed. Her hands stung but she threw one arm up, trying to shove her attacker off her back. She was able to roll over, and she screamed again when she saw what was on top of her.

It was the seven-headed Rat King, the gold crowns glistening in the moonlight and the streetlamp up the road. How was this possible? Was she dreaming? Clara thrust another arm out, trying to shove him off, and a burst of pain shot to her shoulder, followed by a wave of dizziness. Her hand wasn't moving properly; her wrist was broken. It must have happened when she broke her fall.

The Rat King cackled the way he did when he got a hit in the game, as though he was stealing Clara's coins and health right here on the pavement. His mouths were open and drooling, and his beady eyes glinted with glee. He snapped at her a few times, and she only just managed to bat the offending heads away.

Clara struggled some more, but it was no use. The Rat King had her pinned to the ground. She tried rolling from side to side, hoping she could toss him off, but no luck. She tried to strike him a couple more times with her uninjured arm but had to pull away before he bit her.

The screech of tyres momentarily distracted the Rat King and Clara looked up, too. A white car pulled up on the other side of the road. Clara sagged in relief. Help was here! Someone had seen her! She didn't have to fight off the Rat King alone.

The driver got out and ran across the road to her.

"Clara!"

She knew that voice. It was Max Drosselmeier. And he was carrying… a sword? It shimmered the same way the Rat King did, like it wasn't completely real. This had to be just the shock of being attacked. Or a dream. Video game characters didn't just show up in real life, and neither did the weapons to defeat them.

Max was shouting at the Rat King but Clara didn't take in what he said. She was just relieved when he dragged the creature off her, and she was able to crawl away. She propped herself up on a nearby garden wall. She was shaking all over now and didn't think she had the strength to stand. Sweat dripped down her nose and chunks of her hair matted to her forehead. She had no idea whether it was from the heat or the shock. She didn't care at this point.

She watched as Max attempted to fight the Rat King. He might have been good with a sword inside a virtual reality, but in the real world, he was awkward and clumsy. After all, he was a game developer, not a knight errant.

The Rat King started performing one of his spells, and a blue streak of light beamed towards Max. He managed to deflect it with the sword, but another light, green this time, followed soon after. The Rat King was beating him. And what would happen if he won? Clara remembered the way his avatar had burst into a cloud of pixels when he stopped playing the game and the Rat King had beaten him. Was that going to happen to his real body? It didn't bear thinking about.

As Max's situation became direr, Clara's heart hammered inside her chest. Not knowing what else she could do to help, she looked around for something she could throw. There was nothing, so she cast around for her handbag. She spotted it nearby, and worked herself onto her knees to crawl over to it, stopping whenever a new wave of nausea came over her. She couldn't be sick, not now. She had to help Max.

The biggest thing in it was her sunglasses case, and she couldn't see that being much use. She flopped down to the ground, defeated. For a moment, she was tempted to just close her eyes and wait for everything to be over. But then her gaze fell on her sandals. They had solid two-inch heels. It was worth a try. If she could hit the Rat King with one of them, it might at least distract him enough for Max to regain the upper hand.

She fumbled with the buckle, acutely aware of how much time she was taking to undo it with only one good hand. She glanced at Max. He was covered in sweat and his shirt was sticking to his back. The Rat King had backed him a few metres down the street. But he wasn't defeated yet. Clara took a breath and kept working on her shoe. It finally slid off and she raised it above her head, lobbing it as far as she could.

The sandal came into contact with the Rat King's shoulder, just below one of his heads. He stumbled, the spell he had been creating dissipated between his claws. Clara smiled weakly. It was all the celebration she had the strength for. She just managed to watch Max use the distraction to drive the sword through the Rat King's insubstantial form and see both the Rat King and the sword disappear before she passed out right there on the footpath.

****

Clara opened her eyes and immediately squeezed them shut again. She wasn't sure where she was but the light was white and too bright. She groaned.

There was the sound a chair scraping and then she felt the weight of someone leaning on the bed next to her.

"Clara?"

She eased her eyes open again. "Max?"

Max breathed out. "You're awake. Good. That's good. Clara, I'm so sorry about what happened. I should have been more careful."

Clara tried to cast her mind back. What *had* happened? She had memories of being attacked and a fight and… no, that couldn't be right. She tried to move and her arm throbbed. When she glanced down at it, she saw it was set with a splint and a bandage.

She narrowed her eyes at Max. "I'm going to need an explanation. How did you know what was going on? For that matter, what *was* going on?"

"I, uh… Okay, hear me out on this. Sometimes when I play the Veritas, I somehow… bring stuff out of the game with me."

Clara raised her eyebrows. "I know I'm probably high on painkillers right now, but could you repeat that? I thought you said that you can bring your video game characters into the real world with you."

"I know it sounds ridiculous, but it's true. I'm not sure how it works. Sometimes I've managed to consciously do it. Most times it just happens. That flash you saw when I shut the system down the other night… that was the Rat King."

"Okaaaay. And the Rat King came after me because…?"

"I've been out of town the last couple of days. I guess he wasn't able to find me… but were you near the Drosselmeier Industries building today?"

"I was in the city. I walked past."

Max nodded. "So he was able to pick up your signature and follow you, since he hadn't come across me first. But I realised he had escaped as soon as I was back this afternoon. I was able to pull the magic sword out of the game but as you saw, I'm no fighter in real life. Thanks for your help with him, by the way. Throwing the shoe. It really helped."

"You're welcome… I guess. You know, I'm just going to assume that I fell and broke my wrist and passed out and this whole thing is a hallucination. You're probably a hallucination, too. There's no other reason why you would be at my bedside."

Max chewed his lip. "I guess that's fair for now. Maybe I should talk to you again in a few days. Once you're up and about." He turned to go but Clara grabbed his hand with her uninjured one.

"Just in case you are telling the truth," she said, "is the Rat King gone now?"

Max hesitated before replying. "I'm not sure. He disappeared after our fight, but whether that means he's gone… I mean, that's just what he does when he's defeated, so maybe he's recovering somewhere."

"What if he goes after someone else? Someone who knows nothing about him?"

"I don't think he will. The fact that he didn't show his face until he picked up on you suggests that he's not interested in other people. I guess he sees us as his opponents."

"Well, that sounds awesome." Clara frowned.

"I know. I'm sorry. I'll make sure nothing else happens to you. I promise."

Clara yawned. There was a part of her that wondered how exactly Max planned to protect her - was he going to just follow her around until they were sure the Rat King was gone? - but it was overpowered by the part of her that wanted to go back to sleep.

Max noticed her fatigue and stood up. "I'll let you rest," he said. "I guess you'll be taken in for surgery soon. Your parents are on their way. Josef was able to contact them."

"Cool," Clara replied. She attempted a thumbs up but was already falling back to sleep as Max slipped out of the room.

****

It took three days for Clara to convince her parents that she didn't need to stay with them any longer, and that she could return to her own house for the few days between now and Christmas. Max had found her keys after she had passed out and had put all her Christmas shopping inside while waiting for the ambulance. She needed to get it all wrapped before the family gathering on Christmas Day.

Once she'd finally put an end to her father's fussing and pushed both parents out the door, she put on a playlist of Christmas songs and sat down directly under the air conditioner with her gifts and wrapping paper. She cranked the volume up and sang along.

With one arm in a cast, wrapping took twice as long as usual. The wrapping paper wouldn't stay where it should, and sticky tape kept sticking to itself. She was relieved she hadn't purchased any oddly shaped gifts; the standard rectangular boxes were challenging enough.

After an hour or so, she was off in her own world, so the sound of the back door slamming made her jump out of her skin. She tried to stand and stumbled, forgetting she couldn't lean on her plastered arm. She supported herself on an armchair and pulled herself up.

"Hello?" she called.

The house was an old design, with the laundry between the kitchen and the back steps. As she went through the kitchen, Clara silently opened a drawer and pulled out the rolling pin. She didn't think she could actually attack someone with a knife, even an intruder, even in self-defence, but the rolling pin was solid enough if she had to defend herself.

"Is anyone there?" she called.

She could hear movement in the laundry. She knew that she should just push open the door and face whatever was there, but she'd already been attacked once this week.

"It's probably just a possum," she told herself. Old houses like this one had possums running about in the roof all the time, didn't they? But then she gasped as the door handle moved downward. A possum couldn't do that.

Clara swallowed and took a step back. The door opened and behind it was the Rat King, his noses twitching and his heads turning in different directions as he followed different scents.

Clara didn't have time to react before all seven sets of eyes latched onto her. She froze as the Rat King moved towards her. She tightened her grip on the rolling pin in her hand, but the Rat King was beginning one of his spells, the green orb forming between his paws. She only just leapt out of the way in time and the spell sailed past her. How would she even get close enough to get a hit in with a stupid rolling pin?

She needed to get back to her phone. When she had woken again at the hospital, she'd found a slip of paper on the bedside table with Max's number on it. She'd added it straight to her contacts. Once she'd been discharged from hospital, she had put the Rat King's first attack down to shock and heavy painkillers, and she assumed that Max wanted to stay in touch so he could get some proper feedback on *Operation: Sugarplum*.

Now she knew the real reason he had left his details, but her phone was still in the other room blaring Christmas music. Should she run? Or should she go slowly? The Rat King had already seen her. It wasn't like she could avoid attracting his attention.

She made a break for it. The Rat King came after her, his claws slipping on the tiles. She grabbed her phone from the table and tried to find Max's number. Her hands shook and her fingers slipped. The phone display rolled back to the top of her contacts.

"Argh, come *on*!" Clara shouted, whether at the phone or at herself, she couldn't say.

She looked up and the Rat King was nearly on her. He reached out and batted the phone out of her hand, then raised his claw again. Clara was so terrified all it took was a slight push for her to fall backwards onto the couch.

Now that he could reach it, the Rat King was grabbing at her neck. Clara had dropped the rolling pin when she reached for her phone so she just tried batting away his arms. Two of his heads snapped at her and she shrieked. She threw herself into the back of the couch.

She batted his paws away again, but it occurred to her that he didn't seem to be trying to hurt her. He wasn't snapping and clawing at her the way he had the first time he attacked.

No, he was trying to get hold of the necklace she was wearing. It was a string of dark blue, glittery beads. In this light, they weren't much, but they caught the sun and sparkled when Clara wore them during the day.

Realisation dawned on Clara. In *Operation: Sugarplum*, the Rat King stole users' coins and gems if he defeated them. This was what he was trying to do now. She whipped the necklace over her head and tossed it at him, hoping that would make him leave her alone. He caught the necklace in his claws and moved away, but unlike when Max had fought him the other night, he didn't disappear. He started looking around, ferreting under chairs and the coffee table, looking for more.

Clara wasn't about to hand over actual money to a creature that shouldn't even exist, but she did have some costume jewellery she could part with. She just hoped it would be enough. While the Rat King had several noses under her TV cabinet, she sprinted for her bedroom and pulled a bundle of necklaces with gaudy faux-crystal beads in various sizes and colours out of her jewellery drawer. Some were more gem-like than others, but she hoped that a few of them would satisfy the Rat King.

She glanced at the bedroom window, wondering whether she was stupid going back to the Rat King. Maybe she should just climb out and run away. But somehow she didn't think that would help.

She hung a couple of the necklaces from her wrists, letting them dangle below her arms. She returned to the living room and the Rat King sat back on his haunches, watching her approach. Clara waved the necklaces at him and he eyed them for a moment and then pounced, snatching them from her arms. If she hadn't still been scared out of her wits, she might have laughed at the fact that the Rat King put a necklace around each of his own necks.

"Is that what you wanted?" she asked. She wondered if he could even understand her.

The Rat King strung a last set of beads around his leftmost head and chattered to himself.

And then finally, he vanished.

Clara stood where she was for a few minutes before moving further into the room and sinking onto the sofa. Her phone was still playing Christmas music from the floor. She leaned over and picked it up, shutting the music off. The house was still now, and Clara's breathing was loud in the silence.

Eventually, her hands stopped shaking for long enough for her to write a text to Max. *Rat King was here* was all she wrote. Only a minute after she pressed send, the phone rang, and Max's name came up on the screen.

"Are you all right?" he asked without preamble.

"I'm fine."

"I thought you were staying with your parents."

"I persuaded them to let me come home. They were fussing. It was annoying."

"You're sure he didn't hurt you?"

"Yes, I… he took some of my jewellery and left me alone. I think he saw them as gems, like in the game."

"Of course." There was a pause while Max thought about that. "Look, Clara, I was thinking after your attack. The first one, that is. It seems to me the only way to get rid of him is to lure him back inside the game, and then defeat him once and for all in there. Are you free tomorrow afternoon?"

"Yes."

"Can you come back to the DI offices? I'll make sure they know to expect you. Hopefully with you being there, and with the game operating, that will bring him back. I've reprogrammed the game so we can skip straight to the final boss battle. That final defeat should lock him into the game."

The 'should' in Max's final sentence didn't fill Clara with confidence, but what did she know about defeating virtual characters who pop out of their world?

"Okay," she said. "I'll see you then."

***

Despite enjoying their games and knowing the head of the company, Clara had never thought she'd set foot in the Drosselmeier Industries building once, let alone twice in a week. She showed some ID to a security guard at the front and was issued with a visitor's pass, and then led back to the same lab where she had originally played *Operation: Sugarplum* with Max a week ago. Max was already there, fiddling with one of the VR suites.

"I had someone make some adjustments to the equipment," he said. "You should still be able to use your left hand to play, even with the cast on."

"You rebuilt it in a couple of days?"

"Well." Max shrugged, almost bashful. "Three days. My team can move fast around here when we need to."

"Does your team know you can pull stuff out of the game?"

"Sort of. A couple of them have seen me do it. Some of them are aware but sceptical."

"And they didn't question you when you wanted them making dramatic changes?"

"I did most of the reprogramming myself, so they didn't really need to know much about it. The game still exists in its original form; we'll be using a derivative today. You've actually made me wonder whether the gloves were a bad idea, anyway. Why limit gameplay to those who have five fingers on each hand?" He motioned to the chair. "See what you think."

Clara lowered herself back into the same chair she had used last time. She looked to her left and saw the new equipment. Instead of a glove, it was more like a mitten, without separate slots for each of her fingers. It wouldn't help her to hold things in the other world - she couldn't move her fingers enough to hold anything - but at least she wouldn't be playing one-handed.

Max was already logging into the computer, so she got herself comfortable and slipped on the headset. A moment later, the purple and black home screen for *Operation: Sugarplum* opened in front of them. Max hit 'play' straight away.

"Come on," he said to Clara, and started running down the path.

No creatures jumped out at them, wanting a fight. In fact, the way was remarkably clear. Clara discovered why when they arrived in front of the Rat King's castle. In the clearing in front of the drawbridge, a large crowd of non-player characters was gathered. Clara saw the Redcap and other non-player characters she had fought with Max the first time they had played. There were elves, goblins, even a centaur or two. Clara turned to Max.

"The NPCs seem to have forgotten what their job is."

"Their job has changed," Max replied. "They're on our side now."

"We have an army?"

"That's right."

"And is the Rat King back?"

"I don't know. Let's go and find out."

With a wave of Max's hand, the drawbridge started to lower. He and Clara led their new army over the moat and into the palace grounds. There was a flash up above, much like the one Clara had seen when the Rat King escaped into the real world. In its wake, the Rat King stood on a parapet, surveying the various creatures as they flooded in behind Max and Clara.

The Rat King screeched, and Clara gasped as dozens of rats poured out of the lower levels of the castle. Some of them ran on all-fours like regular rats. Others walked upright like the Rat King, carrying daggers or spears.

"Max!" Clara yelped. "What do we do?"

"Fight them!"

Clara looked down. She still had her spellcaster's wand but now there was also a dagger at her other hip.

Clara pulled the dagger from her belt. She swung it at the nearest rat and it fell away from her with a squeal before disappearing. Now that she was using a physical weapon, she was glad she was in a game that didn't show any blood. She swung at another rat and it vanished just like the last.

They were slowly moving towards the large oak door ahead, their army swelling behind them. When they reached the top of the stairs, Max held out an arm in front of Clara, indicating for her to stop. As she watched, the oak doors parted, revealing an ornate staircase ahead.

"Let's find him," Max said, and Clara saw him stand up a little straighter. She readjusted her grip on her dagger and nodded. They began to make their way toward the stairs and the doors clanged shut behind them. Only then did Clara realise that they were making the rest of the trip alone.

Their way was lit by lanterns in sconces along the walls. The flames flickered, casting odd shadows on the walls and constantly making Clara jump. There were odd noises, too: creaking beams in the ceiling and the sounds of doors slamming somewhere in the distance. It put Clara on edge.

"Should I be bracing for a jump scare?" she asked.

"No," Max said. "If everything goes the way it should, he's waiting for us to come to him. He's guarding the tower with the princess."

Something occurred to Clara then. "If you were able to make all these changes to the game, why didn't you just… delete him all together?" Max frowned.

"I thought of that," he said. "But when I went to do that, his code was gone. I guess because he wasn't in the game. There was nothing to delete."

They were following a long corridor on the second floor and Clara assumed they were aiming for the stairs she could see at its end. But then Max stopped and examined the tapestry hanging on the wall beside them, before grasping part of the fabric and pulling it aside like a curtain. Behind it was a wooden door, its plainness stark in contrast to the rest of the wood panelling Clara had seen in the palace so far.

"How is anyone supposed to ever find that?" Clara asked.

"We're not playing the full game," Max reminded her. "When you play right through, there are plenty of clues about finding your way around the castle. Come on."

He ushered Clara into the narrow staircase hidden behind the door. It was even darker in there, and as they began their ascent, Clara had to keep one hand on the wall to feel her way. When she tripped on a stair, she fell forward and gave a cry. She righted herself and wondered how she could have possibly felt the lurch in her stomach that comes just before a fall, when in reality she was sitting down and just moving pedals with her feet. She shook her head. The Veritas was a bit too realistic.

Finally, the stairs came out at a small, round landing. There was another lantern in a sconce on the wall, and in its light, Clara made out the figure of the Rat King. Her breath hitched, her previous encounters with him flooding her memory.

Max touched her arm gently. "It's okay," he said.

Clara nodded, not trusting herself to speak. She kept her eyes fixed on the Rat King. She didn't trust him not to try something sneaky when she wasn't looking. She was surprised to see one of her necklaces was still around his neck, though the beads were now geometric shapes and the colours had altered themselves to fit in with the game's design.

The scene paused and Clara and Max were presented with a series of options. They included "Give yourself up", "go back for more supplies" and "fight now." With a glance at Clara, Max selected "fight now" with a tap of his hand.

Immediately the scene changed. No longer were they in the tower, but in a grand arena. The Rat King stood to one end, and rat minions filled the stands behind him. Clara and Max were together at the other end, and when Clara looked over her shoulder, she saw that their army had reappeared as their cheer squad.

"Clara," Max whispered. "I'll distract him. You get around behind him. Use a powerful spell and finish him off."

Clara nodded, and Max immediately stepped forward, his sword raised high in one hand.

"Hey!" he shouted. "Over here!"

The Rat King turned all seven heads towards Max as Max charged towards him. The Rat King began a spell, a blue orb of light growing between his paws. Clara inched her way toward the edge of the arena, trying not to be seen. Max dodged a spell and darted closer to the Rat King, trying to strike him. The Rat King leapt back, hissing at Max.

Max lowered the sword, taking a moment to regain his balance. The Rat King was already starting a new spell, a green ball of light this time. Clara didn't know what difference the colours made, since she and Max had both managed to avoid being hit by any so far, but she wasn't intending to find out.

Clara made her way halfway around the arena while Max continued to demand the Rat King's attention. She opened her spell menu and chose the most powerful one she had, worth 100 points of damage as long as the Rat King wasn't shielded against it. Provided he was still fighting Max, she would be able to hit him with the full brunt of the spell.

She was just about to head back in towards the Rat King when several of the rats in the stands behind him started kicking up a stink, screeching and cawing, gesturing madly at Clara.

The Rat King turned two heads in her direction. He bared his teeth and hissed, bounding towards Clara. Clara changed course, running back the way she had come. She heard Max call her name and glanced over her shoulder, just in time to see a blue beam of light streaking towards her. She threw herself to the side, but she wasn't fast enough. The spell hit her squarely in the back and she went sprawling to the ground.

She felt the impact of the fall thrum through her headset as well as up both arms. Her broken wrist throbbed. She squeezed her eyes shut as her head spun, and when she opened them again, she found herself surrounded by a black void.

"Uh, Max, what's going on?"

"Hang on. Just getting you back in."

"Did I die?"

"You did. You'd go back to your last save point usually, but we don't have time for that."

While she waited, Clara waved her hands in front of her face. She couldn't even see them; it was so dark. She rotated her view a few times to see if there was any light but there was nothing.

"There!" Max exclaimed. Suddenly, with a burst of colour, Clara was back in the arena, still on the ground. She took a moment to get her bearings. After the darkness, the bright colours took some getting used to.

She clambered to her feet again. This time, she decided she would get close to the Rat King before selecting any spells. Max was closer to the Rat King now and he got in a couple of blows with his sword. The Rat King's health bar went down a little, but they still needed Clara's spells to do most of the work.

She ran towards the Rat King and when she was close enough, selected a spell again as fast as she could. She traced the pattern quickly, trying to remain as accurate as possible. As the spell's beam of light hurtled towards the Rat King, the rats in the stands started screeching again. But as the Rat King turned, the spell hit him square in the eyes. He stumbled backwards, his health bar nearly empty. The amber spell he had been working disappeared and the rats in the stands screamed and hissed.

Max ran forward and thrust the sword into the Rat King's body. He pulled it out and the Rat King stiffened as his health bar drained. He shimmered and then burst into a pile of gems as tall as Clara's avatar. Clara and Max didn't need to collect these; they flew straight into the sky and their inventory rose by two thousand.

Bells pealed in a tower above the arena and a gate lifted to one side. From the passage beyond, a young woman in a long flowing dress raced out into the arena, her hands outstretched towards Max and Clara. She wore a tiara on her head and her hair was in a braid that reached her waist. She bowed to Max and Clara when she reached them.

"Noble rescuers," said Princess Sugarplum. "I am indebted to you for your actions here today. Pray, what can I do to thank you?"

Max bowed in return. "Thank you, your Highness," he said. "Knowing that the Rat King no longer troubles your kingdom or ours is payment enough. We seek nothing further, but simply wish to return to our homes."

"Very well. Safe travels, noble heroes."

The Princess bowed again, and with a wave of her hand, the arena faded. They were back in the tower, but the Rat King no longer guarded the locked door. It was open and the room beyond was empty.

"One last thing to do," Max said, beckoning for Clara to follow him back down the stairs. They exited the castle the way they had come. Their army was waiting for them at the bottom of the stairs. The creatures burst into cheers and applause as Max and Clara stepped out onto the stairs, and over the scene of their leaping and clapping, the words "The End" faded in. Underneath were the options to play again or quit the game.

Max selected the quit option with the tip of his sword and the scene turned black. Credits started rolling in white text. When they finished, Clara pulled her hands out of the gloves and removed the headset.

"Is that it, then?"

Max nodded. "That's it. He won't bother you again."

Clara pulled her hands out of the gloves and removed the headset. She sank back into her seat, took a deep breath and let it out in a whoosh. She hadn't noticed how tense she had become over the past few days, not knowing whether the Rat King was going to come after her again. She could already feel the weight off her shoulders.

Max stretched out in the chair next to her and laced his hands together behind his head. He looked over at Clara.

"How do you feel about Chinese food? I can order us some noodles to celebrate."

Clara hadn't realised how hungry she was until he mentioned food. Her stomach rumbled loudly. She laughed and Max grinned.

"Celebratory noodles sound great," she said.

***

By Christmas afternoon a couple of days later, Clara and her brother had consumed more than their fill of ham, prawns and salads, and were spread out on couches and the floor under the air conditioner. Clara had received a book she'd been wanting to read for ages, so she had curled up on the couch and started on it; she was already five chapters in. Her father, Henry, was setting up a new phone and her mother was sending Merry Christmas texts and Facebook messages to friends and more distant family.

When the knock came at the door, they all looked around at one another, questioning. No one had been expecting guests.

"Henry, can you get that?" Clara's mother asked, getting up and making a beeline for the kitchen. As Clara's father went to the door, Clara could hear the sound of her mother hurriedly collecting plates from where they had all been left on the table, and scraping scraps into the bin before putting the plates in the sink.

Clara tore herself away from her book and went to stand at the kitchen door.

"Mum, whoever it is, they're not going to care you haven't done the dishes," she said.

Her mother placed the last plates in the sink and waved dismissively at Clara, who rolled her eyes.

"We've got visitors!" Henry's voice boomed down the hall. Clara turned to face the living room again and saw Josef Drosselmeier. Behind him came Max. For a moment, Clara wondered if they were there because the Rat King had somehow returned, but she quickly decided they looked too relaxed for it to be that.

"Merry Christmas, Marie!" said Josef, handing a bottle of wine to Clara's mother, who had joined her in the doorway. "I hope you don't mind us dropping in like this. We just wanted to make sure Clara is still doing all right."

"I'm doing fine," Clara said. "Already counting down the days until I get the cast off, though."

"Shall I open this now?" asked Marie. "Who'd like a glass? Josef? Henry?"

Both men answered the in the affirmative. Clara raised her hand. Max declined but requested a soft drink. Marie returned the kitchen to find glasses and pour. Henry indicated for Josef and Max to find themselves seats before joining Marie in the kitchen.

Clara motioned for Max to join her on the couch. "Have you been taking some time off for the holidays?" she asked.

"We take two weeks off over Christmas," Max replied. "Sugarplum is just about finished, but my team will start storyboarding something new in the New Year," Max replied. "A horror game this time. Set in a land of dolls."

Clara pulled away from him dramatically, holding up her hands. "I am never playing that with you. Given what you can do."

"Well, if it's any comfort, I'm going to be steering clear of testing games in development. After what happened, it's just too much of a risk when I don't understand the ability."

"And no one wants to be chased down the street by a hoard of creepy dolls."

"Exactly. But in the meantime, I'm going to try running some tests to see if I can figure it out."

"What sort of tests?"

"Trying different scenarios. See when I can and can't remove things. Try to work out how the Rat King got out. That hadn't happened before."

"Well, let me know if I can help."

Max smiled and nodded. "Thanks. I will."

Marie and Henry returned with glasses of wine and Max's soft drink and handed them out. Max held out his glass and Clara clinked hers against it.

"Merry Christmas," she said.

"I got you a present," Max said, setting his glass on the floor and retrieving a gift bag that sat near his foot. Clara looked inside and saw a stuffed toy rat. She let out a loud laugh and pulled it out to show the others. Josef gave her a knowing smile but her parents looked confused. She shrugged.

"Kind of an inside joke, I guess," she said.

Henry looked between Clara and Max and raised an eyebrow.

"You two have inside jokes now?" he asked.

Clara gave Max a small smile and he smiled back. She nodded at Henry.

"Yeah," she said. "Something like that."

***

About Emily Wrayburn

Emily has been writing since she was six years old, though she has trouble ever completing her projects. The initial idea for a modern-day Nutcracker retelling came to her back in 2013, and she is somewhat surprised that she's managed to not only finish it, but also plan a sequel (watch this space!). She is also the author of A More Complicated Fairytale, available from Amazon, and maintains both the blogs A Keyboard and an Open Mind (for book reviews) and Letting the Voices Out (for writing rambling).

Epica Intermission

It be a true shame your visit won't be longer. Between such wondrous tales and the placing of the bottles upon the mast, there shan't be much time to get to know one another and I should wish to hear your adventures.

A seafaring journey of the likes what brought me to these waters is a sure way to learn the intimates of even the most distant souls. Crammed together like apples on a horse cart, with relentless and ferocious waves ensuring no real chance of space to gather one's thoughts, the lives of others soon become all there is to know. Imagine then the loss upon waking to discover nothing but rotting wood and shadows?

Aye, it brings an emptiness of the heart that an eternity of poetry shan't ever capture, but while you are here there is hope yet for a vagabond scoundrel such as myself! I can sense by the light in your eyes this moment is just as special for you as for me, so what say we reach overboard for another glowing scroll to hold back our eventual goodbye a little longer?

That's the trick, you've got it. Ah, I see this one's particularly bright and heavy in the hand. The parched paper is warm to the touch, and judging by the winking of the words it be matters of the heart to hold forth this tale…

The Last Day of Christmas

By Andrew Roff

To all the elves toiling away in the workshop.
You guys are the real heroes!

It was the best of hams, it was the worst of hams. When Juliette saw it pulled glaze-sticky from the barbeque on Christmas day, and carved into slices so big they covered both of her palms, the whole family had set happily to work. Now, as the new year approached, the meat that remained was slimy. And everyone was sick of eating.

It was the final day of the test, and her dad was sunk deep into the sofa when the doorbell rang. Juliette's grandparents on her mother's side, in town for a late visit, had not been expected for another half hour yet.

"Come *on*," said dad, rubbing at the skin above his cheek. The kids had stuck gold tinsel along the top of the television, but the upper-right corner had come unmoored, and now it was hard to follow the play when the ball was hit to fine leg.

From the kitchen, Juliette's mum must have heard, and she came to the stand in the doorway. "It's once a year."

Near dad's feet, Juliette was playing with the new Lego set she'd got from Santa. Libs, the oldest, had yesterday declared Lego to be kids' stuff, but even so she was helping to rearrange the town Juliette had built. In the far corner of the room, a plastic tree sagged under the weight of too many baubles, angels, decorative school projects from the last week of term, and a rope of Christmas lights that didn't shine any more when you flicked the switch. Toby, the middle child, was in his room gaming. Muffled gunfire sounds turned his closed door into the skin of a drum.

When Grandma and Pop shuffled in, the whole family assembled. There was hugging and the usual commentary about how tall the children had grown. Juliette's mum smiled hard and led everyone out the back.

The pergola took up almost a third of the yard. Cream brick tiles, set at diagonals, ran from the brown brick exterior of the house to the sharp concrete edge of the swimming pool. Overhead, translucent plastic, corrugated, warped the sun and took away its sting, but cast distorted half-shadows. For Juliette, the pergola meant sitting on a canvas fold-out chair and reaching her arms upward toward her plate.

In the middle of the space, their long table was draped with the same red cloth that had served the family through the Christmas season. A wipe-down had restored it to working order, but stubborn discolorations mapped a history. It was hot and still too early for lunch, and Juliette gazed at the pool like it was refuge, but the children knew they were expected to remain while the adults talked.

Pop claimed the head of the table, and Gran lowered herself into the chair next to him, facing back toward the house. Juliette ran to a spot down the other end, between her brother and her sister.

"How's Juliette going at school?" The question, from Gran, was directed at Juliette's mum.

"Her handwriting's come along. Got her pen licence this year."

Juliette knew this was a dumb thing to be proud of—her siblings had told her as much—but even so, she beamed when Gran reached over, clasped her hand and said, "Congratulations."

"You been watching the cricket?" Poppa asked Toby. The boy looked down and shook his head.

"He's not much of a one for sport," Juliette's dad replied.

After that, no one spoke for a while. Mum stood up. "Let's have some music." She squeezed between her chair and the wall, over to the CD player perched on the window ledge, the window open a crack to let the power cable snake inside. Juliette's mum was slender like Gran. Libs had the same build, and with them here together it was like a time-lapse of one person, but Juliette and Toby took after their father. Puppy fat was how everyone referred to it in Juliette's case.

Libs aimed a dark look at their mother. "If she plays Little Drummer Boy again I'll fucking lose it." She said it quiet, so that mum couldn't hear, but Gran's face collapsed like cracked plaster.

"Time for presents!" Poppa announced. He disappeared inside, and returned carrying a large plastic bag. He moved slowly, and as he passed Juliette she heard the rasp of his heavy breath. "For you," he said to Libs, holding out a parcel wrapped in butchers' paper. "From me and your Gran. Happy Christmas." He planted a kiss on the top of the older girl's head while she sat still as a stone.

When he was done, Libs tore at the paper to reveal a make-up kit. There were lots of different things inside a clear plastic case, and Juliette wanted to pull everything out to see what was what. She couldn't tell whether her sister liked the present. Libs was fifteen now, and getting good at the adult trick of hiding her feelings.

"Just what she needs," said mum.

Toby's present was a long triangle-shaped box, about the length of a ruler from end to end. Even before he tore the paper, Juliette was sure what it would be. And yes, so it was: a block of chocolate. "Toby Toblerone," Pop rumbled, looking pleased with himself.

"Thanks Pop. Thanks Gran," said Toby, but it was Juliette's eyes that grew large.

She had eaten a Toblerone once, a smaller bar, perhaps a year before. She didn't remember the exact taste of it. But looking at the honey-coloured box, she recalled vividly the feeling of the triangle piece yielding as she chewed. The chocolate was rich, and there were—what—crunchy bits inside. Crunchy and then sticky against your teeth.

Lost in thought, she didn't notice Pop until he was behind her, reaching his arms around to place a large package on the table. "For you, princess," he said, and kissed her head. Juliette could feel the puff of his breath in her hair. His hand on her arm felt warm and wet.

The size of the present was encouraging. But when she unwrapped it, removing the sticky tape carefully like she'd been taught, she found a doll.

"The woman at the shop said it's very lifelike. You can feed it," said Gran.

"You can practice being a mummy," said Pop.

Juliette scrunched paper in her hand. Dolls were for babies, and she was almost ten. Gran and Pop should have known that. Her mum should've told them.

"Thank you," Juliette said quietly. She looked at her mother, who nodded and winked. For a few seconds that almost made everything better, but she glanced again at the doll, and the injustice filled her right up. Even a make-up kit like Libs got would have been better, and as for Toby's gift—

"Can I have some of your chocolate?" Juliette asked Toby.

"It's mine," he replied firmly. Toby was a good brother most of the time, but he was a hoarder. This year his Easter chocolate had lasted into October, tormenting Juliette until mum threatened to chuck it in the bin.

"*Please,*" Juliette begged.

Mum flashed dad a look, and dad said, "We're about to eat." He marched the yellow box inside. Toby nodded as if justice had been done.

"What's for lunch?" Pop asked.

"I thought we'd put out some cold plates, and everyone can make their own."

"Crackling, and gravy? Roast potatoes?"

Mum frowned. "We did all that on Christmas day."

Juliette said, "I don't want any more ham. It smells funny."

Mum put down the stack of plates she'd been distributing. "I'll make you a peanut butter sandwich."

***

After lunch, Toby took his bike from the garage and wheeled it out the front. Libs disappeared into her room with her new present. She'd asked Juliette whether she wanted to come and watch her try the make-up. Juliette had liked being invited, but she shook her head. She watched the adults for a minute, and clutched her doll upside-down by the foot, dragging it off the table as she stood up. "Are you going to play with baby?" Poppa Bert asked. Juliette nodded, looking at the pattern the bricks made under her feet, and ran inside.

When she'd shut the flyscreen door she held still, checking for any sign of her sister. Hearing nothing, she tossed the doll hard at the sofa. Sweeping into the kitchen, Juliette began with the fridge, but it was too full with leftovers. She couldn't see past the stuff at the front, and it would be hard to shift things in and out. She turned her attention to the walk-in pantry.

She slid the door shut behind her and found the switch for the light. It was cool, and the sounds of her family were not as loud as her own breathing. The shelving formed a U-shape, and there was plenty of space to turn around. Suspended from the ceiling was a too-bright globe that left after-images when Juliette looked up. She scanned the lower shelves, half hidden in shadow, pushing aside bags of rice and flour. Jars of disgusting curry paste. When she couldn't find what she was looking for, she planted her foot on the second shelf off the ground, grabbed at one of the vertical rails holding everything together, and levered herself upward, hoping that the shelf would hold her weight.

When she stretched tall, her eyes could clear the top shelf. There!—next to a half-drunk bottle of clear alcohol. She leaned out and grabbed for the box. Her hands closed around it, but she'd shifted too far and she had to jump clear of the shelf she was standing on. Her feet hit the pantry floor with a slap, and her head ended centimetres away from the hard metal edge of a rail. But in her right hand, raised in triumph, she held the Toblerone.

Juliette stood perfectly still. She heard her grandfather's foghorn laugh, but no sound of chairs scraping over brick. No footsteps.

Examining her prize, turning it over in her hands and feeling the weight inside, she saw a new problem. You were meant to tear a serrated cardboard tab to open the packaging, so that one end of the box would hinge. But if she did that, there would be a gap. Later, anyone who looked would see the foil glint. Would be able to tell what had been done.

She sat cross-legged, resting the Toblerone on one end against the linoleum floor. Her head blocked most of the light, but that didn't matter. Cautiously, she tested the edges of upturned end with her fingernails, running along the three sides of the triangle in turn. Each side was about the length of her ring finger, and one edge wasn't sealed. If she could pry away another side, perhaps she could extract the chocolate, take a piece, and then fold the packaging closed, with no one the wiser.

When she pulled at the cardboard, it started to rip. It was glued too firmly. So she left the box on the floor and ran back out to the kitchen, keeping low behind the benches. In the second drawer next to the sink, she found scissors.

Returning to her cave, door closed over, Juliette eased a blade through one of the triangular points at the end of the box. Wiggling it in and along, she cut a breach in the cardboard. When she withdrew the scissors, the gap she'd created was hardly visible. She had formed a flap, and when she tugged it open she could see silver, and when she tipped the box over, the block slid out as if it was eager.

She peeled away foil, exposing a single wedge of chocolate. In her left hand she held the box, and her right thumb slid down between the end piece and its neighbour.

Juliette paused. She was nine. She understood that some resources were in short supply: time on the computer, toys, the attention of a parent. Chocolate. She thought about Toby. She had fought enough battles, and she knew the feeling of losing something precious.

She wiggled her thumb, just testing, and the piece came away more easily than she expected. The wedge dropped to the pantry floor. Her hand went to reach, but Juliette stopped herself. She stood up, and packed foil back inside the box. She tried to fold closed the hinge she'd created, but she must have bent the cardboard too far. When she took her fingers away, the flap unfurled.

The air felt stuffy in this dim place, and Juliette started to shake. She wondered if she could stick the flap back down. There would be something like glue—golden syrup?—here in the pantry. But then the sounds from outside changed. The scrape of a knife over crockery.

There was no more time. Juliette replaced the Toblerone where she'd found it on the top shelf, making sure that the tampered end faced back towards the wall. Jumping down, she snatched her prize from the floor. And then there was another noise, much louder: a crash of spilled cutlery and shattering glass.

Everything happened then. She peeled away a streak of foil and stuffed the chocolate into her mouth. The taste – she remembered it now. It filled her mouth, the piece was too large, and she mashed down with her teeth; she was taking quick breaths through her nose but it was hard to get enough air. Tears welled and ran down the sides of her nose. And she heard the flyscreen door slide open.

She fled into the kitchen as dad ran in, snatching the cordless phone from its cradle on the wall. Snuffling, turning her face to hide her full cheeks and her tears, Juliette swerved into the lounge room.

When she looked outside, she saw her Gran lying on the bricks, and mum crouched over her, shouting something. Pop stood by, holding his hands to the sides of his head, and as Juliette watched he bent down to retrieve a broken bowl. The tablecloth had been pulled so that it hung like a matador's cape. Half-uncovered like that, the grey wood of the table looked shabby and wrong. Gran's head rolled, moving funny, and mum was screaming now.

Libs appeared at Juliette's shoulder. She must have heard the noises, too. The older girl made a huffing sound and wrapped her arms around her chest.

Behind them, dad was reciting their address. He sounded angry. Juliette turned to look at him and when she caught his eye, he stopped talking down the phone. He walked over to Libs and squeezed her shoulder. "Take Juliette," he said. "Go to your room and stay there 'til I get you."

Libs nodded and turned to face her sister. But Juliette was quicker, already in motion, skirting the coffee table. Grabbing her doll from the floor, she bolted down the hall to the bathroom. Inside, she switched the lock.

Ignoring her sister's calls and the jiggle of the knob, Juliette washed her hands. She sobbed, swallowing the last melted fragments of her prize. Even the lingering aftertaste of the chocolate was better than anything she could remember eating. A dot of foil that had stuck to her thumb disappeared down the plughole. She spat brown saliva into the sink, and worried that Libs might smell chocolate on her, so she brushed her teeth. She remembered the scissors she'd left on the pantry floor.

After she'd dried her mouth, she stood facing the wall, running her fingers over the rough edge of her blue towel. Little Drummer Boy sounded in her head: *pa rum pum pum pum.*

When she was ready, Juliette opened the bathroom door and walked down the hall. She kept her eyes ahead until she was inside Libs' bedroom. Stepping over piles of discarded clothes, noticing the makeup kit opened, contents spilled over the dressing table, she joined her sister on the bed.

Ignoring the heat of the day, the girls made a space between the mattress and the sheet, and settled in to wait.

***

About Andrew Roff

Andrew Roff was the winner of the 2018 Margaret River Press Short Story Competition. His work has appeared in Griffith Review, Overland, Southerly and Going Down Swinging, among others, and he was shortlisted for the Wakefield Press Unpublished Manuscript Award at the 2016 Adelaide Festival Awards for Literature. He lives in Adelaide.

Epica Intermission

I know what you're thinking dear guest, for I have been burdened by the same thoughts for so very long. How does an entire crew of masters and convicts simply disappear, leaving only yours truly on a ghost ship lost in time and space? That there is some serious tomfoolery at play is a fact that requires no evidence before the court. Perhaps when your visit upon these decks comes to an end you might hunt for an answer, and with it a way to free me of this endless night so that I can finally stumble upon Australia's sun burned soil?

Then again, you may come close to the answer and determine that better my fate remain than meddle with a force of such witchery. Fear not strange friend, for there'd be no blame here. Just think, were it not these strange turns of events we might never have had the chance to share such a special Christmas!

I think this bottle is yours to pluck from the deep blue waters. Excellent, now carefully slide out the scroll and let me see where imagination hopes to take us next. Well, well, well, perhaps something in the dark depths has been listening to our thoughts, for these words just may bring us closer to the answers we both seek…

Whispers of a Christless Angel

By Darren Kasenkow

*Dedicated to the mysterious architects, for they
are always watching...*

The following is a Christmas tale unlike many before it that have echoed across the bustling cities and dusty plains of Australia. Due to legal reasons the truth or veracity of the series of events woven together can neither be confirmed nor denied, and where required names have been changed to protect the guilty. What can be said however is that deep within the warm glow and high spirits of the festive season, when the shackles of daily grinds and constant struggles rattle to the ground so that for a brief moment the world is filled with wonder and swells with the promises of new beginnings, darkly wonderful things can happen.

The year was 1979. Enthusiastic scientists around the world were marvelling at the first cosmic photographs of Jupiter's breathtaking rings, the United States Embassy was invaded in Tehran with a show of unrestrained aggression, cinema goers around the world were shocked at the introduction of a chest bursting alien and Trivial Pursuit became a staple for household dining tables across the globe, leading to many a frustrated dice roll and never ending battles pitting brother against sister and siblings against parents.

In Australia the sun kissed residents of Esperance basked in the spotlight of the world when the space station Skylab came crashing down into their quaint seaside town, bringing with it a flurry of excitement and a brief respite from the usual sense of isolation that came from being so very far from anywhere. Sports fans across the country dipped their heads in shame and wallowed in bitter beers when the English snatched the Ashes in far too fine a fashion, Mad Max introduced the world to a post-apocalyptic outback leather clad hero with a love of souped up engines and a stinging taste for revenge, and all across the land girt by sea kids escaped the scorching heat of summer playing chasey beneath backyard sprinklers, risking almost certain tears launching down bone crushing slip and slides, or hiding in the shade turning fingers purple while learning new yoyo tricks. Oh, and a little organisation called the Federal Police was quietly introduced to the politically charged criminal landscape.

Though true it could be said the origins of this Christmas tale actually began on a pleasant metropolitan beach all the way back in 1951, it was the summer of 1979 when the quiet, heart breaking crescendo of what was a long and sinister chain of events came to bear witness beneath the burning stars of the Southern Cross. It was also a long, dry summer that continues to echo across the soul of a city to this very day, and so stands as a perfect place as any to begin…

The Client.

December was as hot as anyone could remember in the quaint southern city of (*redacted*). Had you asked most people they would've been quick to tell you it just *had* to be an all-time record, and that if it got any hotter there'd be exploding tyres all around. The fact that only the brave ventured the sun baked streets for any length of time left the central shopping precinct a festively decorated yet strange ghost town, and on this particular day just a week or so before Christmas those offices that hadn't already closed for the year hummed with the sound of struggling air conditioners, a sound that had truly become the electronic symphony of the season.

In one of these offices, nestled behind a paper laden desk with a rotating fan that did all it could to spread the cool air coming from the far wall, a man by the name of Clarence Turner sat. First impressions would suggest a slightly overweight figure who might once have projected a dashing confidence, with a thick moustache that curved down to the edge of his full chin and a rough-skinned face that almost made the permanent absence of a smile somehow captivating, but a closer examination of his distant yet calculating brown eyes hinted at a man who had seen more than he should have and damn well knew it. Just two days before he'd celebrated his fiftieth birthday in an empty lounge room with long neck beers and far too many cigarettes, and on this December day he was struggling beneath the weight of the ever present question of why he even bothered.

With a frustrated sigh he loosened his cheap tie for the third time and emptied what was left of his now warm TAB with one heroic gulp. It was his second already that morning and as far as he was concerned there'd be plenty more if the heat kept up which, of course, it would. He'd heard the weather report on the radio driving to work and so had made sure to grab as many bottles as he could hold before stepping through the squeaking office door.

Clarence was a private investigator. It wasn't what he wanted to be and it sure as hell wasn't what he'd planned to be, but the sign painted on the frosted glass said so none the less. His licence was barely two years old, banged out on a typewriter with a set of crooked keys, stamped with a green blur of ink and handed to him a month or so after moving from (*retracted*), but then again it might as well have been a lifetime ago.

You see, before moving cities to start a red eyed, carpet stained new life, Clarence had been a defence lawyer whose courtroom trajectory had begun with unlucky citizens for clients and had ended with stone faced, hardened criminals purchasing his skills to combat the sharpened teeth of the justice system. While not as well known as some of the flashier lawyers that held court in town, he had nonetheless garnered a strong reputation as a man married to his job with an obsessive attention to detail that could find any chink in the prosecution's armour. This particular skill had proved to be his undoing however, not to mention a devastating end to his legal career, when he'd managed to save what would be his last client from a lengthy prison sentence regardless of the fact that even the greatest of fools had plainly seen he had been guilty. Shunned from a city that had cursed the blood soaked ramifications of what had proven to be his final courtroom success, all that had been left to do was move under the cloak of night like a wounded bird leaving its nest and try to remould something from the left over ashes in a place where nobody knew his name.

And so it was on this stinking hot day in December, that the routine of waiting for his assistant to poke her head through his door and confirm yet another day of no calls was suddenly broken. Barbara, a red-headed and loyal trooper in her mid-thirties who had brightened the reception area with her smile since the first day his name had been stencilled on the glass, would usually soften the failure of his back page advertisements with some cold ice for his TAB and a fresh newspaper, but not on this day. On this day she burst into his office wide eyed and brimming with excitement.

"There's a lady here to see you!" she declared with a loud whisper and proud thumb pointed over her shoulder. "She says it's very important that she speaks with you."

Clarence wiped at echoes of the previous night's beer that trickled from his forehead and stared back in surprise. Resting on the desk before him pages of an electronics magazine that he'd already read three times rustled against the breeze of the tired fan, and though he was about to study the specs around the world's first push button shutter speed control on the new Pentax one more time he managed to lift his bloodshot eyes from the article.

"Are you sure it's not a debt collector?" he asked, a flash of concern tightening his dry throat.

"Quite sure," Barbara smiled. "You know I can spot them a mile away. If she was a debt collector the door knob would've already hit her in the ass."

"Then I guess you'd better show her on through."

Suddenly aware of his appearance he neatened up his tie as best he could and stuffed the magazine into a drawer as Barbara waltzed back into the reception area. The last thing he'd been expecting that day was to be playing host that was for damn sure, but as he brushed back his thick grey speckled hair with sweaty fingers he couldn't shake the thought that maybe another hook was about to latch deep into his wallet. After all, just because he'd moved states didn't mean the lawsuits had any intention of giving up the thrill of the chase.

Barbara reappeared and ushered in an immaculately dressed lady that appeared to be in her mid-sixties. She wore shining silver hair in a perfect bun held together with a golden peacock pin, was graced with a soft smiling face that shone with an understated combination of lipstick and foundation, and held small, proud shoulders back as she peered through silver framed glasses at the sparse furnishings of the office.

"How can I help you?" Clarence asked by way of introduction.

His unexpected guest settled into the cracked, orange vinyl seat and slowly smoothed her tartan skirt.

"Yes of course," she laughed, "that would be the best place to start." Her hands fell still as she studied him with curious hazel eyes. "I'm sure you must be extremely busy and probably have far more important tasks to worry about than my little problem, especially with Christmas around the corner, but I wasn't sure just where else to turn so thought there'd be no harm in at least trying. Oh, I'm Bernice by the way, Bernice Edwards."

Suddenly the power to the building dropped away with a mechanical shudder, silencing the air conditioner, and stilling the fan. Beams of late morning sun through the small office window became the only source of light as the stifling heat was quick to reach out from the fresh shadows, while the sudden quiet that fell across the desk revealed the once inaudible ticking of the scratched plastic clock that was barely hanging to the wall. Clarence sighed and hoped the sweat stains on his shirt weren't as bad as they felt.

"Sorry about that, seems we can't make it through a day without at least a blackout or two." He did his best to smile but barely managed a curl along the edges of his moustache. "I appreciate you stopping by Bernice. I'm sure we can find some room for you in our schedule, so I'd be interested to find out what's brought you here today."

Resting beside his feet was a small ice cooler with a taped together handle. He reached down into what was now a cubeless pool of water, wrangled one of the last bottles despite slippery fingers, and then promptly presented it as though it were a well fought for trophy.

"TAB?"

Bernice eyed the offering but shook her head politely, prompting him to replace it with a soft splash.

"I don't mind sitting in the dark so much Mr. Turner, the days are long and there'll be plenty of light when I step back outside. As for what brought me here today, well, it's kind of funny really. I'm part of a small group of lovely ladies who dabble in a little publishing you see, and we'd very much like to find a particular gentleman who seems to have… *disappeared*." She pronounced the word as though describing a magic trick that had left her in wonder. "I was excited to see your advertisement in the newspaper and thought to myself, now here's a man who will be able to help us. I would have called but looking someone in the eyes while you speak is so much more dignified, don't you think?"

Clarence nodded quietly as another drop of sweat trickled down the edge of his jaw. He wasn't sure what to make of the woman, couldn't quite read her as easily as most clients that strayed into his office, sparse as they were, but then she had only just sat down. Though she seemed polite enough, spoke with quick confidence and yet maintained a calming, maternal like smile, behind her alert hazel eyes there was definitely a hint of yet to be revealed trouble.

"This man your little group would like to find, is he an author or something?"

"Oh no, nothing so gallant as that. He's a well respected judge, or at least he was, who agreed by correspondence to help with a historical project we were in the process of putting together. Don't get me wrong, it wouldn't matter so much to us ladies if he chose to simply change his mind, but it so happens that this man accepted a somewhat substantial advance for his services before no longer answering the phone or responding to letters. I'm sure you'll agree it would be best for the money to be returned." For the first time since gracing the office Bernice's smile slipped away. "Being a single mother in these modern times isn't easy Mr. Turner as I'm sure you can appreciate, and our humble little publishing company is a way to help ease the struggles of single mothers with the weight of the world against them. Our staff have no financial support beyond this business, and without the return of our advance that was made in good faith I'm afraid any future publications might very well be made impossible."

"Clarence."

"I beg your pardon?"

"Call me Clarence."

"If you insist, I'd be happy to." Her smile returned at the suggestion, this time less maternal and more reflective of a child receiving a surprise bag of sweets. "So tell me Clarence, will you accept our offer of employment?"

"I'm sure I could shuffle things around a little. Of course, I'll need a few details to work with and an upfront part payment, but unlike other investigators my fee comes with a guarantee. After all, finding people that don't want to be found has kind of become my specialty."

"Then I do believe Mr. Turner, oh, I mean Clarence, that we have ourselves a deal." Suddenly power to the building returned, the air conditioner once again humming an ode to its struggles and the fan whining back to life as shadows that had been clawing across the desk were quickly chased away by the light of the bare overhead globe. "I've prepared some documents that should assist your investigation, and of course I've included my contact details should you have any further questions." She smoothed the lines of her skirt one last time and gracefully rose from the chair. "I can't tell you how much this means to us girls. After all, sometimes the task of finding balance in the universe must be made a priority, wouldn't you agree?"

Clarence wasn't quite sure how to respond to such a strange statement, and so chose instead to stand and offer his hand after a quick wipe against his pants. Though her smile was as prominent as ever he couldn't help but notice the promise of trouble still smouldered behind her eyes.

"I'll need a couple of days to get things rolling but I'll be in touch as soon as I have something." He reached across and took her soft hand in his. "Barbara will help with the contract before showing you out."

"Contract?"

"Don't worry, confidentiality is our priority. We just need a signature here and there for our records, that's all."

"Of course, I understand." She released her hand and extracted a pink envelope from her purse, placing it carefully upon the desk. "Christmas really is a time of miracles isn't it?"

The question was left to hang in the air as she shuffled out of his office and closed the door behind her with a soft *click,* leaving him with a quiet exhilaration that came with a well overdue payday.

He fell back into his chair and opened up the envelope. Inside he found a single typed document on paper that was clearly expensive based on the gold gilding around the perimeter, and as he began to read through the contents he reached for his warm TAB and indulged in a long mouthful.

At the top of the page was the name of their company, *Afterlife Publications,* a choice of name that struck him as somewhat odd considering the spiel he'd been given about the struggles of single mothers, while beneath the logo of a sword wielding angel rested a concise summary of the man whom he was now tasked to find.

Richard Varley.

Former Supreme Court judge with forty two years' service to the state. Paid an advance in the amount of two thousand three hundred dollars for consultancy services in relation to historic legal cases for an upcoming book exploring the evolution of crime and punishment in Australia. Just three days before the first scheduled interview all communications ceased, and listed address appears to be no longer occupied. No known record of current whereabouts and, the document pointed out, *friends and associates currently refusing to shed any light on the sudden turn of events.*

Clarence took another swig and opened up his notebook, scribbling down some of the details before glancing up at Barbara's sudden entry. Confusion scrunched the delicate lines around her eyes as she rested a hand on her hip, her head tilted to the side as she expertly raised one eyebrow. He recognized the stance, and knew instantly that something was wrong.

"She was a sweet old lady," Barbara sighed, "but there's definitely something strange about her. She signed off the contract as *Summoning Angel Of Vengeance,* but hold onto your hat because it gets weirder. Under the section for confidential alternative contacts, instead of names or phone numbers she drew a bunch of weird looking pentagrams."

"Say again?"

"Oh I said pentagrams alright, at least I think that's what they were anyway." She shook her head with a growing look of confusion. "Then, as she walked out the office, she turned over her shoulder and said it would be best if we could resolve the matter before the Christmas Eve full moon. I mean, I know things are getting desperate and we need any client we can get our hands on, but something tells me this old lady comes with an extra serving of crazy."

"You just might be right," Clarence assured her as the sound of passing sirens wailed beyond the window, "but as long as her cheque doesn't bounce I'll be happy to look past her eccentricities. Besides, nobody walks in here without some sort of secret they want to peel open."

"Even sweet old ladies?"

"Yeah, even sweet old ladies…"

The Lawyer.

The following day Clarence hit the city streets early in an attempt to beat the torturous heat. His destination was a cafe whose main source of income came from sleep deprived lawyers preparing for battle in the courthouse next door, and though the sun was still rising across the baking city skyline the coffee machines were already working overtime when he navigated his way through the crowded outdoor tables.

And that wasn't an easy feat with a cane.

His right leg hadn't worked properly since an angry mob had shoved a disgruntled spokesperson with a baseball bat his way. The sudden display of athletic skills he'd received a front row seat to meant a cane had become an essential part of his wardrobe. Considering it had been shattered in four different places, it was a miracle he could walk on it at all. He'd already suffered through three surgeries, each accompanied with hollow promises of near superpowers, but the damaged nerves and fractured bones had proven to be a jigsaw that would forever be marred by missing pieces.

With suspicious attention suddenly drawn to his presence he peered through the smeared shop front window and searched for the man who just might have the information he was after. When he spotted him dining alone in the far corner, a calculated and strategic position directly beneath the air conditioner, Clarence shuffled through the door and quietly cursed the cheap bell that announced his entry.

Sean Gow glanced up from his newspaper at the rhythmic sound of a cane approaching his table. He was a strapping young attorney, with perfectly gelled black hair and chiselled features of the kind that proved exquisite genetics and old money enjoyed an eternally symbiotic relationship, and yet unlike other hungry ladder climbers he had no need for arrogance. His success was all but ordained from the moment he first put on a suit, and to compensate for the express lane that upper society deemed an inherited right he spent his energy mastering the intricacies of the legal system and being the best he could be rather than wasting time with rash displays of confidence. So it was, that as much as Clarence wanted to hate him, he had to admit he carried integrity of the kind that was so very rare in a field that took pride in gaming the system.

When he reached the table he pointed down at the empty chair and waited for what would be an obviously regretful invitation. Sure enough, Sean folded his newspaper and looked around the cafe with visible unease before shrugging his shoulders and nodding ever so slightly. Grateful to take the weight off his leg, Clarence took a seat and savoured the cool air blowing against his face.

"I had a feeling you'd be here," he said matter of factly.

"Actually I was just about to leave," Sean replied, "so I sure would appreciate you telling me why you're sitting there because I doubt very much you've popped in for coffee and toast."

"You always did like going straight for the heart of the matter, I'll give you that."

"I've got court in fifteen minutes. I'll need five to find my client and remind him to keep his mouth shut and another five to sort out my paperwork for the judge. Considering I'll need to squeeze in a last minute deal attempt with prosecution somewhere in there, I figure you've got about two minutes to tell me why you're here."

"Shit, you really don't like me do you?" Clarence asked with a shake of his head.

"Actually," Sean sighed while placing the newspaper neatly into his briefcase, "truth is I don't have any judgment one way or the other. What I do have is a lack of time and a strong belief that our business was finished."

"Don't worry, I'm here for something different." Clarence removed a slip of paper from his top pocket and placed it down onto the table with a tap of his finger. "It's pretty simple really. I've got a client who's real interested in catching up with a judge by the name of Richard Varley. She seems to think he's gone missing but it's probably nothing, you know how these things go. Still, it's a pay cheque, so I figure you being part of the court furniture you might be able to shed a little light on his whereabouts."

Sean suddenly slammed his briefcase closed and stared across the table with a steeled expression that was both surprised and worried. Clarence could sense the sudden shift in his composure, so he leaned in a little closer and was sure to lower his voice.

"Judging by the look on your face you know the guy I'm talking about."

"I don't know who your client is, but you might want to reconsider cashing that cheque. Richard isn't a judge anymore and the best thing you can do is forget about finding him."

"Actually, my client's nothing more than a sweet old lady and as far as I know she's just after some money owed to her. All I want to do it talk with him to see if we can't work something out."

"I don't think you're listening." Sean scanned the busy cafe and was growing visibly nervous, enough so that when he continued he lowered his head in an effort to guard his words. "Richard is officially a ghost okay? If you start trying to dig around for him the only thing you'll find is trouble, and I'm talking the kind that can shut you down quicker than a gavel makes a grown man cry so do yourself a favour, grab that cane of yours and hobble away."

Clarence felt a tingle of trepidation at the dramatic warning. If it was anybody else he would've dismissed it as a bad attempt by a power hungry lawyer to protect the judge from unwanted intrusions into his privacy, but it wasn't anybody else.

Sean was a straight shooter. He may have been blunt and he sure as hell didn't waste time with pleasantries, but his ability to approach situations with a clinical objectivity was the reason Clarence had hired him when he first moved to the city. You see, he'd needed a solid lawyer to fight a lawsuit lodged against him by a mob that just wouldn't let go. That also meant Sean had discovered the reason for his change in residence and career, but as much as the revelation had sickened him he'd stuck to the clear merits of the defence with a clinical professionalism. And won. So if he determined a warning was warranted, it was a warning worth listening to.

"I'm not looking to cause a stir mate, but if I walk away from this one she's just gonna find someone else to do the digging. You know I need a pay day, so I figure maybe this judge is worth the risk. Like I said, I just want to talk with him."

"You asked me if I know where Richard Varley is, and I'm telling you he's nowhere." Sean might have been trying to put an exclamation point on the conversation, but there was a sudden glint in his eyes that hinted at a pained resignation. "Jesus Clarence, I thought you would've learned by now that sometimes the right thing to do is as muddy as a bruised confession."

He scanned the busy cafe once more, carefully watching the caffeine wired patrons, then swiftly produced a pen from his inner jacket pocket and scribbled something down onto one of the napkins resting by his discarded coffee mug.

"I've got a client facing serious prison time and I don't plan on being late." He stood with a sudden sense of purpose and grabbed his briefcase. "What you did back then caused a lot of pain for a lot of people, but it doesn't mean there's no good left in you. Something tells me you'll find it, if you're willing to dig deep enough."

The cryptic declaration was left unanswered as the lawyer with the curt warning marched through the crowd and out the door, leaving Clarence to stare down at the table while curious eyes began to watch his every move. Maybe they knew who he was, knew what he had done considering word didn't take long to travel the late night court halls, but for the moment it didn't matter. What *did* matter was the napkin.

He slid it close and studied the penmanship. The neat cursive writing was impressive to be sure, but he wasn't certain what to make of the prose. There was a name, *Ray Ivanov*, and an address for a business, *Big Blue Charters*. It was in a part of the port section he'd never ventured, but that was about to change.

Feeling the weight of the room closing in he slipped the napkin into his pocket, grabbed his cane and began to shuffle his way through the tables. He made a point of keeping his eyes to the ground, and when he stepped outside beneath the blue sky furnace he couldn't help but wonder what kind of trouble the old lady had brought him. He was far from anybody's fool, knew that it was a little too convenient that a missing judge case would fall in his lap considering his previous role in a life growing hazy in the distance, but then trouble had always been a mistress of unrivalled devotion that was there for him even on his loneliest of nights. Truth was the relationship was the only one that had held tight when all others had crumbled away, and that meant the least he could do was honour his lover by doing what he did best. He would find out what this trouble was all about.

The Fisherman.

It was mid-afternoon when he rolled his tan HX Holden station wagon to a stop by the edge of an all but empty wharf, where rusting bollards and splintered slabs of timber protected the ocean from mostly abandoned sheds that creaked and groaned in the sea breeze.

Clarence counted only two boats quietly bobbing in the water, stubborn and weathered vessels waiting for adventures that would probably never come, and when he stepped out of the car he could smell the loss of hope in the air. He'd never been out this way before, but had read about the wharfs and once thriving businesses that were mercilessly forgotten when a fancy new marina had been established much closer to the city. Mere years before the area might have been crackling with the kind of electricity that came with high spirited cruises and hard drinking anglers, but now it seemed nothing more than a salt encrusted ghost town where even seagulls were a rare sight, and he was already starting to wonder if he was in the right place.

The cane burned hot in his hand as he moved along the cracked concrete and eyed the various signs that had long ago given in to the elements. He passed shed after empty shed but then, just as he was about to turn around and head back, he spotted what he was looking for.

Big Blue Charters.

This sign had at least enjoyed a fresh lick of paint at some point judging by the minimal rust and the fact that he could actually read more than a handful of letters, and as he headed for the entrance he was greeted with a wide open cavern with a long belly of dark shadows. From somewhere deep inside there came a series of sharp hammering noises accompanied with sporadic curses that echoed along the tin walls, and for the first time since turning off his engine he realized he wasn't the only sign of life by the water's edge.

Clarence stepped into the darkness and, once his eyes had adjusted, was confronted with a small maze of overflowing work benches and a floor scattered with fishing nets and floats. The smell of fresh weld and motor oil was thick in the air and reminded him of distant times almost forgotten when he'd been allowed to spend time with his dad in the shed, even if those times had been short and cruelly uncomfortable.

He called out an authoritative hello and seconds later the source of the hammering and curses emerged from the shadows of the far corner. Dressed in stained jeans and a sun faded flannelette shirt that looked as though careful breathing was all that kept it from disintegrating once and for all, the guy was clearly startled by the sudden visit judging by his defensive stance with hammer in hand. A filthy baseball cap kept the top half of his face hidden but a thick grey beard that reached down to his chest ensured Clarence that he'd weathered a king's ransom of fishing seasons.

"Is there something I can do for ya?" he asked with a simmering suspicion.

Clarence offered a half-baked disarming smile and shrugged his shoulders.

"Just hoping for a chat."

"A chat huh? Won't do you much good. Boat's in need of repairs and once she's back to health I'll be shuttin' down and moving on, so if you're looking for a charter for you and some mates you won't be finding it here I'm afraid."

"Then I guess it's my lucky day," Clarence gruffed as a hot wind whipped through the shed, "I don't have any mates and I've never been one for fishing."

"Helluva sad state for a man to be in I say. Guessing you must be here to sell me something then," he mused with a scratch of his beard. "Hate to say it but you're barking up the wrong tree there as well, I'm not what you'd call the customer kind and I've got far better things to do with what little money I've got."

"I hear you Ray. It is Ray isn't it? Thing is, I'm not here to buy or sell anything. Like you I'm not much of a customer and I'm sure as hell no salesman."

"Then what the hell are you?"

"A collector of information I guess you could say. The name's Clarence, and it's my understanding you might be able to help with what I'm looking for. I've just got a few questions and then I'll be on my way."

Ray stepped forward and studied him as though he were an odd museum exhibit. For several moments there fell an uncomfortable silence, but it was eventually broken when the fisherman chuckled to a punch line only he knew.

"Figured it was just a matter of time before someone wanted to know something." He turned and made his way through the benches towards a doorway in the far wall. "Might as well step into my office," he grumbled over his shoulder.

Clarence too weaved his way through the benches but his eyes were drawn to several large wooden crates, each with their contents exposed to the corrosive salty air. Then with a shift of his gaze towards the rear of the shed he noticed the outline of a car draped beneath a large tarp. Part of the front grill peaked out from the shadows, and even in the low light he recognized the model.

Stepping into the office was like stepping into a bomb blast with a slapped together desk resting in the middle. Torn nautical posters littered the walls, countless boxes of fishing junk were piled up high across the floor and a collection of rods hung suspended from the ceiling at odd angles, their rusty hooks dangling down as though part of some demented chandelier. On a drawerless filing cabinet in the corner an old transistor radio struggled to add a little atmosphere as *I Will Survive* crackled from the speaker, though truth be told the popular hit didn't have much of a chance.

Clarence joined Ray at the desk and did his best to get comfortable on the upturned milk crate that substituted for a chair. His host sighed heavily, scratched at his long beard and then pulled a proverbial rabbit out of the hat, only the rabbit in this case was a half full bottle of whisky that was quickly followed by two dusty glasses.

"You don't have mates and you don't like fishing, but if you tell me you don't like drinking I won't have much to say."

"One's too many and a thousand's not enough," Clarence assured him, "so make it a triple."

"Now you're making sense." Ray laughed and poured their drinks with a heavy hand. "For a moment there I was ready to step back out and grab my hammer." The brief flash of humour disappeared as quickly as it had come. "You've got until the end of this bottle to tell me what the hell it is you want."

Clarence gulped down the cheap whisky in one fell swoop then slammed the glass down for another. He had no intention of ever coming back to a ghost town like this so figured he'd better make the most of it, and as he watched his host tilt the bottle once more he opened his wallet on the desk to reveal his credentials.

"In case you hadn't worked it out already I'm a private investigator looking for someone in particular. Inside my pocket here there's a napkin with your name on it, and I'm guessing that means you'll to be able to help me do my job today."

"A private eye huh? Fancy that. Wanna tell me who it is you're looking for?"

"Yeah, sure, a judge by the name of Richard Varley. Now I don't know why I was given your name or what you have to do with any of this but I'm here now, enjoying I might add your bartending skills and exotic seating, so if you know where he is or someone that does I'm all ears."

Ray stared down into his glass with a concerned look that assured an internal battle, while on the radio *I Will Survive* came to an end and *Born To Be Alive* began. He slammed down his drink, poured another, and looked straight at Clarence with red blazing eyes.

"I don't know where this judge of yours is. Hell, if you asked me what he looked like I wouldn't even be able to tell ya so best drink up so comin' here ain't a complete waste of time."

Clarence nodded politely enough but propped his elbow and balanced his glass in the manner of someone who had very much settled in for a session.

"Hate to say it Ray but a man who pours a drink like that probably knows something they wished they didn't, and I wouldn't be here if the information I got didn't come from someone who hasn't beat around the bush a day in his life so the way I see it *you've* got until the end of that bottle to tell me what the hell's going on here. Until then, I'm not going anywhere."

"Bad things can happen to a man wanting to know what shouldn't be known."

"Yeah," Clarence responded with a slide of his empty glass forward for another, "you're probably right, but then bad things happen to good men too and it's never an easy thing to carry it on your own."

"You really wanna open this door?"

"Even if it means ripping the hinges off."

Ray let out a long sigh and looked deep into his glass as though somewhere between the whisky and dust a chance of retreat lay in wait. Unfortunately whisky and dust was all there was, and so he lowered his eyes even further as an even heavier sigh signalled a shift in the mood of the room.

"Listen mate," he said reluctantly, "all I know is I chartered a bunch of fellas back in January for some tuna fishing and it ended up being one of the worst bloody days of my life. Came with a curse too, cause ain't nobody booked a charter since."

"I'm not sure if I follow…"

"Yeah? Well you're gonna regret trying to if we don't call this an end to things."

"This milk crate is mighty comfortable if you ask me."

"Then I guess we're both about to find out what it's like to be stuck in a storm with no port." He shook his head with disbelief and gripped the glass tight. "There's a spot out past the horizon I like to take clients with big cheque books, the kind that not many fishermen know about where a reef pops up from the deep water and a hook can barely touch the water before you're on. Weather turned to crap that day let me tell ya, rain showers so thick you couldn't see your hand in front of your face, but we dropped anchor by the edge anyway 'cause I don't do refunds for things I can't control." Suddenly Clarence could sense both fear and shame creeping into his voice. "Anyway, the storm cleared a bit and I spotted another boat by the other end of the reef, real fancy boat this one and not the type to be out that far, and I could just make out someone dropping something big over the side. Whoever it was must've seen us and decided to hightail it outta there but, being a nosy bastard, I grabbed some binoculars to check out the vessel's name."

"And?" Clarence asked, his attention now very much captured.

"*Age of Innocence* was her name. Didn't mean much at the time but like I said, it was a bit weird to see someone else out that far."

With a visible wince he paused to empty what was left of the bottle into their glasses. For the first time since they'd started drinking Clarence could see his hand was beginning to shake.

"Tell me something," he continued, "you being a fancy private eye and all, I'm guessing you must be pretty familiar with death?"

Clarence looked the fisherman in the eye and wondered where the hell a question like that came from. He'd never been asked anything like it before that was for sure, and now that it echoed across the chaos of the office the mood had most definitely shifted gears yet again.

"I think you've been watching too many television shows mate. People usually hire me to see if their partner's shacking up with someone else, or maybe I'll get an insurance agent wanting me to make sure somebody's injury is legit, so in answer to your question no, death isn't quite part of my job description."

"Then here's to new experiences." Ray leaned forward and gently tapped his glass against Clarence's. "Now, you know the name of the boat but you don't know what it is I found."

"I'm still listening."

"Yeah, and you still can't see the storm headed your way."

"Maybe I need those binoculars of yours."

"Yeah, maybe you do." Somewhere outside a rising wind gust rattled the tired frame of the shed, issuing a series of creaks and groans that could almost have been mistaken for whining animals. "I wish it never did, but curiosity got the better of me. If we were closer to shore maybe I wouldn't have paid much attention but we weren't, so we pulled in our lines, motored over to the other end of the reef, and then while the fellas cracked open some tinnies I grabbed a hook line and did a bit of dangling. You see, whoever it was on that boat mustn't have realized the reef was there. It's deep sea all around but at that particular spot the water's only chest high, and on a clear day you might've been able to tell but with the crazy weather and all you'd have to have local knowledge to have an idea of the depth."

"Fishing secrets I'm not much interested in Ray so tell me, what did you find?"

Clarence suddenly noticed the sauna like heat of the office as he sipped his whisky and waited for his answer, though for reasons he couldn't pinpoint he was strangely unsure of whether he actually *wanted* the conversation to go any further. Years of confidential testimony had taught him that true confessions could be the most difficult of words to hear, and something told him the fisherman was about to let out some serious demons. It was impossible not to recognize the pain that had become clearly etched across his face.

"I hooked onto something heavy," he began. "There's no forgetting when I pulled it up because the worst lightning that ever shone my eyes tore open the sky about the same time."

Obviously never one to reveal his entire hand, he reached down into a box against the wall behind him and pulled out another bottle. This time however his hand was shaking so badly the neck rattled against the glass and sent a healthy soaking of whisky to splash across the cheap, warping desk.

"It was a hessian bag," he continued with obvious disgust. "Heavy enough that I had to use one of my chains 'cause there was a bunch of cinder blocks tied to it. When I finally got it onto the deck I grabbed a knife and cut it open, and that's when I found out the Devil is real."

"The Devil?"

"Ain't nobody else gonna destroy something so beautiful and dump it in the ocean to rot away." He dipped his face in a futile attempt to hide a glint of tears. "She was just a little kid, with these big blue eyes that seemed to stare straight into my soul and long blond hair that was tangled around her neck, and the only thing she had on was a pair of Snoopy socks and some kind of bracelet."

He stopped to take in several deep breaths before continuing, his stooped shoulders projecting an air of exhausted defeat.

"Her stomach had been cut open real deep. I'm talking deep enough to see things no man should see. And there was some kind of pentagram burned into her chest, like a branding done with sick twisted metal or somethin', and for the first time in forty years I puked my guts up good and proper." He forced his hands down onto the desk in an attempt to stop the shaking. "No doubt about it, the Devil had ventured to sea and now someone's little girl ain't never gonna see another day."

Though the heat of the room was tinkering on the edge of being unbearable Clarence felt a shiver ripple along his skin. On top of the filing cabinet the old radio had mysteriously switched to a low static fusion of white noise, while the mental image of a dead girl in a storm way out at sea began to bleed across his now racing thoughts.

"So let me get this right," he managed with a suddenly dry throat, "you're telling me the judge I'm looking for was on that boat?"

Ray lifted his face and smeared away the tears. His expression shifted to one of frustration while the shaking in his hands dropped away, and judging by the way he shuffled his frame to the edge of his milk crate and stole a glance towards the door the conversation, it seemed, was coming to an end.

"It's dangerous to put words in another man's mouth. I'm not saying it was the judge and I'm not saying it wasn't, but the way I see things you came here with nothin' and now you know the name of the boat and what I pulled from the water, so doing what you do for a living should mean the pieces can be put together." He leaned forward and tapped the empty whisky bottle. "Nothing left to pour means our little chat is over."

"What about the other one?"

"That's gonna help stop the little girl's eyes from sending me crazy so doesn't count."

"Fair enough mate, but there's gotta be more so I really need you to tell me everything. The cops must've been involved and one way or another you must've found out just who was on that boat."

"I've already told you too much. I tell you any more and they'll hang me out to dry."

"Oh shit," Clarence blurted out as the penny suddenly dropped, "the '79 XD Falcon sitting under the tarp out there that looks like it came straight from the showroom, the brand new boat engine parts in those boxes… you're being gagged. Somebody's paid you to keep quiet."

"Now you listen and listen good. The only reason I told you anything is because knowing the Devil got a free pass is eating me up from the inside ready to leave nothin' but a bag of bones, and every day it's getting harder and harder to convince myself I at least tried to do the right thing. In case you haven't noticed ain't nobody coming round here no more, the banks were chasing me down for mortgage payments I couldn't make and my damn boat was one storm from being a wreck dive so I took what I had to. Only thing left to do now is finish the repairs, head north as far as I can and never look back."

He slammed a fist down onto the desk, kicked away the crate then marched towards the door with fresh bottle of whisky in hand.

"You can show yourself out," he said almost apologetically over his shoulder.

Clarence sat stunned as the radio crackled back to life with the opening bars of Little River Band's *Lonesome Loser*. There was no point chasing after the broken fisherman with medicine clasped tight, he'd made it pretty obvious that his brief flash of hospitality had come to an end and besides, a few more swigs and there'd be no telling what the pain would do should he be backed into a corner.

Overhead the lights flickered and suddenly he was all too happy to leave. The atmosphere in the sauna-like office had become eerily foreboding, as if an invisible wake simmering with anger at his presence had begun amongst the boxes, and so there was nothing to do but to head back out to the wharf where ghosts of forgotten times mixed with the cracked, burning concrete.

When he slipped back behind the wheel he took one last look across the smooth surface of the ocean, fired up the engine, and knew that his investigation was about to take him to dark places that would surely have him wish he never took the job at all.

The Time Machine.

The early evening sky was a dark molten red when Clarence stepped into the quiet of the city library. Thankfully it was open late during the hot months of summer, a place of non judgment and treasured knowledge that had served as a sanctuary of sanity for him so many times, but on this night it was different. After a sea breeze adventure that had come with whisky stinging revelations, he was quite sure sanity played no part in the tapestry thread he was trying to pull.

Though conversation was never more than cordial, the staff were familiar enough with his requests to use the microfiche room, and when they ushered him through he was relieved to see nothing but empty chairs. For Clarence the machines were akin to magic, with the logistically simple yet beautiful boxes giving him the power to shut out the world and traverse back in time through tiny snapshots immortalized on film stock. To be a silent witness to places and events that had since passed was almost meditative, and though he didn't always find what he was looking for there was something to be said for the way the silence of the sanctuary tried valiantly to ease the anxieties of the day.

The first thing he did was search the January newspapers for any articles surrounding the discovery of the girl's body out at sea, but it didn't take long to come up with nothing. He moved on to February, then March, and still not a single paragraph had been written about the tragedy. There was always the chance that the fisherman had been lying of course, a sad trait he'd learned could afflict even the noblest of clients, but then if it was a lie it was also one of the greatest performances he'd ever seen and besides, the whole idea of bullshitting was to try to throw him *off* a lead. Unless he was sorely mistaken, he'd been given one.

Still, it was quickly becoming apparent that his search for confirmation of the murder wasn't pulling up a damn thing. The fact that Ray's silence had been bought and paid for was most likely the culprit, but it was hard to imagine that such a heinous murder didn't even warrant a mention. Sure an investigation into the crime itself could be covered up, but there should have at least been mention of the initial find or an outcry from the heartbroken family. It just didn't make sense that a little girl's dead body made it to the morgue without garnishing at least a little attention.

With frustration overtaking any sense of meditative gains he rubbed his eyes and began scrolling further back in time to see if anything jumped out. He had no idea *what* might catch his attention of course, but the plates had a way of revealing secrets and patterns if you just gave the machine enough of a chance. It was a strong enough working theory most times, but on this evening it proved to be nothing more than a butterfly in the rain.

It was time to switch tactics. He trawled through the drawers, switched up the plate, and was suddenly transported to a magnified world capturing the hallowed pages of the Australian Police Journal. A staple of the thin blue line since 1946, he had spent many an hour deep in its pages when the court room had still been his temple and the truth of high calibre crimes could be found resting somewhere between a cop's report and a client monologue.

Slow and tediously, article headline by article headline, he floated back in time. When his eyes began to strain midway through 1977 an attention grabbing combination of words jumped up through the hazy screen and gave his heart a quick jolt of adrenaline. *Supreme Court Judge Missing*. And, just like that, the sting in his whisky shot eyes didn't seem so bad.

Though the article was short and didn't seem to want to reveal too much, it was enough to confirm that esteemed Supreme Court judge *(redacted)* had been officially listed as a missing person seventy two hours after failing to return to his family home. The clinical prose reiterated that police had been unable to determine if foul play was a factor and would no longer be pursuing the matter. Considering it read more like a shoplifting report and less like a high profile crime possibility, it couldn't help but emanate from the screen with a smell fishier than Ray's unkempt office on the edge of the wharf.

With the tang of the fresh scent sharpening his senses he scrolled back even further, and when another headline jumped out like a blood stain on a wedding dress the back of his neck turned cold. *Search For Senior Police Officer Called Off.* This time the year was 1974 and, just like the previous article, any real detail had been left on the editorial floor. All that could be garnered was that a Constable (*redacted*) had taken a short leave of absence only never to return, and that following a lack of sustainable leads all further investigations would cease.

Clarence broke away from the machine and stared up at the ceiling. If the previous article had smelled a little funny, he was quickly surmising, then this one had a stench strong enough to strip the paint job off a new car. If there was one law that was never broken it was that cops looked out for their own regardless of which way the moral compass swung, and there wasn't a chance in hell they'd just walk away from a missing colleague. The fact that the decision had even been published probably had more to do with the family than the need to broadcast a desire to let the matter come to rest.

And so his search for missing persons continued, and so too the discovery of articles that didn't seem quite right. There was a corporate lawyer that simply didn't show up to court one day in 1973 and was never seen again. Next a Labor Party MP in 1971 whose sudden disappearance was made even more cryptic when his warm, half-filled coffee cup had been discovered still sitting on his desk. Then, in the dizzy free love of 1969, there were not one, but two cases discontinued and both once again involved senior state politicians.

By the time the magic machine had transported him back to 1953 his cramped hand had scrawled eleven names into his tattered notebook, each and every one an investigation that had been ceased, and though it was impossible to say whether the strange series of events had anything at all to do with the judge he was looking for there was no denying that something sinister seemed to be festering beneath the facade of the city.

Clarence had seen and heard enough for one day. Besides, there was a fine number of longneck beers calling from his apartment with a subtle yet irresistible song triggering a yearning for the lonely comfort of the couch that was always happy to cradle a blackout, and so he made his way back through the aisles of books and lamp laden tables with a sudden growing thirst. Through the front entrance doors he could see that the dark of night had arrived, but he suddenly brought his cane to a halt while remembering the contract folded in his back pocket.

With an exhausted sigh he turned and spotted a young librarian quietly sorting through a pile of returned books. Sensing someone vying for her attention she looked his way and smiled politely with an understated beauty, the kind that enhanced the calming ambience of the room but could silence a front bar in seconds.

"Sorry to bother you love," he said with a slight twinge of embarrassment, "but I don't suppose you have a witchcraft section?"

Popcorn and Literature.

Sleep wasn't easy for Clarence that night but then it never really was. Some might say he had mastered the art of passing out and truth be told they would probably be right, after all he was a man with a lot on his mind and an ever growing collection of empty bottles on the floor that were chipped and scarred with futile attempts to forget. Unfortunately however, he had embarked upon an investigation that was about to spiral into a series of events that would change his life forever, and perhaps also the very city with festering secrets bubbling up from the belly of her abyss.

Sitting at his desk the following morning with a cold TAB to ease the foggy remnants of the previous night's consumption, he flicked through his notebook and pondered what his next move would be. A summer storm was beginning to build outside and the sudden rise in humidity was stifling.

If he could somehow wrangle a few more clients he might be able to replace the damn air conditioner, but for the moment the old lady with the strange signature was all he had. Considering what he had managed to read in the early hours after midnight, before his head had grown heavy and the beer had blurred his vision, there were definitely some serious questions to be raised around his only client.

He slammed the notebook closed and tried to focus on the task at hand before any truly dark and bizarre thoughts filtered their way into the heat of the office. Lucky then that Barbara made her first appearance for the day, bounding in through the door with a flushed face and small bundles of envelopes clutched in her hands.

"Sorry I'm late. I had the car halfway down the bloody driveway before discovering a flat tire and then when I got going again I landed straight into a traffic jam thanks to some moron hitting a power pole." She paused to clear the hair from her eyes, took a deep breath, and dropped her bounty onto the desk. "I picked up your mail but you might want to open it later, nothing but overdues judging by the return addresses I'm afraid, but you've got today's paper, the latest copy of Popular Electronics and I picked up a new magazine I thought you'd be interested in."

"Slow down," Clarence winced with hands raised in the air, "my head's already spinning this morning."

"I can tell by how red your eyes are," Barbara smirked. "Did you get the licence plate of the truck that hit you?"

"Very funny."

"So there were two calls to the office yesterday afternoon. One was from our sweet little old lady who wanted to know if anything had come up, and the other was from a lawyer that said you'd know who he is. Left a really weird message too."

"Message?"

"Hang on, I scribbled it down."

Barbara spun on her heels and dashed back to the reception area before again bounding through the door with a scrap of paper wedged between her fingers.

"*Midday screening of And Justice for All*," she read out loud. "*Front row. Don't be late, and don't try to call me.*" With a raised eyebrow she placed the message beside the envelopes. "Is that supposed to make any kind of sense?"

Clarence leaned forward to examine the instructions to be sure he'd heard right. If it *was* from Sean then it was definitely out of character, and if it wasn't then lunchtime was about to come with a whole heap of risk.

"That's the million dollar question." He gulped some more TAB then reached for the newspaper. "I'll need you to give Bernice a call and see if you can't arrange a meeting for tomorrow, then maybe shop around to see if there's any cheap deals on new air conditioners. Don't worry about the message, I'll take care of it."

"What are you planning to do?"

"Well, the plan is to browse a little literature and then I guess I'm off to the movies."

"You might want to splash a little water on your face first."

"Trust me," he replied with a hint of a grin, "I intend to do just that."

Barbara gave him a sympathetic look and then quietly made her exit. Outside there was a low rumble of thunder, and Clarence knew the storm wasn't far away. With a pained sigh he opened the newspaper and flipped straight to the cinema listings, scanned the session times and locations until he found what he was looking for, then grabbed his cane and hobbled out the door.

***

The bookstore was nestled on the corner of a busy street deep in the heart of the city, where the hot summer breeze carried the noise of blaring radios from late morning traffic and weekday shoppers bustled and browsed for items that would bring a brief moment of happiness. With the storm clouds overhead growing thicker and more menacing by the second, the day felt as though it had become a stifling grey chamber void of any direct sunlight and offering no way out for those trapped inside.

Clarence pushed open the door and was hit with a cold blast of air rich with the smell of books old and new. It was a familiar scent with origins that stretched back to the first bunch of pages bound together with blood tainted leather, and one that in an instant brought back memories of midnight sessions poring through legal volumes in the hope of finding something, *anything*, to strike back at the system.

Sitting at the counter with head buried in a book, the owner seemed oblivious to the handful of customers casually fingering spines and flipping through pages as though the rush of ink would help make a decision. He looked like he was in his mid-thirties, carried a distinguished air thanks to an expensive silk shirt that was tucked into black pants that would have been more suited to a fancy dinner, and wore a striking gold medallion that hung perfectly around his neck.

Not in the mood to scour the inventory, Clarence wiped the sweat from his face and stepped up to the counter as cracks of his cane hitting the hard wood floor echoed across the room. The sound, it seemed, managed to break through and grab the owner's attention.

"What can I help you with today?" he asked with open book still in hand. "If you've come looking for a copy of *The Dead Zone* I'm afraid we're all sold out."

"Never was one for horror," Clarence replied, "too much make believe rubbish if you ask me. Actually, I'm looking for any books you might be carrying by a particular publishing company."

"Is there a certain title you're after? I pride myself on having one of the best selections in the city, so if you've got a name there's a good chance I stock it."

Clarence threw a purposeful glance across the shelves and adjusted his cane to ease the pressure on his leg. He could see by the way the owner stood and held back his shoulders that he *was* proud of his collection, and considering how engrossed he'd been in his own copy of the latest Stephen King novel he was obviously a passionate reader who'd created his own little wonderland.

"Sorry mate," he said as another rumble of thunder rattled the front windows, "I don't know any book names but if you've got anything by *Afterlife Publications* I'd love to see them."

The owner scrunched his face while gently massaging the medallion as though it would trigger some sort of revelation. He closed his eyes for several seconds, nodded in answer to a silent question, then opened them again with a satisfactory grin.

"*Afterlife Publications*, yeah, I remember their books. It's been a few years since they've released anything new, but I might still have something in stock." He shifted his fingers from the medallion to tap the side of his head. "I can remember what's gone out on the shelves back to the first day I opened, but what gets sold or lost in the organized chaos is another matter. Time to fire up the new machine I guess, and see if the future really does link us back to the past."

Clarence moved up to the counter and watched him shuffle to a glowing green monitor and shiny new keyboard. Suddenly a voice erupted from the back of the store, drawing his attention with a snap of the neck to a tall kid wearing a glitter speckled KISS shirt.

"Hey Derek!" the kid called out. "*Zen And The Art Of Motorcycle Maintenance*, is it any good?"

Derek looked up from the digital green lettering and grinned at the totally random interruption.

"Mate, it'll change your life if you're ready to slip inside the mind of a man going insane. I reckon it's my last copy, so I'll do you a good deal if you're ready to take the plunge."

"Sounds totally groovy man, I might take you up on the offer."

The kid returned to his browsing and Derek brought his attention back to the screen. So too did Clarence, who was now very interested in the machine that the book specialist was using.

"Is that what I think it is?" he asked while peering over the counter.

"If you're thinking the new TRS-80 you'd be right. This thing is the future man, all I have to do is type in what I'm trying to find and it'll search through a database I put together. Took months to do I can promise you that much, but streamlined efficiency always comes with a price."

"So you can really use something like that for business?"

"Like I said, it's the future."

His face contorted with both concentration and determination as he tapped away at the keyboard and studied the screen. After a minute or two he slapped a hand down onto the counter and muttered something inaudible. Visibly frustrated, he looked up at Clarence and shrugged his shoulders.

"Problem with the future is the present isn't always ready." He turned on his feet to stand before a number of drawers built into an orange wood cabinet and paused as if deep in thought. Suddenly he raised his hand with a finger pointed to the ceiling. "I think it was 1976 or 1977. I remember because it was a local publisher and I was surprised I hadn't come across them before."

He plucked out two glossy catalogues from one of the drawers and promptly slapped them down onto the counter. Concentration creased his face as he frantically flicked through the pages of the first before promptly discarded it to the side, then scoured the pages of the second until confirming his find with a proud nod.

"Here it is," he declared, spinning the catalogue for Clarence with a finger tapping on the prize.

And there it was indeed, a full page advertisement in crisp black and white displaying three feature releases available for wholesale order. Clarence leaned down a little closer to read the titles. *A Journey That Begins At The End*, *Questions For God* and *Sins Under The Moon*.

"I'll take all three."

"Passion for the written word, I like it. Let's see if we can't find them."

Derek marched his way from behind the counter and led Clarence along row after row of books covering every possible genre. In a flash he darted down one of the aisles, squatted down, and began running his fingers along the various volumes. The ritual continued until he reached the bottom shelf and suddenly extracted a slightly dusty hard covered edition.

"Aha!" he laughed while jumping up to his feet. "I knew it would be down here somewhere. Looks like *Sins Under The Moon* is all I've got though. It's the last copy too, so if you're wanting to take it I'll do you a good deal."

"Sounds like you give out a lot of good deals."

"That's why my customers keep coming back."

He handed Clarence the book and wandered off to chat with the Kiss fan about the essence of reality and the truth in beauty, leaving him to stand there in the quiet cool and examine the dust jacket with an anticipation that came with the possibility of discovering a piece of the puzzle he was quickly becoming lost in.

The cover was understated to say the least. Besides the title and an author's name he didn't recognise, there was only a faded silhouette of what appeared to be a cross split in two set against a barely visible moon. When he flipped to the back cover however, there was no mistaking the face that stared back from the black and white photo. She was definitely younger, with hair resting upon her shoulders and dazzling earrings lit by a camera flash, but there was no mistaking the smile of Bernice Edwards.

Clarence balanced his cane against the bookshelf, adjusted his weight to minimize the pain, and opened the cover to study the inside blurb. Why she had used a different name he couldn't understand, but as his eyes fell upon the brief description of the tale that could be found deep within the pages he knew that his only job in nearly six weeks had become far more than a missing person's case. Not only that, but it seemed there was a whole lot more to his client than he could have imagined.

***

Back in the car the first drops of rain had begun. Distant rumblings of thunder had become bone shaking cracks of violence along the dark heavens, hot humid air forced its way in through the air vents, and the drive to his midday rendezvous just several blocks away was a frustrating crawl amidst piercing headlights and the glowing red of constant brakes.

Against all odds he found a park just a street away from the entrance, and by the time he stepped up to the booth for a ticket his shirt was pasted to his skin and trickles of sweat dripped down from his fingers onto the cane. One thing he was sure of, humidity was in no way a friend.

Ticket in hand he turned and studied the foyer. Apart from a young couple balancing popcorn and drinks by a poster for *Kramer vs. Kramer* and the gruffy middle aged woman that had taken his money, the place was empty. He hadn't expected anything different though because as far as cinema time was concerned it was still early, a simple fact that was almost certainly the reason he'd been summoned to such an unusual venue for a meeting.

There was no need to stop for anything at the candy counter. He'd grabbed a flask of bourbon from the glove box when he'd stuffed his newly purchased book in there for safe keeping, a stash that always managed to come in handy at the oddest of times, and the idea of food wasn't exactly vying for his attention anyway. As things stood something was about to go down, and the sooner he found out what the better.

He checked his ticket, cursed under his breath at what the cinema number meant, then slowly made his way up the red carpeted stairs stained with patches of well-trodden gum and crushed popcorn. Not a soul could be seen when he reached the top, and he took a moment to rest his hand before heading along the small hallway and into the double doors for his first movie in years.

The soft glowing darkness was soothing on his eyes. The only other person in the place was seated high up in the back row, a scruffy looking guy with long tangled hair and stained suede jacket casually smoking a cigarette with bare feet stretched out. He seemed unfazed at the intrusion to what had almost been a private viewing and barely paid attention as Clarence navigated the steps and settled into the middle of the front row.

On the screen a series of advertisements began to slide by, prompting him to take a few long sips from his just in case flask as the tension of the moment began to grow exponentially. Now that he was sitting down there was no denying his nerves were sizzling on a proverbial knife edge, and until he knew what the hell he was doing there all he could do was take another sip as the opening credits of the movie brought disco infused saxophone to vibrate across the chairs, followed by the appearance of a lady of the night being led away by a uniformed cop.

Transfixed by what was happening on the screen he almost didn't notice the movement to his left, but when a figure from the dark suddenly fell into the chair beside him there was no mistaking who it was.

"Didn't expect to be meeting a legal eagle like you in a place like this," he said somewhat startled.

"Wasn't planning on meeting you at all," Sean replied with a cold tone, "but guilt got the better of me so let's keep our eyes on the screen and voices low."

There was a moment of unease as they watched Al Pacino's introduction, with both men harbouring a knowledge that the day was about to go through a significant change. Unlike Sean, Clarence still didn't quite know how, and if the already heavy mood soaking the seats weren't weighing him down he might've actually enjoyed the irony of watching a loose cannon lawyer deal with a crazy judge on the screen, but it was a wait that needed a resolution one way or the other and even another shot of bourbon wasn't going to put him in the mood for some bullshit movie.

"If it's guilt that's got me sitting here smelling some hippie's feet you should probably get right to the point like you always do."

"Ray's dead."

It took a second for the statement to process, but when it did Clarence squeezed his hand tight around the flask as shock flushed his neck and face with a rush of hot blood.

"What do you mean dead? What the hell happened?"

"What happened? I'll tell you what happened. I made the mistake of giving you a name because of some pie in the sky ideology that had me believe shedding a little light on something that doesn't belong in the dark might fix a bad situation, and instead I get a high level cop storming into my office last night telling me Ray's lying in his shed with three bullets to the head. Oh yeah, it was also made way too clear that if I fuck up one more time I'll be extended the same hospitality."

"Bloody hell…"

"My bet is it'll be in tomorrow's papers as just another botched drug robbery. Either way the fisherman's gone, and now his reputation is shot, making anything he might've said worthless."

Clarence could hear a rare wavering in the lawyer's voice and took a chance by handing him the flask. He was surprised when he brought it to his lips and took a long mouthful, and took the opportunity to voice the obvious concerns.

"If Ray's dead then I have to assume they know I paid him a visit, but what I don't understand is why they went straight to you. There's no way anyone in that cafe knew what we were talking about and they sure as hell didn't see what you wrote on the napkin, so why come to you? How do you fit into any of this?"

"Because!" Sean spat through clenched teeth before attempting to calm down with a deep breath. "I was the one they had make sure the court sealed documents were in order and then they had *another* lawyer file a gag order on me to make sure it was all locked down tight. I haven't slept properly since and by the time you ambushed me in the cafe I was already planning to pack up my briefcase and move the practice to the other side of the country."

"So it *was* the judge on the boat," Clarence sighed before grabbing back his flask.

"This is as bad as it gets Clarence. You said your client just wants money owed but even if that's half the truth she's started something that neither of us can get out of. There's no making this one right, no hope of back door style justice, and as of now any belief I had in the system is nothing but a sour memory."

They were powerful words and Clarence knew it. Sean had postponed his wedding not once but twice to take on big cases and was as dedicated to the courts as any truly great lawyers before him, and for him to declare his belief in the system as gone was akin to a parent suddenly losing all love for their only child.

Any step forward was going to be tricky. Clarence thought long and hard while their dire situation was seemingly mocked on screen by a crazy judge in an out of control helicopter, and had no choice but to face the promise he'd made when the first strike of the bat had shattered his leg that he would spend whatever days he had left choosing right over wrong.

"I just need to know one thing," he said low and cautiously, "do you actually know where the judge is?"

"No," Sean replied with certainty. "As far as anyone's concerned he's retired and moved on. Only a handful of people know what happened and until yesterday Ray was one of them. Safe to say you can add your name to the list now, and the reason we're here smelling a hippie's feet is so I can tell you to shut up shop and lay low. I'm taking a leave of absence next week and when I get back it'll be to start packing boxes, and if you don't want a headache that won't go away you'll do the same."

"I'm going to do what's right this time mate," Clarence assured him with conviction, "and something tells me you want me to otherwise you would've left me flapping in the wind back in the café and we wouldn't be here right now."

"Then you'll probably die."

"Probably still means there's odds both ways." He took another sip then handed what was left to his shaken companion. "Now listen. From here on in it's on me, but I need one last thing from you. What was the name of the cop that grilled you yesterday?"

"Are you kidding me? I tell you that and I'm basically sitting here committing suicide."

"You've got serious standing in this city and old money behind you. Trust me, they'll try to rattle you but they'll think twice about doing anything worse if they can't really prove anything. Fact is a dead little girl has got us here, and I don't know about you but I reckon we both got into law because of innocent victims like her, so even if the system corrupted me and is starting to do the same to you doesn't mean we can't strike back. Now tell me, who was the cop?"

"Senior Sergeant Anthony Saxby."

"Works in the city station right? Just do me one small thing and then you can wash your hands of all this mess forever. I want you to reach out to him Friday morning, no earlier, and tell him you've just found out there was someone else out on the water that day. Tell him there was an anonymous message on your answering machine so you don't have anything else for him, no name or nothing."

Sean turned to Clarence with simmering fear in his eyes. It was a look that was usually found on clients when they learned they were about to go away for a long time, but this time the fear was etched in a man who had once been a poster child for integrity.

"What the hell are you planning to do Clarence?"

"I'm planning to make things right somehow."

Blood For The Rain.

Rather than head back through the now pouring rain to the office he squeezed his way into the library car park and headed straight for the microfiche room. He was quite a sight, what with hair plastered across his face and cane dripping with water, but then nobody in the main foyer seemed to pay him much attention anyway.

He wasn't interested in any investigations closed for no reason this time. Instead he made some rough calculations in his head, settled into the cockpit of his time machine and traversed the magnified landscape of local newspapers back to 1949. This time he had a good idea of what he was looking for, but it wasn't until March of 1951 that an article reached out to him as though having been waiting for a new witness after so many years.

Partial remains found washed up on a metropolitan beach on Thursday have been identified as belonging to a nine year old girl reported as having been abducted just days earlier. Witnesses say the gruesome find was tangled in clumps of seaweed after an overnight storm ravaged the coastline.

Clarence swallowed hard and dared to move forward in time. His eyes burned and stomach churned as disturbing headlines jumped out from the long stored microfiche that now seemed so eager to reward its gift of a brief moment to live again, and by the time he reached the summer of 1976 his tattered notebook had marked down the dates of sixteen young girls that had been classified as abducted or missing. Not one of the articles, however, offered a name or any indication of who the unfortunate victim might be.

With head beginning to swell from troubled thoughts tumbling one after the other he shut down the machine that had become less magic and far more haunting. He had all he needed, at least for now, and so marched his way back through the library with a little extra force that sent the sound of his cane to reverberate across the foyer. This time, it quickly became apparent, there were quiet whispers and startled eyes that watched him leave.

The savage heart of the summer storm had arrived, sending down rain with such force that at times his tension filled drive back through the city streets came to a complete standstill until he could see the road ahead once more. His wipers did all that they could but were little more than a feather swatting a dragon, and as he crawled his way closer to the office he cursed the fact there was no underground parking or, to be more accurate, no dedicated parking at all. Because he hadn't wanted stairs his real estate options had been limited, and so his ground floor space came with the luxury of having to fight for a park as close as he possibly could each and every day.

But both the storm and the streets were determined to give him no quarter. The only park he could muster was three blocks down and that meant he was in for a soaking. Running was out of the question that much was for sure, so with a frustrated resignation he stepped out onto the footpath and into the torrential grey of the day.

With not so much as a breath of wind the concrete steamed and his clothes grew hot and wet. He did his best to seek cover beneath small shop fronts or cafe umbrellas on his journey but ultimately it was a fool's quest, and so he simply gave up and splashed his way through the ever growing puddles until he began to pass the alleyway that ran alongside his office.

In an attempt to calm his growing anger he tried to remember how many TABs might be left in the cooler. Considering the start to the day a beer seemed a whole lot more fitting, but the indulgence in the cinema had already begged him for more and this time there'd be no heeding the call. From this point on he'd need to keep razor sharp.

Suddenly the back of his neck was hit with an almighty force that sent his cane flying and the full weight of his body sprawling forward, but just as he was about to land face down in the muck soaked puddles strong hands from behind wrapped around his shoulders and dragged him into the growing darkness of the alley. Before he knew what was happening he was thrown to the ground behind the filthy dumpster that never seemed to be emptied, followed by a crunching rubber sole to his jaw.

His heart surged and he tried to look up through the stinging rain but his eyes were forced shut when his own cane began pounding into his legs, hit after hit that brought shock waves of pain and a very urgent and sudden need to defend himself. The hits kept coming though, and were quickly joined by heavy boots that cracked the side of his jaw and smashed into his ribs.

Face down in soaked garbage he still couldn't see what the hell was happening and knew bones would start breaking any second, so with a desperate groan he freed an arm that was trying to cover his head and reached down towards his waist. Another solid kick ignited a swirling galaxy of stars but just before he thought he was done for his fingers found his only chance. It was, as the alley as his only witness, a grip that would have made Dennis Lillee proud even on his slowest of days.

He rolled over, pointed a faded silver Colt Python up into the grey abyss and pulled the trigger. The second the bullet tore through the belly of the storm the beatings stopped, while adrenaline had his finger heavy on the trigger ready to fire again and the searing pain suddenly muted in the distance. As his eyes were finally able to focus the sight above him began to emerge and it was not the kind to bring any hope to the day, if the day had dawned with any hope to begin with, and his adrenaline was quickly infused with survival fuelled anger.

The metallic smell of gunfire momentarily overpowered the stench of the garbage already embedded in the rising steam. Standing just an arm's length away with wild eyes peering down at him were two tall blokes that would've made the Cop Shop cast and crew proud. Obviously comfortable with their chosen social stature they both wore wispy moustaches better suited to a pimply faced teenager, had long hair that looked more like seaweed draped around their necks, and both had worn out jeans and blue singlets that proudly displayed arms covered in random images that could only have been scribbled with a jail house tattooing rig.

"Never bring a cane to a gun fight," Clarence snarled while shuffling his back against the dumpster.

"Now you listen here mate!" the wanna be Cop Shop extra on the left barked. "We're only gonna tell ya once. Keep ya bloody nose outta business that ain't yours or you'll be swimming with the sharks got it? And don't go pointin' that thing like you're Dirty Harry or something 'cause we both know you ain't gonna use it."

"Yeah," his social twin added, "you ain't gonna use it, and you ain't gonna be using this either."

With the savagery of a small dog growling through a fence he snapped Clarence's cane across his knee and threw the now useless pieces down to the alley floor. Meanwhile, the wanna be extra leaned forward and brought his face as close as he could to the barrel of the gun, an either a brave or stupid attempt at intimidation considering the actual logistics of the situation, and pointed a rollie stained finger at Clarence's face.

"This is no joke okay? Some real heavy people aren't happy with what you're doing so ya better pull ya head in 'cause it's real bloody easy to go missing in this city and ain't no one gonna start lookin' for ya."

High above the alley a vicious roll of thunder rocked the darkened sky. Clarence could taste the blood that streamed down from his forehead to mix with the rain and dirt, and watched the dedicated crim messengers slink back out onto the city street like filthy mice that had snatched the cheese without setting off the trap. The sudden flash of violence, thankfully, was over as quickly as it had begun.

There was no point trying to salvage what was left of his cane and the garbage around him hardly had anything that he could try to use, so it took a good five minutes to stagger the hundred or so metres to the office entrance. The bones of his leg were on fire, making every wincing shuffle a self-induced torture that promised even more pain to come once the adrenaline began to wear off, but if Clarence was anything he was as stubborn as a politician looking for a pay rise and eventually he stumbled in out of the rain.

Behind the brown and orange desk Barbara jumped to her feet with a handheld tight against her mouth. Considering suspicious spouses were their main, albeit infrequent, clients, she of course had seen Clarence the worse for wear after a minor dust up or two, but his appearance this time raised the bar to a whole new level.

Soaked to the bone and barely able to stand, his face and torn shirt were caked with blood and his left eye was bruised and already beginning to close. There was clear swelling around his neck and she was shocked to see that his hand was still wrapped tight around the gun that he had been so apprehensive to own just six months earlier.

"Jesus Clarence," she finally gasped, "what the hell happened?"

Clarence staggered the few steps to the green vinyl couch and collapsed down with a sharp groan. He did his best to stretch out his damaged leg and wiped some of the hot blood from his eyes.

"Just a couple of thugs earning their beer money." Despite the state he was in and perhaps as a slight show of defiance, he looked up and managed an almost not there grin. "There's a few things I need to take care of, so I won't be in the office for the next couple of days."

"I think I need to drive you to the hospital."

"It's okay," he assured her, "not much they can do about a couple of bruised ribs and a leg that was already a mess."

"You're starting to scare me Clarence. What on earth are you planning to do?"

"Well, looks like I'm going to spend some good old fashioned private eye time in the car, do a little more digging into our sweet old lady client… and shop for a new cane."

Driver's Seat Discoveries.

And spend time in the car he did. Or, to be more accurate, *lived* in the car, made obvious by the fact that the floor was hidden beneath an abundance of crushed beer cans and empty Styrofoam burger containers that came together with a chaotic jingle every time he took a corner too fast.

His term of solitude had begun late afternoon beneath the same storm that had borne witness to the alleyway carnage. With his latest book purchase resting against the battered cooler in the passenger seat he'd located his mark and settled in for the job. Sure, his swollen closed left eye made using binoculars a task drenched with curse worthy frustration, but still he managed to find a way to watch the understated doorway from his position down the street.

The *Afterlife Publications* address was hardly making itself known as a business. Located on a main road on the outskirts of the city, nestled between a rundown dry cleaners and Vietnamese grocery store, there was nothing to indicate what might lay behind the wooden door and rain smeared window made void by thick red curtains on the inside. Still, with his leg on the verge of agony and a steady stream of warm beers broken with the occasional swig of bourbon, it was an address he grew to know over the next couple of days.

On each afternoon he followed one of the women that emerged from the plain wooden door home, parked just the right distance away to maintain his observation capabilities without detection, and spent the night quietly sipping bourbon or beer while waiting for the first glow of dawn. There were times when the pain in his leg offered a brief respite and the crushed ribs pinching his lungs let him breathe without gritting his teeth, as there were moments when an extra stinging mouthful from his flask hushed the growing storm of thoughts, but sleep did come in small pockets. They were brief moments to be sure, yet each little slip into the abyss was enough to recharge his need to know.

And the glow of the dawn did indeed bring with it a knowing. On three different evenings he followed three different women from *Afterlife Publications* home, and each surveillance that had him aching with pain and wedged behind the wheel for hour after hour had eventually gifted him with the same revelatory, and somewhat haunting observations.

The first woman had appeared middle aged, her plump figure made all the more feminine with crisp white jeans and a high collared blue top that carried an air of both business and casual. Her house had been at the base of the hills with a long, tree lined driveway that was almost medieval in structure, and the street had proved to be a quiet one with barely a passing car to light up the interior.

The second mark had been a little older. She had driven a sleek white convertible Volkswagen Beetle with little regard for the intrusion of road rules and had stopped to accrue a bottle of wine and bread stick before pulling into to her beach front home. Clarence had watched her enjoy the crimson red sunset from the comfort of her porch, wine glass in hand and cigarette resting in ashtray, and until the darkness had come there were tense moments when he thought she might have noticed the one eyed, battered man parked nearby.

On the third evening he had watched a slim, beautiful woman in her late twenties step out through the *Afterlife Publications* door and into a taxi. Even from where he'd been sitting he had seen the sadness on her face, a stark contrast to her flared silk green pants and matching floral shirt that radiated a promise of carefree happiness that belonged at a colour lit roller disco rather than a stifling, traffic filled street.

The follow had been a tricky one. Whoever had been behind the wheel was obviously a traffic veteran, for the taxi had raced along the streets taking side street after side street to avoid banked up stop lights before breaking free to head high up into the foothills. The eventual drop off proved to be in a breathtakingly beautiful suburb that Clarence had previously never visited, with sparkling views of the city lights that had seemed a perfect fit for the last glowing reaches of the setting sun. That's why it had been strange when, as he'd peered through the binoculars, he caught another glimpse of the woman's face and there were definite tears rolling down her cheeks.

While the other two houses had been far from shabby, this cosy home had been the kind that most people would drive past simply to indulge in a little dream, and when the night had fallen Clarence himself had dared to imagine what it must be like to live in such extravagance high above the populous with nothing but raw nature beyond the back windows.

On the first two nights he'd spent leaning back in the driver's seat with the window wound down to let any hint of breeze in for relief, the arrival of midnight had marked an unusual event on both occasions. Through his bloodshot eye he had watched the curtain drawn windows slowly illuminate with the soft flickering flames of candles, one after the other until he had lost count and long, dancing shadows had stretched out across the front lawns. Both times the candles had burned until dawn, and both times he sensed strange movements beyond the curtains that didn't quite make sense and had left him unsettled until the morning sun had pierced the cracked vinyl of his interior.

When midnight had arrived on the third night however, the windows of the double storied house had remained dark. At least, that had been the case until lonely headlights had washed across the street just after two a.m. Clarence had slid down as low as he could behind the wheel, forced to grit his teeth when his leg had no choice but to bend sharply, and watched as the two previous women he had followed came to a stop in the driveway and had entered the house as though visiting someone in the middle of the night was completely normal. Not long after they had disappeared through the front door, the lighting of candles had begun. When dawn finally came, so too did dark thoughts that itched at the base of his spine.

And so it was that, after sneaking back to his apartment for a desperate shower and change of clothes, Clarence found himself back in the heart of the city watching a bustling police station while the ever present heat ignored the fact that it was still early morning. With the sound of rush hour traffic streaming through the open window, he sipped a bitter coffee and quietly struggled to make sense of what he had learned.

When Bernice had arranged his services she'd mentioned that the publishing company staff had been single mothers, but he had surveyed each of the three women as they'd made their morning departures to work and in all instances there was not a child to be seen. It was almost certain that each lived alone, not counting the third mark's strange visit in the middle of the night, and all three burned a treasure trove of candles until dawn. Something wasn't right that much was for sure, and Clarence had every intention of sitting down with his client to decipher just what the hell was going on. First though, there was a gamble he'd put into motion and it was time to see if it was going to pay off.

The minutes ticked by and the heat continued to rise. Parked far enough away that his exhausted and battered face would be nothing more than a blurred shadow, he was still able to squint through the binoculars and see both the front entrance and a good portion of the rear of the building, where squad cars sat sizzling in the sun awaiting their eventual chariot masters.

At approximately 11:03 the first part of his gamble came to be when he spotted Sean stepping out of a taxi by the front steps. Clarence hadn't been overly confident that the lawyer would follow through with the request, so much so that he'd left him a midnight message from a pay phone just to be sure, but there he was making his way through the front doors wearing his always crisp suit.

He shoved the rest of the coffee down his throat and leaned forward. The reality was he no idea what Senior Sergeant Anthony Saxby looked like; hell he couldn't even be sure he that he was even in the bloody building, but if he was, and if Sean passed on the lie that someone else had been out on the water that day, there was a good chance he'd be making an appearance soon enough.

The swelling in his left eye was going down and if he squinted just the right way he could make a little use of it. As he rested his weight against the wheel he cursed how hot it had already become, but the stinging burn across his chest was soon forgotten when Sean emerged from the entrance with a flustered look across his face. Clarence brought the binoculars closer to his eyes to watch the lawyer for a moment or two before another taxi appeared to whisk him away, then shifted his line of sight to the rear car park.

For several long minutes there was only a lone seagull picking at a discarded fast food wrapper to be seen, but then he shifted his leg to ease the pain and saw movement that signalled his gamble just might have paid off. The blur of passing cars pulsed across his vision as he adjusted the focus and targeted the uniformed officer that had suddenly appeared, a tall and intimidating figure with a stern, scarred face that was visibly red with anger and who was obviously very much in a hurry.

Clarence threw the coffee cup to the rubbish strewn floor and started the engine. It was a hot, steamy Friday morning in the city and there was one last mark to follow. If his hunch was right that the judge would want to know of any weakened threads in his silent web as soon as they surfaced, the fuming cop slamming the door of the XC Falcon equipped with sirens and official decals was going to ensure the week ended with an answer to his now very big problem.

And so the mobile surveillance began. Sergeant Saxby proved to be a literal bullet in the traffic, racing between slow moving cars that were all too happy to get out of the way of an obviously urgent cop and ploughing through orange lights with little regard that came with racing across a busy intersection, forcing Clarence to do his best to maintain a strategic distance without losing sight or fear of imminent impact.

It seemed Saxby had decided that his sudden departure from the cop headquarters wasn't exactly official police business. Unaware of the station wagon emulating his every turn he pulled into a residential address, dashed inside for a brief few minutes, then bound back out with his uniform replaced by brown slacks and a high coloured purple shirt before jumping into an HG panel van and tearing back into the traffic. The destination was still to be determined, but it was clear he wasn't planning on wasting any time getting there.

Clarence followed the vehicle for the next two or so hours as it pushed through the city traffic and sun drenched suburbs, before eventually bursting out onto a barren country highway like a gallant horse breaking free to chase the eventual sunset. An occasional road train helped to keep his presence both understated and less the star of the show in his mark's rear view mirror, not to mention ensuring his sleep deprived attention to the bitumen remained sharp thanks to the unpredictable swerving of thundering monolith like road trains, while a growing threat of deathly curious kangaroos kept his fingers pressed tight around the wheel.

And so it came to be, that beneath a scorching late afternoon sun beyond the reaches of the city that the journey of private investigator Clarence Turner began to sound the opening notes of a slow, simmering crescendo. Just when he thought the drive was never going to end the panel van made a sharp turn by a dust caked roadhouse, and then travelled down a short road that twisted along a series of new, well to do homes built upon the banks of the Murray River. It was too risky to follow close behind, and so he casually parked by a boat ramp where several sunburned anglers sat on flimsy deck chairs beside empty eskies and still rods, painfully got out the car, and did his best to look like just another tourist taking a break from the featureless drive.

Though he looked like he'd just stepped from a world class bar room brawl nobody threw him much more than a cursory glance. It was bitter luck he'd take any day, and as much as every step brought with it an eruption of pain up through his leg and across his spine, he reached for the binoculars and limped up to the shade of an old tree that offered a view along the quiet street.

Deep in the hot wind he could hear the creaking of the door signalling Saxby's exit, then watched through one good eye and one bad as the cop that had strayed so far from base marched up a cobblestone driveway and battered a meaty fist upon the solid steel front door. For a quick panicked moment Saxby peered back towards the boat ramp and almost seemed to be staring straight through the binoculars, but then the door to the riverbank home opened and he was no longer interested in a bunch of down on their luck fishermen.

Clarence risked a painful step forward for a better view and was rewarded with the sight of a grey bearded gentleman with neatly combed hair looking Saxby up and down with a healthy dose of contempt. It was the kind of look that he'd had seen far too many times as a lawyer on the wrong side of an objection attempt, and that could only mean one thing.

It was the judge.

And taking into account the brand new campervan parked beneath the carport and the fact that cardboard had been taped across the inside of the windows, two things were evident. Even out here the level of privacy didn't quite meet the judge's standards, and even if they *could* be met he sure didn't seem like he was planning on hanging around for long anyway.

The cop and the judge indulged in a short and visibly strained conversation that only they could hear, then promptly disappeared inside. Clarence had to work on the assumption he had only a scarce few minutes and quickly shuffled back to the car, a fresh squirt of adrenaline tingling the tips of his fingers. He never had been a fan of the river, and so he would get what he came for, adjust his mirrors and get the hell out of there.

Keeping with the theme of being a man that was always willing to push his luck, he turned down the street and drove past the property to ensure the final detail was obtained. The shiny new letterbox that was obviously a newcomer to the battering of a hot summer sun proudly displayed the number six. Clarence couldn't know it then and there but the number would prove to come back to sting the soft and vulnerable parts of his soul when the nights were fitful and dreams fragmented, and so it was with a raspy curse that his attention was instead drawn to the fact that the quiet street terminated just beyond a small rise.

He swung the car around with a soft screech of the tyres and in an instant saw that he'd pushed his luck a little too far. The front door to number six opened with a start as he raced past, and for a long searing second his eyes locked with those of a startled and oh so very angry Saxby.

With the clinking sound of empty bottles colliding on the floor he couldn't get back onto the highway quick enough. A check of the mirrors as he opened up the engine on the long straight showed that for the moment there was no panel van to ignite the anxiety already growing deep inside his gut, and with the late afternoon sun beginning to dip along the horizon rich in deep reds and searing oranges soaking across the heavens he turned on the radio and hoped for the best.

But, as you can probably imagine, the best wasn't to be, for not more than thirty minutes later and just as the second chorus of *Don't Bring Me Down* had begun there came an accelerated movement in his rear view mirror. Considering up until that moment he had been alone on the molten-like glow of the highway, the sudden increase in traffic could only mean one thing.

The panel van roared past, swerved sharply and came to a thundering halt, forcing Clarence to slam down on the brakes with gritted teeth and a dragon like tail of smoke erupting from his rear tyres. The panel van had hardly come to a stop before Saxby kicked open the door and marched up to his window.

"Get out now ya mongrel!" he barked, face flushed red and hand resting on something hidden in his waistline.

Clarence too reached down and rested his hand on the Colt wedged beneath his leg, suddenly aware that the last light of day had just turned considerably nasty.

"Don't think I'll be doing that," he said with a strained calm. "Too bloody hot to be standing out there with the flies."

"Listen here mate," Saxby hissed as he leaned in close enough that Clarence could smell the pungent tang of cologne and sweat, "turn off that fucking engine and get out here right now or I'll make sure the flies will have at ya sittin' there like a bloody mug."

"The way I see things," Clarence replied carefully, "we've both got our hands on a bad way to spend Christmas which means you keep going the way you're going and we both hit the night as roadkill."

Saxby eyeballed him hard and tried to spot any signs of a bluff. Then, with a strange fear washing across his face, he leaned in closer while extracting the hidden leverage from his waistband.

"Sorry mate but you shouldn't have stuck ya nose where it don't belong..."

Clarence felt the hot vinyl roof close in as time slowed, but as his hand ripped the gun free leaving him sure he'd moved a split second too late and his brain was about to play host to a steaming round of lead, the interior became awash with a sudden ripple of flashing blue and red lights.

Saxby replaced his gun while Clarence risked a glance into the side mirror. Behind him a lone police officer was casually strolling their way, his patrol car quietly idling as the first bugs of dusk flapped and dived into its headlights, and as he stepped up closer his gruff, weather-shaped features appeared neutral yet very much alert.

"Any reason you blokes are stopped on the highway like a couple of rabbits that don't know which way's what?"

"Our bad officer," Clarence replied with head slightly out of the window. "Shoulda' waited for the next turn off. Just catching up with an old mate is all."

"Is that right?" the officer responded with growing suspicion. "Helluva place to be shootin' the shit that's for sure. Sitting out here with your lights off, this time of evening? Trucks come through and I'll be spending the night scraping you off the bloody road."

"Didn't mean to put you out. If it's alright with you I'll be on my way and let you have a quiet night, I can catch up with my mate another time."

Hoping his part in the conversation was over Clarence nodded politely and ever so slowly began his departure with one eye on the road and the other on his mirrors, and as the bitumen rumbled below with the sweet growing of distance he could just make out the blue tinged silhouette of the officer accepting something from Saxby. Then, when the bright lights of a road train washed away the vision and began to follow his sweat soaked journey, he figured he just might make it back to the city.

And he did, arriving into the chaotic Friday night traffic with the knowledge that not only had he located the missing judge, but he'd also come far too close to fashioning his very own roadside grave. Such that it was that, on a steamy night just days from Christmas, when all around decorative lights of every colour could be seen and people shopped and drank and laughed, Clarence pulled over to the curb, limped his way into a dirt smeared phone booth like a wounded dog seeking refuge in its kennel, and made the call that forever would change his life.

Bernice picked up after only three rings.

"Hello?"

"It's Clarence."

"Clarence? Oh I've had such trouble trying to reach you. I can't tell you how many messages I've left with your assistant Barbara, not to mention my worried calls to your answering machine…"

"Bernice," he interrupted, "let me talk."

"Oh, yes of course, I think that would be best."

"Good, because I need you to listen very carefully. The parameters of this case have taken a very sharp turn and I'm afraid it may not be resolved the way you'd like. You said in my office you prefer dealing with things face to face, so this is me calling to say we need to meet right now."

"Why of course Clarence, after all it's I that's been waiting for you."

Pretty Scars.

The small gravel walkway to the door was cushioned either side by an array of tall, well-watered shrubs and palm fronds that seemed to want to reach out and smother Clarence as he struggled his way along. A large, antique styled doorbell awaited his touch with a soft glow that wasn't quite green and wasn't quite blue, and as he pressed down on the cool plastic he heard the distant sound of warm-toned bells.

Next came the echo of footsteps upon a polished floor, the jingling of unlocked chains, and then his one and only client Bernice appeared before him. She wore a long sleeved cardigan despite the heat, its elegant cut soft beige in colour, and a tartan skirt that reached down to her quaint white shoes. This time her silver grey hair was let loose to fall down upon her shoulders, and as she peered at him through glasses that reflected the shadows of the night he couldn't help but notice she wore no makeup to soften the inevitable reaches of time.

"Oh am I happy to see you," she began with a childlike smile. "The days seem so very long when you're waiting for something special to arrive and it can leave one feeling like a child again, wouldn't you agree? There's no greater thrill than opening one's presents at Christmas."

"I'm not here for festivities Bernice," he said with a sigh, "I'm here for business."

"Why of course you are!" she replied as though there were a million other reasons for him being there. "And I'm sure you don't want to be standing out here listening to me babble on so please, do come inside."

With a growing unease that had begun when he'd first stepped onto the gravel pathway, and a glance up revealing all the second story windows of the old house alive with a shimmering dance of deep orange candlelight, he followed his host down a long corridor and into a spacious living area. From somewhere above there came the softest of chanting, and while it affected Clarence with a slight chill he shrugged it off as a curious taste in music.

Lit only by a tall lamp in the corner and the globes of a small Christmas tree resting against the wall, the room had the appearance of a time capsule from the 1920's. There was a large cabinet that looked as though it belonged behind the bar of a cabaret club, four high backed, velvet padded chairs seated around a cast iron table, and hanging from the ceiling a chandelier sparkling with a hundred or more glass diamonds that sent ocean like reflections across the wallpapered walls.

At Bernice's invitation he lowered his aching frame into one of the seats and indulged in a long, deep breath. The air was cool and carried the fresh scent of pine needles. As she took a seat opposite, he couldn't help but notice the cabinet was adorned with black and white photos of a little girl with long curly hair and dark, almost haunting eyes.

"If you don't mind me saying," Bernice began, "you look quite a state, and anyone with less tact might even suggest a good shower would be in order."

"It's been a rough few days."

"I can see it has." She offered a polite smile while clasping her hands upon her lap. "I know it's been barely a week since you so graciously accepted our job but I just have to know. Did you find him?"

For the first time in what felt like years Clarence managed to laugh. Restrained at first and definitely apologetic, but it didn't take long for the self-imposed restraints to fall away as the laughter grew louder and louder, each deep breath sending lightning bolts of fire across his bruised ribs and aching chest. His host simply sat and waited for the moment to pass. It didn't take long however for the pain to steal away the sudden outburst.

"I told you when we first met that my services come with a guarantee so yeah, I found him, but I came here tonight to tell you that I'll be giving you back your deposit. I'm not the man I used to be Bernice, so I'm not going to do anything that's going to lead to more bloodshed. I know you don't want to hear it, but I won't be telling you where the judge is."

Bernice held her smile but the lines around her eyes drew tight as she allowed his declaration to sink down onto the hardwood floor.

"I imagine it must be hard carrying such a weight on your shoulders, to wake each day knowing just one decision, just one brief moment in time, caused so many innocent people to die." Her voice was sympathetic, her eyes searching and observant. "Of course, a lawyer must do what a lawyer must do, but it must have been oh so very difficult to watch a man you set free batter his already abused wife to death, gun down her family, then ignite a fire that burned with the screams of women and children."

"You weren't there so don't you dare sit there and judge me," Clarence said with obvious threat.

"Oh please don't think I'm judging, I only bring it to light because you *are* a changed man and you have my utmost respect. You were a victim of a system crawling with snakes and, unlike so many before, you've managed to purge yourself of the insidious venom. Now, whatever troubled thoughts are leaving your head heavy or chest tight tonight I want you to know one thing." She reached across the table and placed a delicate hand upon his knee. "Giving me the judge isn't spilling more blood my dear friend, it's a special gift that you can give to help cleanse the system."

Though Clarence's face was flushed with anger her soft touch somehow quietened his heart and eased the muscles around his jaw. Besides, the recent days had already taken their toll and what little fight he had left would be best kept in reserve, but that didn't mean he'd just sit there with no response.

"And what about you?" he asked. "What exactly were you planning to do with the information?" He could feel her hand growing warmer by the second. "I read a little of your book, read how your daughter was taken from the beach when you turned your back for just a minute only to be washed up on the rocks days later. I also know the suspect in the case disappeared a year or so after the investigation, an investigation that did nothing but slam doors in your face with every question you chased. What I'm trying to figure out now though, is how you fit into this mess the judge has made because as far as I can tell what happened to your daughter was back in 1952."

"You don't have any children, do you?" Bernice asked as she leaned back in her chair with a sadness in her eyes that assured no answer was needed. "Yes my daughter was snatched from me on a beautiful beach not far from here, murdered by a man under the protection of a sickening justice system too scared of truth seeing the light of day, but research doesn't mean you have any idea whatsoever of what it means to truly lose something."

"The suspect, he was a judge too wasn't he?"

"Yes," she said with a hint of venom, "he was but one tendril of a serpent that has slithered beneath this city for oh so very long, rising up when hungry to feed on all that is beautiful. I know you've learned what there is to learn Clarence, so we both sit here knowing that innocent little girls have gone missing time and time again over the years. It's safe to say we also harbour knowledge that in almost every case a high powered figure has been involved, sometimes a politician, other times a priest, a judge or a filthy rich business magnate with money to bury all that seeks what is right. But make no mistake, this serpent has many changing faces and hides in a society where sharing the ultimate secret is the greatest of power, and the beast has reared its ugly head once again."

Clarence sunk deeper into the chair as his host's description of a secret society filled with influential kid killers pierced deep into his already uneasy state. Fortunately or unfortunately however, he was a man adept at reading the lay of the land even if the only view was from the gutter, and on this night just days from the Christmas full moon, with his leg shattered, ribs bruised and face swollen, he knew damn well she was right.

"Yeah," he sighed, "from what I can tell there *is* something going on with the men who wear suits and disappearing little girls, and yeah I know this judge of yours has something to do with the body found in the ocean and nothing to do with any moneys owed." He rubbed his jaw and winced at the sharp sting that brought water to his swollen eye. "What happened to that little girl breaks my heart, believe me it does in ways you can't imagine, but I can't in good faith play a role in this anymore. If I hand over the address something bad will happen to you and I don't want to have to carry that on my shoulders. I'm sorry, but I'm afraid that's the way it's going to be."

"Why Clarence, please don't apologize. I understand, truly I do." A smile that he would expect to see on someone who just scratched a winning ticket lit up her face and ignited a twinkle in her eyes. "Surely you'll at least indulge in a nice glass of wine with me before our business concludes?"

"Our business *has* concluded, and that means it's time for me to go."

"But I insist."

"And I decline," he stammered, though as he tried to rise from the chair his arms seemed unable to follow through with his wish.

Across the table Bernice shook her head with defiance, her eyes growing darker by the second and lips pulling tight across her teeth.

"It could be taken as quite rude to ignore a gracious offer at such a festive time of the year, but then I can see your body is oh so tired and I suspect you're not going anywhere for now."

In an attempt to prove her wrong he tried to rise once more, but again his muscles refused to aid in any form of sudden movement. Maybe she was right. His body *was* tired and the chair increasingly comfortable, so all things considered perhaps a stiff drink was just the medicine he needed. After all, oblivion on his couch was all that awaited, and he didn't need to grace it with the knowledge he'd made an enemy of an old lady already haunted by her own demons.

"Considering the circumstances," he said with an uncomfortable sigh, "I guess one drink won't hurt."

"Absolutely wonderful. *Oh Teresa!*" she suddenly called out across the room. "*Please do come and join us. Oh, and bring some glasses and the wine from the cabinet.*"

Startled at the sudden request Clarence turned his tension filled neck and was surprised to see a light flicker to life in a kitchen beyond a bricked archway. He was even more surprised however, when from the kitchen emerged the same beautiful woman he had followed on his third night of surveillance, this time wearing faded blue jeans and a somewhat strange black top that covered her arms and floated down to her knees. The sadness he had seen from the car could still be found in the delicate features of her face, but as she placed the wine and glasses upon the table and took a seat, he could see that she was doing her best to hide it.

"Teresa is one of *Afterlife Publication's* most valued family members," Bernice explained. "She's also preparing for a very special Christmas."

"It's nice to meet you Mr. Turner," Teresa smiled while delicately filling the glasses, "believe it or not I've heard a lot about you."

Clarence chose only to nod his head and watch as his two hosts raised their glasses and closed their eyes for the briefest of moments.

"To the wonders of the beyond!" Bernice declared before indulging in a long sip of the rich burgundy liquid. "And may those wonders bring peace to aching hearts."

Increasingly uncomfortable as the mood seemed to be shifting by the second and reflections of the chandelier continued to shimmer along the walls, Clarence figured he'd drink the wine and make a quick, albeit polite exit. He brought the wine to his lips and quietly hoped it would help soothe the sickening fire along his leg.

"I can't help but ask," Bernice continued with the twinkle in her eyes growing stronger, "does a private investigator like yourself look forward to Christmas?"

Clarence took a long gulp and, for the first time, noticed something odd poking out from the edge of Bernice's sleeve.

"To be honest I've never cared much for this time of the year, but then I'm probably the odd one out. Guess I'm just not good with tinsel and wrapping paper."

"It is such a strange time isn't it? We decorate trees with pretty ornaments while ignorant of pagan origins, open presents supposedly delivered by a jolly man in red in order to celebrate a theoretical messenger of God's birth, a man whose horrific torture just months later will spawn strange rabbits with the gift of laying chocolate eggs, and wonder why there is a hollow feeling when the festivities have passed."

"That's one way to look at it I suppose." Clarence could feel his muscles slowly relaxing as the wine warmed the inside of his belly. "Sounds to me like you're not much of a fan either."

"It's the religious confusion that troubles me," Bernice revealed with a soft shake of her head. "Are you a religious man Clarence?"

"Can't say that I am."

"Then it's safe to say you're a *cautious* man, and a fine attribute it is to have. You see, we view religion as a wonderful gallery of different attempts to explain those mysteries that lay hidden in wait deep in our every cell, our every dream, our every *thought*. To be religious, it seems, is to admit you've stopped at one particular piece of art when there's a whole gallery to explore, a truly sad choice made even more upsetting when it comes with the belief all other art works are but unfortunate illusions. Can you imagine, choosing to enter halls filled with our artistic attempts to discover our place amongst the stars and taking only two steps!"

Bernice brought a hand to her heart as though the very thought threatened her pulse. There was an eerie silence that followed the emotional testimony, and for Clarence the silence represented the perfect opportunity to make his exit. Only, his legs seemed a little too heavy to be getting up just yet and besides, the second he leaned forward to give up his empty glass Teresa lifted the bottle and poured him another.

"I really should be going…" he slurred.

"Oh I'm sure you can stay for one more," his host insisted. "After all, I thought you'd like to meet the mother of the little girl who met such a horrendous fate at sea."

The words echoed across the table like sparks from a raging fire caught in a thieving wind gust. Clarence turned his heavy head and discovered a beautiful smile radiating from Teresa's soft glowing face.

"It's hard to put into words sometimes," she said. "The judge taught me that there's a pain so bad, a pain so awful that eternity itself won't find a way to make it better. It's deep inside me and won't let go, but thanks to you the pain can at least find new reason."

"That's right," Bernice confirmed as she leaned forward and once again placed a hand on Clarence's knee, "you're a changed man that's done a wonderful thing."

Clarence didn't feel good at all. The walls had started to ripple and pulse as though made of rubber trying to hold back a torrent of flowing water, his stomach felt cold as ice, and as he tried to swallow he realized he couldn't feel his throat at all.

Still, determined to know what it was that he had seen earlier he reached down to Bernice's hand and pushed back the sleeve of her cardigan. Vivid black ink of various pentagrams and geometric shapes were revealed, a shocking and unsettling collection of tattoos that not only looked so very out of place on an old lady's arms but, carried within the needle thin carvings, was imagery strong enough to stir the awakening of a primal terror deep in his heart.

"I knew it..." he whispered as the chair began to melt and reflections from the chandelier became glowing embers ready to fall and burn.

Bernice shuffled to the edge of her seat and leaned in even closer. The smell of her perfume overpowered his senses and when she spoke he could feel her breath against his blood swollen cheek.

"We admire all of the beauty that the gallery holds," she said close to his ear, "but we believe in the one that *designs* the gallery." She brought her face even closer, the soft skin of her jaw brushing against his. "We believe in the Curator."

Clarence felt his heart pound with the force of a wrecking ball against his chest. His dry mouth fell open and his hands began to twitch. He was about to attempt to lift himself from the chair when suddenly there was a noise that emanated from the kitchen sounding like a low, distorted animal cry.

With all the energy he could muster he turned to look through the archway. Though his eyes were heavy and the air had become a thick sparkling haze that swirled and danced and begged for sleep to come, he could just make out a tall dark shape taking a slow step toward them.

"Who the hell…" he rasped with breath growing shorter and shorter.

"Why it's the Curator," Teresa said with a whispered fear, "and he's come to feast on the serpent."

Visiting Hours.

It was Christmas Eve in the sun baked city of *(redacted)*. The streets were slowly but surely growing quiet as last minute shoppers claimed victory and headed home with arms laden with gifts, stores closed their doors and flicked on decorative lights in preparation for the electrically charged dark of night, and radio stations across the dial broadcast the timeless harmonies of carols that gave ode to the birth of a king and the promise of joy to the world.

And so it was, that in the last hour before dusk on a day so very treasured by so very many that Clarence Turner finally opened his eyes, and when he did so there came a blinding white light that nearly burned straight through the back of his head. It was an unpleasant awakening to say the least, and when he was finally able to focus it was also as disorientating as could be.

He was in a small hospital room that could have doubled as a shrine to the colour green. The walls, the sheets pulled tight across his bruised body, the curtains drawn in an effort to hide what was left of the sun, all were the same sickly shade that left him feeling he had awoken at the bottom of an algae soaked swimming pool.

Shocked at the sudden realization of where he was he rolled onto his side to investigate the strange tapping sound that had drawn him from the abyss. Imagine his surprise when he found Barbara seated on a flimsy plastic chair, quietly enjoying a cigarette while rapping her fingernails against a magazine resting in her lap. When she saw he was awake she flipped the pages closed with a start, stumped out the cigarette into a small foil ashtray and jumped to her feet.

"You sure know how to scare a lady you know that?"

"The real question," Clarence winced, "is what the hell am I doing here?"

"Well, there I was curled up on the couch with a bag of Smiths Crisps, smoky bacon of course, ready for the year ender of Chopper Squad when the next thing I know the phone rings and it's Bernice telling me you've collapsed!"

"Maybe tap the brakes a little? My head's killing…"

"Shit, sorry about that, I guess I'm just glad you're okay. Anyway, I don't know how she got my number, but I jumped in the car and the next thing I know you're slumped on my backseat and I'm racing to the hospital." She shrugged her shoulders and reached down to squeeze his hand. "Doctors think it might be a delayed concussion. You were in bad shape Clarence, totally dehydrated and beyond exhausted, and they say your leg's suffered three fresh fractures."

"Yeah? Well it feels like thirty I can assure you." Despite the confusion at all that was happening he grinned up at the only woman that had an inkling of care for him. "I feel like I've woken up from the dead. How long was I out for anyway?"

"Two days."

"Two bloody days?" he almost yelled. "We should never have let her in the office."

"Who, Bernice?"

"She's not the sweet old lady we thought she was, believe me."

"That reminds me." Barbara spun on her heels and grabbed the magazine from the small fold out table. "This is the new one I dropped on your desk. You need to see this."

She licked a finger and flipped through the pages with a growing urgency. Her brow drew tight and a sigh seeped from her lips but once she found what she was looking for she handed Clarence the publication. With an awkward outstretched arm he looked over what she thought was so important.

Australian Federal Police set to re-open investigation into child killer ring. Links between high profile figures and missing children's cases, both cold and current, will be forensically examined after a high court decision to release previously sealed documents was handed down in a controversial decision just weeks ago in an attempt to locate missing tobacco millionaire…

With blood pressure rising he flicked his eyes down to the photo accompanying the article and felt the thin mattress grow cold. Majestic and proud against a cloudless sky, *The Age of Innocence* sat moored amongst several other opulent displays of wealth, and there, standing on the deck beside the cigarette funded playboy smiling for the camera, was none other than the riverbank loving judge.

He flicked to the front cover, saw that it was the first edition of *Platypus*, issue one of the official Federal Police publication, and knew there and then that he'd landed face first into the perfect storm.

"You know what? This case is just way too bloody big for our little office," he said with not a little spite as he threw the magazine down onto the floor.

"Oh I almost forgot," Barbara replied. "This was couriered this morning." She produced an envelope from her pocket and tapped it against her hand. "It's a little strange considering there's no return sender."

"Probably the start of another lawsuit."

"Legal paperwork on Christmas Eve? You know I just don't get how lawyers can sleep at night."

"With a whole lotta nightmares I can assure you." He snatched the envelope from her hand, threw it down onto the bedside cabinet, then looked into her eyes with a sympathetic frown. "If it's Christmas Eve the last place you need to be is here with me. Why aren't you at home celebrating with a champagne or something?"

When Barbara shrugged her shoulders and lowered her face so he couldn't see her eyes he suddenly wished he could take the question back.

"It's been a week now and he still hasn't called," she said shamefully. "Guess I'll be ushering in another new year with an ad in the personals."

"He didn't deserve you," Clarence assured her. "Screw him, we can have our own little hospital party."

And so as darkness fell across the city they shared childhood memories of innocent times gone, laughed at some of the strange clients that had hired their services, and enjoyed peaceful moments of silence that only true friends could beneath a festive night sky that was always able to weave together the magic of similar hearts beating as one.

Careful not to dampen the mood neither had brought up the herd of elephants in the room but, when an apologetic nurse had explained to Barbara that it was close to midnight and she would have to leave, Clarence felt the sudden rush of knowing that he'd been pushing back all evening. Concussion wasn't what had landed him in hospital that was for damn sure and then, alone in his little room in the ward, he had to face what had happened.

With foggy visions of what he'd seen through the bricked archway slowly coming to the surface he reached across for the envelope. He knew deep in his gut that whatever was inside had nothing to do with a money chase, and when he did finally read the carefully penned contents he knew his stay in the hospital was over.

It was quite an effort to slip back into his filthy clothes considering he could barely stand, and even worse was the fact there were no keys in his pockets and he had no idea of where the hell his car could be. At least his wallet was still there, and though the nurses did their best to change his mind he hobbled to the elevators, rode down to the ground floor, and shuffled into one of the lonely taxis sitting idle beneath the entrance lights.

The Christless Angel.

There's something about the beach that soothes even the most anxious of souls, and on bright sunny days her glittering blue has a seemingly endless magic that yearns to embrace all who are touched by a salty summer breeze.

At night however, when the blue is an ink black abyss with no end in sight and the sand sits cold and coarse, the beach has a different face. At night her waters are home to unseen monsters that feed without mercy, and her crashing waves taunt with a promise of fear for those willing to enter her dark, primal embrace. Free of the warming light of the sun, her true magic rises free from her most mysterious and deepest of depths.

It was on a quiet secluded beach, far from the festive glow of the city, that Clarence came to know there were more mysteries to life than there were stars in the ink black sky. The silent taxi drive had taken more than an hour, and as it had pulled up at the end of a dead end street that marked the start of a sandy track beneath the stars, he'd begun to wonder how much of his sanity would remain come sunrise.

After eagerly accepting payment for the large fare that came with a generous tip the driver rolled off into the night, leaving Clarence to stand beneath a lone, salt crusted light pole as a soft wind carried the sound of lapping waves and the smell of wet sand and seashells. He was pretty sure he was in the right place, and though it was going to hurt like hell he began the cane infused rhythmic trek along the sandy path with the letter clutched tight in his hand.

When he finally staggered over a large sand dune that flooded his muscles with agony, his chest heaving and eyes tearing from the pain, he looked down the beach and saw the outlines of several figures huddled around a fire and forced his legs to move once more. To his right there stretched across the water a mesmerizing, electric blue highway courtesy of a full moon, and in the air he could just make out faint traces of laughter.

Waves crashed and tumbling rocks crackled beneath the stars as he pushed through the sand towards the dancing flames. He could see them clearly now, five women sitting in a circle around the bright red coals, each draped in long black cloaks and each with tinsel tied to their hair. One by one they turned to smile at his arrival, and when it was Bernice's turn to greet his presence he could've sworn her eyes had a light of their own.

He collapsed down onto his knees with a cry of pain, then sucked in a deep breath and held out the crumpled paper of the letter.

"You wanted me to come so here I am."

Bernice broke from the circle, knelt down beside him, and kissed him gently on the cheek.

"It's so wonderful of you to join us," she whispered while taking the letter from his hand. "I've always believed it's important to be around those who care about you at such a special time of the year."

"Care about me?" Clarence gasped. "You drugged me into oblivion and left me to rot in a hospital bed."

"I'm afraid sometimes doing the wrong thing is the only right thing to do. Now come sit with us by the fire, the magic is about to begin."

Clarence was far too exhausted to raise any arguments, and though his head was filled with a dizzying array of questions and strange memories that were bubbling up from realms he thought forgotten forever, he felt a growing sense of calm calling from somewhere beyond distant realms. Besides, the air was becoming cool making the warmth of the flames beckon with a trance like effect.

He dragged himself close as Bernice returned to her place within the circle. One of the women he didn't quite recognize, yet he could see Teresa staring up at the moon with a familiar fear in her eyes and discovered that he knew the faces either side as the marks he had followed. Those same faces watched him silently as the flames flickered and rose higher into the night, their expressions radiating a sense of peace and maternal protection that opened feelings in him not felt since he was a child.

"We must remember," Bernice said quietly to the surrounding ladies, "that sadness has no place under tonight's moon. Any tears will only steal from you the joy of peering behind the veil that lifts for only the briefest of moments. Embrace the wonders of a gallery with no end. Embrace all that is love."

The soothing tone of her voice seeped into the wind and echoed across the sand. Hunched down on his knees with hands barely keeping balance, Clarence felt his eyes grow heavy and thoughts begin to slow. On one hand there was nothing about the moment that made any sense at all, in fact it was verging on madness, and yet on the other hand it was as if his every move since moving to the city was always destined to lead to this. It was all just one big dream, and now the dream was keeping a promise that had been his to unravel from the start.

Through bloodshot eyes he watched Bernice ease the letter into the fire where it was quickly consumed, then reached beneath her cloak to reveal a long, silver blade. Next she drew back her sleeve to expose the intricate tattoos along her arm, the pentagrams and geometrics visibly glowing beneath the light of the moon as the flames danced and her skin warmed against the heat of the moon.

"The serpent has brought each of us a pain that rages with a boundless fury, but tonight its tail lays still."

Her eyes rolled back as the blade sliced deep into her skin. First the blood trickled, then began to flow as she brought her arm over the fire where the dark crimson fluid hissed down onto eagerly awaiting coals. In an instant the wind died and gone was the sound of crashing waves. Besides the tall, proud flames that seemed to swell with the addition of fresh blood, all was still.

Suddenly Clarence sensed movement behind him. Slowly and painfully he shifted his weight to look towards the water. At first there was only darkness, but then, from deep within the shadows, there emerged a breathtakingly beautiful little girl with long blond hair and a dress covered with flowers.

Her little feet barely left impressions in the sand as she stepped up to Teresa with arms outstretched.

"Hello mummy."

Teresa did all that she could to fight back the tears but it was a battle marred with futility, and like small rivers in search of the sea they streamed down her cheeks while she took her daughter's hand to be led off into the night.

Soon another little girl appeared, and then another, and another until left there was only Clarence and Bernice to watch the quiet ritual of mothers being drawn into the shadows that separated the endless abyss of the ocean and the crackling, blood fed flames. What happened in the dark couldn't be known, but Clarence could hear muffled laughter and soft tears of joy. It was truly a dream that he had awakened within, and as light from the full moon continued to shine in Bernice's eyes he focused as hard as he could to bring sound back up through his throat.

"How is it possible…" he barely managed before sinking further into the sand.

"A mother's love can do such wondrous things," Bernice smiled, blood still dripping from her decorated arm. "A devil's serpent may have ways to destroy the flesh, but a love it shall never experience will always prove unbreakable. Now you know Clarence, now you understand that even the most heartbreaking of roads can lead to a place that was always meant to be."

Her words seemed to push through his skin and rise up within. Time had slipped from the confines of physical law, swirling and shifting so that he couldn't be sure if he lay broken in the sand for minutes, hours or if the night had always been forever and anything else mere fragments of illusory imaginations, but there did come a time that the shadows stirred and mothers and daughters returned. For they stood at the edge of the fire's light, shoulder to shoulder with protective arms around the greatest of all love they had ever known, and watched the deserted beach with expectant eyes.

Clarence too followed their gaze along the water's edge and into the dark of night, his senses lost along a stretch of beach where even the light of the moon seemed unable to penetrate. Beside him, Bernice brought the blade to her arm once more, and there came a sharp hissing as new blood rained down upon the coals.

Along the lonely beach the dark began to take shape. Subtle at first, as though wisps of sand were being lifted towards the stars in a silent breeze, but then shapes and shadows became form and the night gave birth to a serpent's tendril. The little girl's mouths fell open with awe, while standing behind them their mothers drew in a fearful breath and knew that the time had come.

Clarence could suddenly smell burned sulphur. It itched the inside of his nose and brought a little clarity back to thoughts that had been caught by the tides that carried dreams to the edge of all things forgotten, and so he lifted his heavy head and watched the forms as the sound of a grown man crying rose and fell.

Bernice began to laugh and the mothers narrowed their eyes with disdain. The crying grew louder, and then the summoned arrived with its fill. Clarence felt the moon spin when the tall, faceless shape he had glimpsed through the archway marched towards the little girls with an enormous, disfigured glistening hand clenched tight around the back of the judge's neck. The Curator stood ten foot or higher with glowing red veins that pulsed beneath tar like skin, and it dragged the sobbing serpent tendril as if he were nothing more than a raggedy doll washed up in the seaweed.

Teresa dropped to her knees and watched her daughter run up to the tall shape of night before lowering her head to look the terrified judge in the eyes.

"You sir are a very bad man," she said in a slow angelic voice, "and very bad men have a special place to go to."

"Oh no please…" the judge gargled, "I didn't know…"

"Shh now. You're on the edge of eternity and you'll need your strength to scream soon enough."

The Curator reached down and gently stroked the little girl's hair, prompting a magnificent smile to curl her delicate lips, before dragging the judge towards the ink black water. Ignoring previous instruction his screams were filled with a terror soaked majesty that came with knowing his soul was about to discover a new bending of time and an eternity of torturous suffering, and his legs kicked and his arms thrashed but still the Curator marched forward.

One by one the little girls kissed their mothers goodbye, then happily danced in the huge footsteps like faeries in a land of giants while following the faceless shape with its bounty. Teresa's daughter, however, hadn't yet joined them. Instead of dancing her way to the water she crouched down beside Clarence and tenderly wrapped her tiny arms around his neck.

"Thank you," she whispered into his ear.

The tips of her fingers were velvet wrapped clouds that electrified his skin with an angelic soft touch. A magnificent warmth like nothing he'd ever felt before exploded within every cell of his body, bringing a rush of euphoria to wash away the pain and agony of damaged bones and muscles. His lungs filled with a long breath of air that rivalled, or perhaps even surpassed, his very first gasp upon his arrival on the planet, and as her tiny arms broke free he could feel every teardrop traversing his warmed cheeks.

The little girl giggled and ran to join the Curator and its clan as they splashed into the returning waves. The judge's screams still pierced the night air, but it was no match for the laughter and squeals of delight that shamed even the greatest of symphonies.

Clarence lifted himself up from the sand, looked at his client's smile one last time, then quietly stepped away from the fire. A particularly vicious scream drew his sharpened attention across the water, where he could just make out the little girls tearing flesh from the judge's face and neck before digging their nails into the open wounds and giggling as his screams were finally muffled with a mixture of blood and stinging salt water, but he didn't need to watch the fun. An eternity of hell was a personal matter, and it was time for him to leave.

He trudged through the soft sand and began the climb up the mound to the track when he suddenly stopped. It had happened so naturally he almost hadn't noticed. His legs had carried him effortlessly, and all the pain was gone.

With a surge of excitement breaking through the confusion he turned over his shoulder, and as his eyes adjusted to the moonlit distance he could see the little girl whose hug had stolen his heart frantically waving her arms. Then, as a warm breeze carried along the sand, he could hear her voice calling out above the sound of the waves that crashed against her flower dress.

"Merry Christmas Mr Turner…"

***

About Darren Kasenkow

Darren Kasenkow is an Australian author of dystopian horror and science fiction... with a sprinkling of existentialism. His short stories have appeared in various street publications and magazines, as well as a collection appearing in the national anthology Paroxysm (Paroxysm Press). His current feature length releases include: The Apocalypse Show, Dust And Devils, See The City Red, and The Hallucigenia Project, which is his latest release and book one of a new dystopian thriller series. Book two, Godless, is scheduled for release in January 2020. To learn more, visit www.darrenkasenkow.com

Epica Intermission

Now that surely sent a tingle down my scurvy wracked spine, and to think such a tale has been hidden all this time! Something tells me this particular Christmas haul is going to be truly special.

Ah, can you see it bobbing in the dark? Another bottle set free from the mysteries of the deep, and this one glowing with the molten orange of a long yearned for setting sun. Placed next to the others they'll be a wondrous sight hanging from the masts for all the stars to see, a gently swaying collection of iridescent treasures to warm the lonely decks with a sprinkling of festive magic. After all, there's no Christmas Tree to be found on a convict ghost ship.

Well I'll be, this looks to be a story ready to stir distant memories of searching for something delicious! Oh, how the tantalizing scents of freshly baked treats would taunt as I shuffled along cobblestone streets with a skinny belly hungry for even the tiniest morsel, but something tells me this yarn holds more than warm pastry and cream…

An Awfully Evangeline Christmas

By Madeleine D'Este

For the Lebkuchen beasts

Evangeline's bedroom window was wide open, in the vain hope of capturing even the slightest whisper of breeze, but the Melbourne midnight air was as still as stone. She kicked her Witney blanket aside. How could it be so unbearably hot? She knew things were topsy-turvy in the Colonies but where were the familiar festive grey skies, dirty snow and the chilblains? She tossed and turned, still sweltering under her thin sheet. Evangeline's first Antipodean Christmas was turning out to be more surprising, and sweaty, than she expected.

Her hankering for chilly old Blighty stopped when she heard a scrape along the roof. She jolted upright and forced open her gluey eyes. Something, or someone, was traversing over the corrugated iron. It was a trifle early for Father Christmas and so perhaps it was one of those strange screeching possum creatures. Evangeline leaned forward and held her breath as she strained to hear.

And then she gasped.

Something was at her window... and it was ghastly.

A face.

A face with red leering eyes.

A face with a lolling purple tongue.

A face crowned with sharp curling horns.

And it was looking straight at her.

Her head scrambled and her heart thumped. She rubbed her eyes and blinked several times but when her vision cleared there was nothing there. Only an empty open window.

Crash!

The sound came from inside the house. The intruder must have slipped inside through another open window.

Evangeline narrowed her eyes. "Burglarising on Christmas Eve," she tutted. "How rude."

She scurried out of bed and grabbing her latest invention, took a position by the door. She gritted her teeth. No one would get away with breaking into 56 Collins Street without a fight.

Muffled voices drifted up the stairs. Was it a whole gang of prowlers? Evangeline gripped the handle of her pink parasol tight. Whatever the number, the rogues were in for quite a shock.

Heavy boot steps clumped up the stairs towards her bedroom and Evangeline pressed the button on the parasol. Once. Twice. Three times and the bayonet sprung from the ferrule. The secret blade glinted in the moonlight.

Crash!

"Bally stair runner," grumbled a familiar voice. "Who put that there?"

"Shhh, Monty. You'll wake them," slurred another, followed by a thump and a bong as someone crashed into Clarence, the grandfather clock.

"Hush yourself, little brother. I am as silent as a church mouse."

Further down the landing, two bedroom doors slammed and Evangeline breathed easy with a little grin on her face.

But the sounds of her inebriated father and uncle did not explain the horrible face with horns ogling through her bedroom window. Was it some type of native monster? Perhaps it was another dream, the result of this bothersome heat. Or was Marvellous Melbourne as dangerous as they warned?

Evangeline shook her head at her own silliness and retracted the blade on her parasol. She climbed back under the sheet and dozed off, drifting into a more pleasant dreamland filled with steaming plum pudding and creamy brandy custard.

***

The next morning, the heat was as thick as treacle once more. Evangeline splashed her face with water but her skin was clammy all over again by the time she fastened the last buttons on her high collared day dress. Mopping her brow, she skipped downstairs for breakfast and let out a sigh as she descended into the cool relief of the high ceilinged rooms on the ground floor. But the Caldicott house, where Evangeline had lived the past two months with her new extended family, was silent. There was no sign of her father, Professor Montague Caldicott the pre-eminent horological-engineer in all the Colonies, or her uncles or Miss Plockton. Even *The Argus* lay crisply folded and unread on the breakfast table. Evangeline shrugged and lunged for the newspaper, taking advantage of the solitude to read whatever stories took her fancy. The constraints of being a proper respectable young lady could make life awfully dull and after seventeen years on the streets of London, Evangeline was more worldly than her new family gave her credit for. A headline in the bottom right corner caught her eye and she pulled the paper closer. What deliciously gruesome stories could she find today?

"There you are, Miss Evangeline," Miss Plockton said, silently appearing at the open door. Evangeline flinched and rifled to the Women's supplement to avoid one of Miss Plockton's scathing glares. Her father's steely-haired personal secretary held a tray laden with toast and floral china. "I shall be right back."

"Is someone ill?" Evangeline said with a tilt of her head as she pointed to the tray. "Surely not at Christmas. What rotten luck."

Miss Plockton nodded solemnly and a grey curl bobbed beside her ear. "The Professor requested his devilled kidneys in his bedroom. He is feeling a little under the weather this morning. A good rest and, God willing, he'll be right as rain for tomorrow."

"Poor Father," Evangeline said as she suppressed a little smirk. Last night's Annual Christmas Supper of the Society of Antipodean Engineers must have been quite the lively affair, if the midnight racket on the landing was any indication.

Uncle Augie bustled into the room. Tall and rotund Augie was not truly Evangeline's uncle but her Uncle Edmund's constant companion. "This dreadful heat. So uncouth," he said as he dabbed his forehead and pounced for the teapot. "Only one more rehearsal. Only one more. With the fire, the rats and this dang heat melting the paint off the sets, this production is more cursed than the Scottish play." He raked his fingers through his fair hair and tossed a brew down his cravat covered throat.

"Uncle Augie, did you see…" Evangeline started.

"And my cast? The worst group of reprobates since my production of Tita in Thibet. And that is saying something." He placed down his cup with a porcelain clang. "But the show must go on. Toodles." Augie swept away, the brass knocker on the heavy front door clanging behind him.

Alone again in the breakfast room, Evangeline returned to her newspaper and the scandals on the front page.

"Now Miss Evangeline."

Evangeline jumped as the uncanny Miss Plockton reappeared. It was not the first time Evangeline wondered whether Miss Plockton owed some of her efficiency to a touch of the fey.

"This is a wee bit unusual but there isnae much time and so much to do before tomorrow. Polishing the silver, dusting the chandeliers, trussing the goose, making my shortbread. Such a lot of fuss but you English do love your Christmas. We never bothered with such frippery in Inverness… but Cook and I are as busy as bees, and I need your help with a wee errand."

Evangeline straightened in her seat and hid *The Argus* on her lap. "Anything to help, Miss Plockton." And any excuse to leave 56 Collins Street without the shadow of a chaperone. Miss Plockton could have saved time and wired an order from a telegraph kiosk but Evangeline kept her mouth firmly closed.

"I know you haven't finished your paper chains for the tree…"

Evangeline turned up her nose at the thought of sitting inside for another day, cutting up coloured paper, not when there was an opportunity to be out and about having adventures. "I don't mind, really, Miss Plockton."

"After a stint in Vienna, your father developed a fancy for continental Christmas treats. Why he cannae be happy with mince pies and pudding, I'll never know." Miss Plockton pursed her lips and fingered the cross at her throat. "But I have ever so much to do, and I hoped you could call into Hellig's for me."

An outing for cake? Even better. "Anything to make Father happy." She grinned, remembering the handful of pennies sitting in her dressing table drawer. Here was her chance to finally try one of the Hellig's famous vanilla crescents.

"I have a list." Miss Plockton handed over a sheet of paper filled with her immaculate copperplate handwriting.

Evangeline secured it in her pocket. "Leave it to me, Miss Plockton."

"And no dilly-dallying," Miss Plockton said with a beady eye on Evangeline.

But Evangeline smiled back innocently. "Of course, Miss Plockton," she replied.

***

After fortifying herself with three more triangles of toast and raspberry jam, Evangeline rushed upstairs to prepare for her outing. She chose a striped day-dress with an accompanying straw hat, and once she was satisfied with her appearance in the looking glass, she finalised her ensemble with another of her inventions. The horridly humid Melbourne streets were the perfect place for a test run of her new brass mechanised fan.

All prepared, Evangeline trotted out the back gate with her wind-up fan and her list. Whistling *O Christmas Tree*, she crossed the cobbled alley and proceeded through the gate of Fang's Fine Laundering, and stepped into a maze of white sheets drying in the sun. She knocked sharply on the back door and Mei poked out her head, a laundry basket in her arms. Her best friend and kung-fu teacher was dressed in her traditional and practical Chinese trousers.

"Merry Christmas. Are you busy?" Evangeline asked.

"Too right." Mei grimaced. "Everyone wants their tablecloths and napkins starched and spotless for Christmas dinner tomorrow."

"Oh no, I was hoping you could join me on a little outing," Evangeline said with a smirk.

Mei wiped her forehead. "I'd love to but I'm needed here. Ma would have a fit if I bunked off."

Evangeline's shoulders dropped dramatically. "What a shame,' she sighed. 'I'm heading to Hellig's."

Mei's eyes widened. "'ellig's? The bakery?"

Evangeline nodded.

Mei chewed her lip and squinted, then dropped her basket and disappeared inside the house. Evangeline chuckled and gently removed her hat. Having decided to use her waiting time efficiently, she tipped her head and leaned all the way over, practicing her back bends against the wall. Her new well-heeled life in Melbourne was making her rusty, only a few months earlier she had earned her keep by tumbling for pennies on street corners. She sighed as her spine enjoyed the stretch, but she quickly recoiled as her fingers touched the brick wall which was as hot as an oven.

Minutes later, Mei returned in a pale green dress, her face flushed with exertion. "Stupid corsets," she said as she shoved coins into her purse. "Let's go."

"I thought your family did not believe in Christmas."

Mei shrugged. "We believe in cake. Ma loves that Hellig gingerbread. Come on."

The best friends left through Mei's front door and headed down Little Collins Street, avoiding the harsh sun by strolling under the shade of the shopfront awnings. Swanston Street bustled with rattling trams, clip-clopping horses and whirring auto-chariots. "Get your pineapples. Get your pineapples," sang a costermonger, while a brass band parped *O Come All Ye Faithful*, and ladies in fine hats, men in shirt sleeves and black-clad housekeepers elbowed through the crowds. Evangeline breathed in the scent of roasting chestnuts, the festive aroma was a brief respite from the overpowering stink of the street as rotting rubbish and horse mess bubbled in the heat.

In amongst the busy determined faces, a little urchin girl with a dirty face caught Evangeline's eye. The girl in a torn dress, no older than four years old, stood in the gutter. Tears rolled down her face as gentlemen and ladies pushed past her without a second glance.

"Mei, stop," Evangeline said and reached for a penny from her pocket. The little girl's expression brought back painful memories, scars barely healed after a few months in Evangeline's new comfortable life. "What's wrong, little one," she said as she bent down.

The girl sniffled and wiped her snotty nose on her grubby sleeve. "It's Gertie. I miss 'er."

Evangeline handed over her white handkerchief. "I'm sure she's here somewhere. We can help you look."

"I dunno where she is," the little girl said. "'e took her."

"Who took her?" Evangeline frowned.

The little girl shook her head and pressed her lips tight.

"You can tell us," Mei said. "What man took 'er?"

The girl glanced from side to side, her blue eyes wide. "They say it's Old Nick,' she whispered. 'Wiv the 'orns."

Evangeline gasped. Horns?

"'orns, you say?" said Mei, her voice shaking. "And a grey beard?"

A scabby-kneed boy rushed up and tugged the little girl away. "Come on, Maisie. Don't say nothin'."

"Stop," called Evangeline but the two children were soon lost in the bustling crowd. She turned back to Mei, her mouth still agape. "Did you see a face too? I thought I was dreaming."

"Last night." Mei nodded. "At my window. A demon with a face like a goat."

"What could it be, Mei?"

Mei shuddered. "I don't know. It didn't look like any demon I know."

"How many demons do you know?"

Mei counted out on her fingers. "Monkeys. Pigs. Dragons, but no goats."

Evangeline shivered, imagining what horrors the horned beast had planned for his small victims.

"Come on. We'd better 'urry. What if they've run out of cake!" Mei took her hand and they dashed towards the bakery.

***

The newly opened Viennese patisserie was the most fashionable bakery in Melbourne and the queue for Hellig's stretched half way down King Street. Outside the shop window, a crowd of middle-aged women tapped their heeled boots and flapped their fans, wafting the baking scent of cinnamon and sugar through the stifling air.

"We should have started out early." Evangeline sighed as she stood on tip-toes to count the number of the hats and parasols ahead of them in line.

"Gives me a chance to work up an appetite."

"Appetite for cake?"

"Right, silly me. It's so awful 'ot in this corset. My mind's going doolally."

"Ah, I have just the solution." Evangeline ferreted about in her pocket and thrust up her new invention with gusto.

"Here we go again…" Mei rolled her eyes. "Have you tested this one?"

Ignoring her insolent friend, Evangeline turned the key mechanism with a series of grinding clicks. She smiled as the leaves of the fan unfolded automatically like a blossoming metal flower and the brass semi-circle began to flap up and down, exactly as she planned. But rather than producing a refreshing breeze, the fan moved with the pace of an elderly snail, and was accompanied by a shrill metallic screech. Evangeline winced and Mei covered her ears.

"Stop that awful racket!" bellowed a tall, bosomy woman behind them and Evangeline hid the fan away in her pocket with another sigh. She would have to find an alternative gift for Miss Plockton before tomorrow morning.

The queue moved a few inches and by Evangeline's estimation, there were only another twenty-five women ahead of them in the queue.

"I hope they don't sell out," Mei said as they shuffled forward.

"Our apologies, ladies and gennelmen. Ve are serfing you as quickly as ve can." Mei elbowed Evangeline with a wink. Otto Hellig was another reason why a trip to Hellig's was such a thrill. "Please accept a little treat as our vay of saying thank you for visiting our little konditorei." The tall, flaxen haired Otto sauntered down the line towards them. Evangeline drew in a delighted breath, straightened her hat and smiled her very best smile.

"Ladies, vhat a pleasure. You are Miss Caldicott and Miss Fang. Am I right?" He grinned, his sky-blue eyes sparkling with mischief and a tray of golden gingerbread trees in his arms.

They giggled behind their hands, exchanging half-shrugs and coy looks, and Mei reached out her fingers for a gingerbread tree.

"Oh no, for such handsome… and interesting… young ladies, I haff a special treat for you." He lowered his voice so the others would not hear. Mei and Evangeline glanced at each other with shining eyes. "A special family tradition for special customers."

Otto clicked his fingers and a serving boy appeared with a round biscuit tin decorated with scenes of snow and a jolly Saint Nicholas. The tin was filled with gingerbread hearts, each with a dab of red jam in the centre. "Lebkuchen."

"Why, thank you," Evangeline said breathily, her cheeks blazing red as she selected a biscuit. To her delight, the underside was slathered in chocolate, unfortunately melting in the frightful heat. She took a bite and dark chocolate, raspberry jam, ginger, cinnamon and cloves exploded inside her mouth.

"Good?" Otto asked with a nod of his handsome head.

"Oh yes," groaned Mei in an almost unladylike way.

"Wunderbar." He smiled.

"Otto!" Another young man with a scowl on his face called from the doorway. His colouring was similar, but Otto's twin brother Leo was as ugly as Otto was handsome. How could they be twins and yet be so different?

Otto waved his hand dismissively at Leo, and winked at Mei and Evangeline. "Ladies, please excuse me. Thank you for your patience, ve vill be vith you very soon."

Mei and Evangeline elbowed one another as Otto strolled away towards his sneering twin brother.

"Otto recognised us. How?" Mei asked.

Evangeline was staring dolefully at her empty hand. "I wonder if they have more inside." She licked the last crumbs and chocolate smears from her fingers before reaching for her handkerchief. Then she remembered she'd handed it over to dry the eyes of the little urchin on Swanston Street.

"Hello, ladies. I am glad you are enjoying our treats." Leo slithered up beside them, his lips exceedingly moist. "Christmas is such a super time of year. Especially for those who haff been good. I trust you haff been nice? And not naughty?" he said, raising a blond eyebrow.

Mei clenched her jaw in a twisted grimace but Evangeline smiled falsely and formally. "Thank you for your enquiry into our well-being, Mister Hellig," she replied, puffing out her chest. 'Of course, we have been good."

"Excellent. I am sure you vill be revarded this Christmas. Enjoy, ladies."

Evangeline shuddered as he skulked away. "He gives me the creeps."

But strangely, Mei said nothing in reply. Evangeline turned to her friend with a frown and saw Mei leaning her cheek against the shop window, her hand pressed against her forehead. "So 'ot," Mei moaned weakly, her face the same green hue as her dress. "When is this cool change comin'?"

Evangeline grasped her friend's arm. "Mister Hellig? Can someone bring a glass of water? My friend. She's…"

But the sinister twin had already disappeared inside.

Evangeline tried to call out again but she lost train of her words and thoughts. The blinking lights, gaudy baubles and grand gingerbread house in the shop window started swimming in front of her eyes. Christmas carols, buzzing flies and the complaints of surrounding ladies rang loudly in her ears. Her knees buckled and she grabbed for the wall, and then everything went dark.

***

Evangeline woke up with a start, her head throbbing like a metronome, her dress damp with sweat. Mei lay beside her, unconscious on the straw-covered floor.

"Mei. Wake up." She gently shook Mei's shoulder.

Mei grunted and her eyes flickered open. "Not again," she groaned as she blinked and took in her surroundings.

They appeared to be locked inside a wire cage in a dim hot room. The cage, like a large chicken coop, stretched along the entire wall, and at the far end of the room, a fire-breathing clay oven belched out a wall of brutal heat.

The piles of straw around them shifted. Evangeline clutched her chest with a gasp. They were not the only prisoners in the cage and one by one, a handful of small dirty faces peeked out from under the straw.

"What is going on?" Evangeline asked.

No one replied. The children kept their eyes lowered and their heads bowed.

"Why are we here?" she said, more insistently this time. "Is this part of the white slave trade?"

"Oi!" Mei elbowed.

"Sorry, all colours slave trade."

"They're goin' to eat us," said a gappy-toothed boy. "For Christmas dinner. Wiv all the trimmin's."

"Don't be silly," said Mei with a gulp. "You've been readin' too many stories. There's nothin' around here that eats children. Except for the *wangliang* but they usually only eat babies. Unless they're really hungry."

Evangeline grimaced. Eating children? Gingerbread? The story was sounding awfully familiar.

The key rattled in the lock and Evangeline scrambled to her feet, but the cage ceiling was too low and she had no choice but to stoop.

"Little kinder. Little kinder," a familiar voice said.

"Krampus," whispered another little voice in amongst the straw.

"What did she say?" Evangeline wrinkled her forehead.

"Something about 'ampers." Mei shrugged. "This 'eat has turned everyone loony."

Evangeline gasped as a man with the head of a goat strutted into the room, curling horns protruding from his forehead, grey and white hair covering his face, a thick dark-purple tongue lolling from his mouth. It was the face from her window last night but this time he held a basket of the delicious gingerbread hearts in his arms.

Mei gawked at Evangeline and mouthed the word, "Leo."

"I always knew there was something off about him." Evangeline nodded. "But he may have underestimated us."

Mei winked back. "Butterfly kick."

"Absolutely. On your count."

The girls scuttled towards the cage door as the goat-headed man approached and Evangeline sucked in a breath. Leo had no idea what he was facing.

"We'll be out in time for supper," said Mei. "One. Two…"

The goat-headed man approached the cage and pressed his horrible face against the wire. But he did not unlock the door, rather he held the basket of gingerbread hearts within reach through the bars.

"Maybe the little blighters were right," Mei said. "They're tryin' to fatten us up."

The warm scent of ginger and spices coiled through the air. Evangeline licked her lips, the taste of the last biscuit still lingering on her tongue. She knew better but for some strange reason she couldn't control herself and her fingers reached out for another heart from the basket.

"Don't be an eejit!" Mei spat.

"But…" Evangeline said, her fingers out-stretched.

The goat-man sniggered. He pulled out a birch rod and slapped Evangeline across the knuckles.

"Ouch, you rotter," she snapped, withdrawing her tender hand and sucking the site of the blow.

"This is what happens to bad kinder." The goat-man laughed.

Evangeline narrowed her eyes.

"How about those powers of yours?" Mei whispered. "You can get us out of here again, can't you?"

Evangeline sighed. Last time they were locked together inside a cage in the cellar of the Lady Alchemist's mansion in East Melbourne, Evangeline had conjured up a strange power to free them, an unreliable power she had not been able to reproduce, no matter how hard she tried.

The door crashed open and another man-sized silhouette stood in the doorway, shouting in hurried German.

"Otto. Save us!" called out Mei.

The goat-man spun around to face her and laughed wickedly. He chortled so hard, he doubled over and slapped his knee.

The other man stepped into sight. Mei and Evangeline exchanged glances, then stared back at the goat-man incredulously.

"Otto?" they exclaimed in unison.

"They are bad, they deserve all they get," said Otto the goat-man in English. "You are too soft on them, Leo. They are all too soft on them. How will they learn if they are not punished?"

"You must stop. You must let them go. They are only kinder." The ugly Leo rushed into the centre of the room. "Look at them, they have nothing. Poor little urchins."

"Bah. They are evil."

"You take that back," Evangeline demanded. "I am not evil!"

"I can see the evil in you. Simmering away. Just below the skin," Otto snickered.

Evangeline pursed her lips and smoothed back her hair. "It's not what you have, but what you do with it."

With a wooden baker's paddle in his hands, Leo hurtled towards his brother. Otto swung around, sending gingerbread hearts flying through the air. He deflected Leo's pathetic blow and with a single punch to the nose, knocked his twin brother to the ground.

Otto loomed over Leo and laughed. "You were always the veak one."

"And you the crazy one." Leo spluttered as blood trickled out of one nostril.

Evangeline shook the bars of the cage but it was locked tight. She clenched her jaw but then she remembered the contents of her pocket.

"Leo. Take this," she called as the unattractive brother stumbled to his feet. She unfurled her metal fan and tossed it across the room to him.

Unfortunately, Evangeline's aim was a little off. She bit her lip as the metal fan soared across the room at surprising speed and collided with Leo's forehead. The sharp brass edge slashed his skin and knocked him out cold. He collapsed to the ground in a heap.

"Knickers," said Evangeline.

Goat-faced Otto guffawed and prodded his brother with the toe of his boot, but Leo did not move a whisker.

"Ah, we haff someone here who is extremely bad. Who needs to be punished vorse than the vorst of you," said Otto as he strutted in front of the cage. "Vhich one of you threw it? Vhich one of you hurt my bruder?"

Evangeline swallowed hard and one of the nearby urchins burst into tears. She glanced around the cage and saw the sea of frightened faces, little children whose only sin was hunger, an ache Evangeline remembered all too well.

She rolled back her shoulders and straightened her spine. "It was me," she declared. "Come and get me, goat man."

Mei elbowed her with a frown but Evangeline shook her head and tapped the side of her nose. Mei winked back.

"You big ugly goat," Mei added with a grin. "Come and get us."

"Ah, the young ladies. Of course." He stood in front them on the opposite side of the wire and Evangeline narrowed her eyes. "But I cannot afford to lose you bigger ones. I need every single one of you to fill our special Boxing Day pies."

"Our families will be looking for us. They know we are here. You will not get away with this."

"But you and your Oriental friend vere seen on a tram heading for Flemington. I distinctly overheard you speaking about catching a dirigible for Hobart Town. Sick of your family's hard rules, you vanted to go off and seek your fortunes."

"I would never…" Evangeline started.

"As if anyone would believe that," Mei scoffed. "'obart Town?"

"No one vill come looking."

His words were like needles, reminiscent of her drunken stepfather, Charlie Drigg, the man Evangeline escaped in London. After all she'd been through, she would not miss her first Christmas with the Professor, her real father. Evangeline gritted her teeth and clenched her fists. "You are wrong, Mister Hellig. So very wrong."

Otto raised a bemused eyebrow.

"You, sir… or goat…whatever you are, you are ruining my Christmas."

"And puttin' us off cake!" Mei added.

"Indeed. You shall not be allowed to get away with this."

Mei whispered behind her hand. "Nice speech, Prime Minister, but 'ow are we goin' to get out of 'ere?"

Evangeline continued to glare at Otto, but muttered from the corner of her mouth. "I was hoping you'd think of something."

"Ballocks." Mei sighed.

The door burst open and two figures stormed inside the bakehouse.

"Evangeline. Where are you?" said a voice with a Scottish brogue.

"Leo," said another female voice with a Germanic lilt and a plump grey-haired woman rushed over to Leo. She knelt down beside and started to gently slap his face.

Miss Plockton darted into the light and flung her wicker shopping basket aside. Brandishing a knitting needle and her gold cross, she charged at Otto and pressed the sharp point of her steel needle against his neck.

"Go away, you silly old woman." Otto swatted Miss Plockton away like a fly.

But Miss Plockton was too quick. The pewter-haired Scotswoman stamped on his instep with her heeled boot. He yowled, hopping up and down and clutching his foot, and Miss Plockton kicked again, slamming hard into his knee with all her weight. Otto toppled to the ground, and she finished the job by stamping her foot across his throat.

"My apologies, Mrs. Hellig. I hope you forgive me for hurting your son," she said, turning to the plump woman as she smoothed away a wayward curl.

"Think nothing of it, he deserved it. And please call me Bertha," Mrs. Hellig said. She rose to her feet and approached her son, writhing on the floor. "What have you done to your bruder, you little vorm?"

"It wasn't me. It was her," Otto croaked, whingeing like a small boy and pointing to Evangeline.

Evangeline lowered her eyes and pressed her lips together. Miss Plockton raised an eyebrow but kept her boot firmly on Otto's neck.

"Get her off me, Mutti."

"This time you have gone too far, Otto."

"I vanted to carry on the traditions in this strange new country. Make sure the kinder grew up good. I vanted to make you proud."

"Vat vill I do with you?" Mrs. Hellig shook her head with a sigh. She grabbed the set of keys from her belt and unlocked the cage. "Come out, little kinder. You are safe now."

The children poured out from under the straw, scurrying across the room and out the open door into the sunshine. Evangeline and Mei leaned on one another as they climbed out, their longer limbs cramped and stiff.

"I am so sorry. So sorry," Mrs. Hellig said, taking their arms as Miss Plockton removed her foot from Otto's throat.

"What will you do with him?" Evangeline asked as Otto curled into a ball, coughing and rubbing his neck.

"I shall give him a taste of his own medicine. Into the cage, Otto! You are the bad one and you know very well how I treat the bad ones."

"Mutti," Otto whined but he dutifully stumbled up to his feet and inside the cage. His mother locked the door behind him.

'Perhaps locking your son in a cage is not such a good idea,' Evangeline suggested. But as soon as the words left her mouth, Mrs. Hellig turned to face her. The plump baker's pleasant expression was gone replaced by a look of pure malevolence which chilled every drop of Evangeline's blood. She inhaled sharply but in the blink of an eye, Mrs. Hellig's fearsome glare disappeared and her face returned to a gentle smile.

"I am sorry again. I hope my boy hasn't spoiled your Christmas. Please, come into the bakery and take vhatever you like. As much cake as you can eat."

"No. Thank you," said Evangeline and Mei replied hurriedly in unison.

"I think I'll stick with Miss Plockton's shortbread for now," Evangeline added.

Miss Plockton nodded, a rare radiant smile gracing her lips. "Let's go, ladies. It's Christmas Eve and there is ever so much to do," she said.

They said their farewells to Mrs. Hellig and Leo, and as they stepped out onto King Street, lightning cracked across the sky.

"How did you know we were there, Miss Plockton?" Evangeline asked.

"I didnae. I forgot something from my list and you were taking ever so long."

Evangeline eyed her dubiously. "But you never forget anything."

Miss Plockton shrugged her shoulders, a twinkle in her eyes which had nothing to do with the lightning. "The Lord rewards charitable work, Miss Evangeline. Especially at Christmas."

Before Evangeline could probe any further, the heavens opened. Fat rain drops battered down upon their heads and the temperature plummeted. They shrieked and covered their hair with their hands as the rain pelted harder and harder on the cobbles.

"Snow?" she gasped as little white pellets bounced at their feet.

"Ow. Is snow this 'ard?" Mei asked as a ball of ice struck her on the nose.

"Hail, Miss Evangeline," Miss Plockton tutted.

The three ran under the protection of a shop awning and watched as the gutters filled with ice pebbles.

"A white Christmas after all." Evangeline sighed.

***

Back at 56 Collins Street, Evangeline changed out of her damp dress and headed downstairs with a growling belly. She found her Uncle Edmund and the Professor with their pipes in hand, taking tea in the parlour. Alongside the verdant Christmas tree twinkling with lights and decked in red china ornaments, the two men looked rather wrung out and wan.

"Ah, there you are, m'dear," her father said wearily. "What have you been up to today?"

She opened her mouth to speak and gazed across at Miss Plockton. Her Father's personal secretary pursed her lips as she poured the tea.

"Nothing particularly exciting, Father. Helping Miss Plockton with a few Christmas errands."

"Very good," her father said as he stroked his enormous black moustache with the fingers of his clockwork hand. "Now where are these famous gingerbreads?"

"No," Evangeline and Miss Plockton interjected in a hurried chorus, sending the Professor recoiling back into the settee.

"They were sold out, I'm afraid, sir," Miss Plockton continued.

"Not to worry," the Professor said with a grin. "I never cared much for gingerbread. Your shortbread is much more the ticket, Miss Plockton."

Evangeline and Miss Plockton exchanged a wide eyed glance, and Evangeline burst into peals of laughter. Miss Plockton stood ramrod straight and bit down on a giggle but a stray tear defied her efforts and trickled down her cheek.

"What's the joke?" said Uncle Edmund.

"Yes, do tell," said the Professor

"Never mind." Evangeline sighed as Miss Plockton dried her eyes and presented a plate of her star-shaped sugar-dusted shortbreads.

"Capital," the Professor said as he crunched into a biscuit. "Magnificent batch, Miss Plockton. I'm beginning to feel markedly better. Just in time for Christmas. Who's for Charades?" Her rotund father jumped to his feet. "I'll go first."

With a buttery shortbread in her hand Evangeline settled back into a red velvet chair and watched the Professor's wild gesticulations in front of the Christmas spruce. This was exactly the Christmas Evangeline had expected. With a few less kidnappings and goat-faced men, of course.

***

About Madeleine D'Este

Growing up in Tasmania, Madeleine now lives in inner city Melbourne surrounded by books. After studying law (and never practising) and travelling the world, Madeleine now lives a double life, immersed in the corporate world by day and writing female-led speculative fiction or podcasting by night.

Madeleine is the author of four novellas in The Antics of Evangeline steampunk cosy-mystery series, Women of Wasps and War (a feminist historical fantasy novel) and The Flower and The Serpent (a young adult supernatural novel due out in late 2019).

Epica Intermission

When the glowing bottles are hung from the masts, their colours stirring ever so distant memories of Christmas trees and childhood wonder, I am always struck by the absence of snow. When the journey was still young there were mutterings amongst the unlucky that our destination burned like a furnace through the months of December and January, though not many believed it to be so. Having now traversed every nook and cranny of Australia's coastline I know the mutterings to have been true, even if landfall is forever too far a swim away and the night eternal. Even from the decking of this cursed ship I can feel the heat rolling across the ocean as if the entire continent were nothing but baking stone in a giant oven.

How can such a land welcome Christmas without snow?

I can but imagine the confusion of those who made it to shore. It must take hostile determination to celebrate a time made for open fires and blessed families when blistering heat encompasses day and night, though perhaps a demon's land it truly is. Maybe an answer is to be found in the prose of the mysterious gifts that float, and as chance would have it here bobs one now!

Please do make yourself comfortable strange friend, for this one looks to take us upon a very unique journey…

Santa Claus Goes Missing

By Natasha O'Connor

*This is for Gerry, who's always believed in my
writing, and always reminds me to have
adventures and enjoy life.*

All was well in the Green Forest. Queen Aeria and King Artus of the Elven kingdom surveyed their domain with satisfaction, pleased with the progress they observed. Green-skinned elves of all shapes and sizes dotted the scene, even though the King and Queen fit the more traditional tall and lithe stereotype.

It had been decades since any kind of trouble had visited, and they hoped that would never change. Every elf remembered the Great Santa Claus Debacle. Unfortunately. Never again.

So, when Mrs Claus came a-knocking one freezing winter's day wild-eyed and blustering, Queen Aeria shook her head and turned the human woman away. Mrs Claus was trouble, and there was no need to give humans any more ammunition to humiliate elven kind.

Of course, Mrs Claus protested, begging on her knees. "Please, Queen Aeria, only you and your elves can help. I have a serious problem with Santa Claus."

Queen Aeria stood impassive as a stone. "You said that last time, and it was some silly, juvenile thing. The answer is no."

Mrs Claus gasped. "How can you say that? The kiddies would've been devastated. Please, I don't know what else to do."

"I must put my kind first. Find someone else to help."

The old lady saw she was fighting a losing battle, and gave up, staggering off with a wail of despair. As soon as she had left, the grim-faced Queen stalked off to the opulent Royal Residence, not noticing her husband hurrying being her.

"Aeria, my dear, what did you do?"

"I saved our people from further indignity by the humans. They already think we are nothing but silly childish helpers for Santa Claus." Aeria tossed her chin in the air.

"That poor woman needed our help. Is your pride that much more important?"

"No, no of course not, but do we also not have a duty to protect our people?" Aeria jabbed at the fire, apparently trying to provoke the fire into spitting out some warmth.

"Protection? From what? We are Elves - a few mocking words will not hurt us. If we can help, we must do so." King Artus gazed at his wife with half a smile, prompting Aeria to growl, but he persevered. "We need to send a search party to bring her back, so we can offer our help."

"No, absolutely not. We cannot let our reputation fall so far no-one will take us seriously again."

"My dear, have you forgotten the first years of our rule? When there was laughter, and merriment, and we did not take ourselves so seriously. Mrs Claus clearly needs our help."

"The answer is still no. If something happened to Santa Claus or Mrs Claus, that is not our concern. We want our other elven kin to respect us enough to trade with us."

"Is that truly your fear, or have you let your pride dictate your actions?"

The Queen cringed, unable to deny the truth of his words, and she felt a twinge of guilt in her belly. How had she let her mother's complaints of her apparent childishness get to her so much? "Very well, I shall organise elves to locate Mrs Claus." Aeria perched on the corner of her throne, hands still clenched.

Before long, a team of tall, fit elves in streamlined gold and black clothes hurried into the Royal Residence. Aeria relayed her orders to the leader and bade them be fleet of foot in their mission.

Deep down, part of her wanted to know what had gotten Mrs Claus in such a lather, even if she would not admit it. When her search party strode into the Residence with Mrs Claus in tow, Aeria marched up and demanded.

"Well?"

To her credit, Mrs Claus looked the Elven Queen right in the eyes. "Good to see you remembered your manners. I wouldn't have come if it wasn't an emergency."

"What has he–"

"Aeria," King Artus laid a hand on his wife's arm. "Let me talk to Mrs Claus."

"If you insist." Aeria had not entirely forgiven her husband for his earlier comments.

"Mrs Claus, what is your emergency?"

"Santa Claus is missing and none of us can locate him. It's the week before Christmas and he might as well have fallen off the planet."

"Are you sure you looked everywhere?"

Mrs Claus shot Artus a withering look. "Yes, we looked all over the North Pole."

"Only the North Pole?"

"Why would he have gone elsewhere? Man isn't silly."

"You need to consider it. Perhaps you should try the South Pole."

"You don't understand! I don't have time to do it myself. Only Santa Claus can drive the Sleigh. I need you, and your team of searchers, to help."

Queen Aeria knew arguing was a waste of time when she saw the desperation in Mrs Claus's eyes. Truth be told, she sympathised with the old woman. It had to be hard being Santa Claus's wife.

"Darling," she said to King Artus. "Maybe we should help. I know I said no before, but Mrs Claus was not responsible for the previous… situation. Besides, Santa Claus may be in real trouble."

"Oh, thank you, Queen Aeria!"

"We had better start preparations to leave immediately." The Queen said. She would coordinate rescue efforts. Not that she distrusted her husband, but nothing would go wrong if she could help it. And this time, the Elves would wear hats to cover their ears. It was cold at this time of year, after all.

***

Queen Aeria, Mrs Claus and her crack team of Elves stood at the door of the Royal Residence a very short time later.

"Queen Aeria," Mrs Claus began. "How do we get there?"

Queen Aeria glanced at the dog sled Mrs Claus had come on and shook her head. "We need elf transport."

"Not the thing that makes people disappear?"

"Yes. If we are to conduct this search quickly, it is imperative we use it." Aeria tried a different tack. "I know non-Elves distrust them, but they are quite safe. My word is my bond."

"I'll have to be brave, then. I can't let all the little kiddies down on Christmas Day."

"Of course. Now, follow me and do exactly as I say." Aeria marched off without another word, leaving Mrs Claus to scamper after.

One by one, the group of six people filtered into the cylindrical building made of carved sandstone. Mrs Claus shuffled onto the transport pad with clenched fists. After a moment or two, she raised a hand.

"Er, Queen Aeria, are we actually going to the South Pole like King Artus suggested?"

"Yes, of course." At that moment, one of the search elves tapped the Queen on the shoulder.

"Your Highness, we received a communication from our brethren in the Great Southern Land that Santa Claus has been spotted. They did not specify where. They did warn us to bring a change of clothes."

"What the Dickens is he doing there? I sent him to get mince pies last Tuesday, not on holiday."

Aeria had to admit, she very much wanted to know the answer, too. "I have a feeling we will find out very soon. Set the dial for the Great Southern Land."

***

It took but a short time for the transport to deposit them at their destination. Despite being royalty, Queen Aeria had never left her kingdom in the cold North and she was curious to explore.

When the small group stepped outside the building, the heat greeted them with a blast, prompting an undignified scramble to remove thick woollen clothing. Aeria blinked in surprise as she surveyed her new surroundings, feeling naked without her woollens. A yellow sun high in a cloudless blue sky blazed down on a baked land completely unlike her home. Scratching her head, the Queen peered at the glowing orb in bewilderment. It was meant to be nightfall, or dark at the very least.

Unlike their transport building, this one was far from civilisation. There was grass, but it was brown not lush green and the trees were a dusty green and they smelt… she sniffed the air, but could not place the sweet but sharp smell. This couldn't be the place...

"We have arrived at the Great Southern Land, your Highness." A search elf informed her.

Queen Aeria did her best to maintain her composure. "Very good. Have we received any more communication?"

"I don't know about you four, but I need a cold drink." Mrs Claus interrupted. "It's as hot as a forge here."

"Yes, of course, water should be a priority. Where can we find our brethren in this parched land, Varta?"

"Our brethren chose to live close to the water, so I suggest we start in that direction."

"Excuse me, not to be a pain." Mrs Claus interrupted again, pouting lips putting the lie to her words. "How are we getting there?"

The Queen began to regret her decision to help. "We will walk there. We have two legs, and the walk will do us good." After all, that's what they would do at home.

Varta swallowed a splutter. "Excuse me, your Highness, but might I suggest we arrange alternative transport? It is rather hot, and we are unused to this climate."

"Bah! We are Elves. We can adapt to any situation."

"That's all well and good for you pointy eared lot, but this old human woman has never left the North Pole. I'm already too hot."

The Queen glanced at Mrs Claus, and indeed fat drops of sweat rolled down her face. "Very well, what are our options?"

"I believe our brethren advised us to stay here and they will collect us." Varta said with the tone of an elf who had previously left out vital information, and was about to receive an ear-bashing.

"Why did you not tell me that when we first arrived? Never mind, we shall wait here, then."

As she said that, a loud roaring sound came from nearby and the small group jumped a mile in the air when some kind of vehicle came charging round the corner. It was covered in rust with some kind of tray at the back and a lion attached to the front and back.

"What is that?" Aeria cried.

"G'day, yer Majesty. That's our ute - sorry she's in a state, sea water'll do that. Welcome to the Great Southern Land - or Australia as the humans call it." A tall, tanned elf with browny-green skin in some kind of sleeveless shirt, sandals, and shorts strode up, grinning from ear to ear, and tossed them some bottles of water. "Name's Utt, by the way. Didn't realise there'd be a whole group of youse. There's cold drinks in the esky - sorry, cool box - if that'd be better."

Aeria goggled, completely speechless for once. Utt had the same pointed ears all elves shared, but that's where the similarities ended.

Mrs Claus had no such trouble adjusting. "Say, you aren't like those stuffy Northern elves."

That jolted Aeria back to life. "Stuffy? You had no complaints before."

Before Mrs Claus could reply, Utt said, "I reckon we all need a cool one, and a sit down. You lot probably aren't used to the heat, right? Plenty of room in the ute for all of youse as long as long as you don't mind the dog. Queen Aeria, you better have the passenger seat, but the rest of youse'll have to go in the ute tray."

"You travel in a human contraption?" Aeria asked.

"Yeah, why not? Just because it's made by humans, doesn't mean it's bad. You'll see: we're more relaxed here. Doesn't make sense not to be when it's so bloody hot."

With a scowl, Aeria sat down, and swivelled to watch her companions clambering into the back. The minute they sat down, Utt slammed his door and shot off down the road.

He glanced at her. "So, word has it you didn't want to help Mrs Claus at first because of the Great Santa Claus Debacle. I gotta know: what happened that was so bad?"

Aeria recoiled, her skin turning a mossy shade of green. She did not want to talk about it. "Nothing you need to know about."

"It can't have been that bad."

"If you must know, we agreed to Santa's little helpers because his normal helpers went on a pay and conditions strike and it became a debacle. Humans, both young and old, came to point and laugh at us. They made us wear silly costumes with bells on and made a mockery of our customs." The Queen trailed off. The memories of how the children had pulled her ears and called her elves rude names still haunted her.

Utt saw the look on her face and said nothing more, letting the countryside roll past. Soon, the sunburnt fields gave way to houses and before long, sparkling blue ocean unfolded like a blanket of jewels

Queen Aeria gazed at the water, stunned by how vibrantly blue it was, and how alive it seemed. Framed by a golden beach and dark green trees, it made the colours of her homeland dull by comparison. How was it one land could present such a contrast?

Utt put the window down, and a cool sea breeze drifted in. Queen Aeria sighed in relief as her skin stopped prickling and her head began to clear. As they drove along, Utt broke the silence.

"I hear you're looking for Santa." Silence. "Good news is, we found him. Bad news is… you'll see for yerrself."

"As long as you've found him, we will take care of the rest." Aeria said, already dreading the answer.

"I admire your optimism, but you're in for a challenge."

Five short minutes later, they arrived at their destination, a two-storey blue house with boards across the front. There were no other houses in sight.

"Welcome to our humble abode." Utt declared. "It's probably not what yer used to, yer Majesty, but we like it."

"Yes, of course." And because she had her manners: "Thank you. It will be fine."

"Glad to hear it. Don't often have foreign royalty in town."

"This is all very different, and not what I expected. You said you knew Santa Claus's location?"

Utt nodded. "We've got him holed up here for his own good."

"What do you mean?" Mrs Claus said.

"He and the sun... didn't get on."

They traipsed into the house through to the kitchen, grateful for the semi-darkness after the bright sunlight. Mrs Claus gasped when she spotted Santa Claus lounging on a sofa, eyes half-closed. He groaned in agony when he spotted them.

"What happened to him?"

"The sun is much stronger here, and he spent far too long under it with no protection. It gets everyone from the Northern hemisphere – both elves and humans." Utt pointed to the bandages swaddling the man who was meant to deliver presents in less than a week.

"Did he say why he ended up here?" Mrs Claus said.

"He mumbled something about the best mince pies, and carrots, and rum, but that must have been the sunstroke talking."

"Oh no." Mrs Claus closed her eyes. "I sent him out for mince pies. I didn't mean for him to get so lost?"

"Will he be ready for Christmas Eve?" Aeria asked.

"Not likely. Somebody else will have to do the deliveries. We can't fly the sleigh, so it can't be our lot."

"You'll have to help again, Queen Aeria, if my husband can't do it."

"No, absolutely not. Not after last time when we became a laughingstock. Besides, we cannot drive the sleigh, either."

"Not trying to tell you how to rule, yer Majesty, given that we're separate clans, but don't you think you're taking yourself too seriously? Life's too short for that. Have some fun."

Queen Aeria choked, skewering Utt with a death stare. "Excuse me?"

"You Northern elves have a reputation of having a board up your arse. What about all the legends of old? Elves still sing about how Agar the Great's parties went on for days, how elves and humans mixed in everyday life. Anyway, if you don't do it, who will?

Utt continued. "We can't let all the human children go without just because we're too proud to help out. Let's get some sausages cooking on the barbie. The food'll help us think and we can talk about what to do while we wait."

A fragment of the Queen's conversation with King Artus prodded her, and she winced. She remembered her younger, more carefree days, running through the Green Forest with Artus, giggling like a child, collecting herbs and spices for weird and wonderful concoctions. When had she started thinking elves were better than humans, rather than merely different?

"Very well. I suppose we could all do with some food."

"Awesome, I'll fire up the barbie while you lot settle in by the pool. Go for a dip if you want - I've got some spare bathers upstairs."

"No, thank you." Swimming was more than Queen Aeria had bargained for. "The sea breeze is good enough."

Mrs Claus stared longingly at the water, but remained quiet.

While they talked around the problem of Christmas Eve, Aeria thought about the problem of Santa Claus. Nobody else knew how to drive the sleigh, even if she volunteered.

There had to be another way. Her mind gnawed at the memory of collecting herbs and spices when an idea hit her so hard so cried out.

"It will not cure him entirely, but he will be able to work." Aeria said.

"What will?" Mrs Claus asked, leaning forward.

"Healing leaves from the Green Forest. There is only a small patch of them, and they will need to be ground into powder and tipped into a warm bath."

Utt smacked his forehead, and groaned. "I can't believe I forgot about louas. Call myself an elf. This is a job for you, Mrs Claus. You'll need to slather him entirely in louas gel."

"If it means he'll be ready by Christmas Eve, I'll cover him in-"

"It's OK, we know what you mean." Aeria cut in, with a grimace.

***

Several days later, Queen Aeria and King Artus stood in front of a roaring fire, the smell of cooking meat drifting into the air. Stars twinkled in the dark sky, despite it being midday. All around them, the elves of Green Forest had gathered, murmuring among themselves in anticipation. An outdoor feast was highly unusual at this time of year.

When the Queen had returned from the Great Southern Land, she insisted on new traditions for Christmas Day. "It may be cold at this time of year," she declared. "But we should celebrate with cooking meat on coals."

It met some resistance to begin with – too cold, too dark, elves had complained. Their complaints were short-lived when King Artus told them "We are elves. We do not let cold and dark trouble us."

Some elves were even brave enough to take a dip in the thermal baths not far from Green Forest. Loud cheers and cries of joy rang out, a sound not heard in those parts for many a decade.

Aeria surveyed her people with a satisfied smile. It warmed her heart to see her people so happy, and she tried not to let a twinge of guilt squeeze her heart. Her gratitude to their elven brethren in the Great Southern Land knew no bounds, even if some of their ways still mystified the Queen.

Better yet, Santa Claus had indeed recovered in time to fly the sleigh around the world, no doubt a miracle that would be talked about for decades to come. If they were lucky, perhaps it would be immortalised in a human Christmas story. And that would be, Aeria decided, a fitting way to remember.

***

About Natasha O'Connor

Natasha (also known as Tash for those playing at home) is an Aussie mum who also works for a radio station doing their pays. I've been writing on and off for as long as I can remember, inspired by the Discworld novels. My one regret is never getting to meet Sir Terry. These days, I write as a hobby, but in a previous life, I was a music journalist. Getting to see bands and review albums was a dream come true for 20s me.

A Final Farewell from the Epica

Look out upon the waters strange friend. How beautiful are the colours of the glowing bottles as they sit proud on the masts, defiant beneath the stars as they bring such beauty to a darkness that herself secretly beckons for a moment of relief from endless swells? Aye, together we have put together such a magical beacon that surely the dazzling light show is only possible at such a special time of the year. True, it is that a year is a measure of time draped with fog, but not even eternity can strip from Christmas the majesty of a cosmic moment that gives us reason to love all that gives both life and laughter.

Here we sit, circling a land that knows no snow when all should be white and innocent. 'Tis a new land, with parched soil to test the strongest of hands and hopping creatures ready to box at the drop of one's hat, and yet her terrain seems to promise such reward for those willing to dance in the embrace of her spirit. If Christmas is anything, it is a time of new beginnings, and there can be no greater beginning than a new country ready to challenge the sweat and spirit of convicts desperate to live. Should there come a time that the brown earth ever touch my sea salt encrusted feet I know one thing for sure – I should be thankful to be a part of a young nation ready to change the world with her newly formed criminal spirit!

Alas, a soft but warm wind is beginning to blow. Don't be sad for the goodbye that it brings, for though I'll watch you glitter into the darkness while stumbling back to a bunk that has only thought for company, I'll rest my head knowing the magical bottle bound tales will bob to the surface sometime again. As for when, who knows? I've learned not to hunger for future tales, especially when this new haul has brought such an array of different worlds to treasure as I close my eyes and succumb to the monotonous creaking. The gods themselves must feast upon the soft flesh of imagination, and should we love the power of words and the worlds that come hither as much as they then we stand beside those same gods to bask in the warming glory of that which it is to tell a story.

I'm afraid the seas are about to grow rough. It's time for me to say goodbye, but there's always the chance you'll be back for another starlit cruise. Don't worry for now though dear friend, this will all be but a dream that shimmers on the edge of the waking light before the echoes of the sails flutter into nothing. It's been a momentous pleasure to discover the gifts of the deep with you, and to stand upon the bow beneath the colourful glow of all that were such wonderful escapes, but now departure is all that remains. As I wave bon voyage from a place of ghosts and forgotten maps please tell the Demon's Land Merry Christmas. Where there should be snow there may be sunburned branches and weary animals, yet I have a feeling this ship will eventually land on the beaches of a country ready to transcend the stars…

Merry Christmas dear reader, and apologies again for the lack of rum!

***

Thank you for reading
Christmas Australis: A Frighteningly Festive Anthology of Spine Jingling Tales.

If you enjoyed our stories, please consider taking a moment to write a review. Even a couple of sentences helps. As independent authors, we rely on reviews and word of mouth. Your support and feedback are greatly appreciated and can really make a difference.

To find out more about the authors and to read more of their work, check out their websites for links to stories books, newsletters, blogs, podcasts, and updates.

And of course you can follow them on Twitter on the #6amAusWriters hashtag. Most of them are there – most mornings…